crets

straight
ed for it
one and

th many
danger,
exy, and
."

Renewals
www.liverpool.gov.uk/libraries
0151 233 3000

Severus

R.267

npathize

with their struggles and celebrate their triumphs."

~ *JT, Romance Junkies*

Look for these titles by
Lynne Connolly

Now Available:

Triple Countess Trilogy
Last Chance, My Love (Book 1)
A Chance to Dream (Book 2)
Met by Chance (Book 3)

Secrets Trilogy
Seductive Secrets (Book 1)
Alluring Secrets (Book 2)
Tantalizing Secrets (Book 3)

Richard and Rose Series
Yorkshire (Book 1)
Devonshire (Book 2)
Venice (Book 3)

Coming Soon:

Richard and Rose Series
Harley Street (Book 4)
Eyton (Book 5)
Darkwater (Book 6)

Alluring Secrets

Lynne Connolly

A SAMHAIN PUBLISHING, LTD. publication.

Samhain Publishing, Ltd.
577 Mulberry Street, Suite 1520
Macon, GA 31201
www.samhainpublishing.com

Alluring Secrets
Copyright © 2009 by Lynne Connolly
Print ISBN: 978-1-60504-330-2
Digital ISBN: 978-1-60504-214-5

Editing by Angela James
Cover by Anne Cain

First Samhain Publishing, Ltd. electronic publication: October 2008
First Samhain Publishing, Ltd. print publication: August 2009

Dedication

To Jean and Kelvin. Thank you for your dining room table and for being so patient with me.

Chapter One

Miss Penelope Makepiece stared out of the carriage window at the imposing sight of the North Front of Swithland House. It was enough to daunt the heart of the boldest young lady, its gleaming bulk looming above them. The traveling carriage drew to a decorous halt before the steps leading to the huge front door.

Here lived her dearest friend in all the world and the man she had made a complete cake of herself over. A shame they were brother and sister.

Penelope waited until a servant had ceremoniously handed down her Aunt Cecilia before she took the gloved hand of the liveried footman and climbed out of the carriage, careful to keep her footing on the narrow steps. Without her spectacles she was apt to trip and stumble, and her aunt did not allow her to wear them in public. Her cousin Toby Makepiece, Aunt Cecilia's only and most beloved son, followed her. His thin brown hair, tied back in a fashionable queue, stirred in the slight breeze that was all this warm day had to offer.

She had no time to study the façade, as the servants immediately led them indoors where the superior butler waited to greet them and conduct them to their rooms. Penelope found that the broad, shallow steps leading up to the Great Hall were not difficult to climb without stumbling.

The Great Hall was one of the sights of Hertfordshire, or so the guidebooks dedicated to that area of the country declared. The eminent artist Sir James Thornhill had decorated the walls and ceiling in the previous century and the result was staggeringly grandiose. The blur of color swamped Penelope's senses.

"Good afternoon, Mrs. Makepiece, Miss Makepiece, Mr. Makepiece," the butler intoned. "I am Hutton, and I have the honor of being Lord Swithland's butler. If you should require anything during your stay here, please do not hesitate to call for myself or the housekeeper, Mrs. Yeovil."

Mrs. Makepiece nodded graciously, and turned at a sudden movement at the back of the hall. Out of a side door ran a young lady, carrying the scent of hyacinth with her. "Antonia!" Penelope forgot all her misgivings on seeing her friend.

"Penelope, it's so good to see you!"

They embraced, Penelope feeling her friend's warmth through the fine silk of her gown. She hadn't seen Antonia for some time.

Antonia drew back, her arms still resting on Penelope's waist, and studied her face. "I'm so pleased to see you in such good looks, Penelope." At Penelope's snort, Antonia raised a dark brow. "What, you don't think you are? A trim figure, dark hair with that hint of fire and your eyes could enchant most men. I've seen Peter Worsley watching you with appreciation, and he's not the only one."

Penelope looked into the smiling eyes and felt better than she had for months. While she didn't share Antonia's delusions about her looks, it did her good to share her thoughts with her friend. "Peter Worsley? I doubt that. He prefers high flyers, and blondes like Mrs. Wisheart."

"You're wrong, Penelope. You might not have the flashy

beauty of the Wishearts of this world, but your kind of beauty will last longer."

Penelope laughed. She knew she didn't show to effect in a ballroom and she'd never seen any eligible male looking her way. Not that she could see anything beyond the end of her nose.

Antonia gave her a sympathetic smile. "I was so sorry to hear about your mother. I haven't seen you since she passed away,"

Penelope nodded. "She'd been ill for some time." It had been two years since her mother's death, but Penelope had not been close to her for some time before that. The late Lady Wimbourne had been too intent on giving her husband an heir to care for her sole living girl child.

"I hardly remember my mama," Antonia confessed. "I think Sev remembers her better." Severus, Earl of Swithland. The rush of emotion she felt at the mere mention of his name no longer surprised Penelope. As she always did, she put the feeling aside. He was not for her. "Papa will arrive shortly. He has a few matters to arrange in Town first, he said."

After making a pretty curtsey to Penelope's aunt and her cousin, Antonia linked arms with Penelope, clearly intending to accompany them upstairs. "Sev is in London on business, but we expect him back any day to attend his house party. You are early, but not as early as some of the guests. No doubt he'll bring some more of his friends with him. Sev hardly ever travels alone." She sniffed. "Always in state."

Penelope grinned. She didn't know how Severus Granville always managed to be surrounded by sycophants and attendants in town. To do him justice, he didn't encourage them, but they clustered around him anyway. She hoped they would keep him away from her.

The remembrance of her girlhood crush stayed with her to torment her in the lonely nights. Occasionally she would remember her declaration of love and his look of horror, justified, since no one could wish for the advances of a clumsy, gawky girl, just fifteen. The remembrance subdued her rising pleasure at meeting her old friend, and she followed her upstairs with a decorous tread.

Hutton led the way up the broad marble staircase and along several elegantly decorated corridors to the guest rooms. Antonia accompanied them, chattering all the way, and followed Penelope into the pretty room appointed to her, plumping down on the daybed at the foot of the canopied four-poster. "Do you like it? I chose it myself, it's near my room and it's one of the prettiest guest rooms in the house."

Penelope peered around, squinting.

"Oh for goodness' sake put them on." A note of irritation entered Antonia's voice.

Penelope grinned. Diving into the pocket slit in her gown, she drew out a long embroidered case and took out a pair of spectacles. She perched them on her nose and gazed around with interest. "It *is* a pretty room. I knew the color was pretty, of course, but I didn't know what the detail looked like." The predominant color was a pale yellow, enhanced by plaster bows and the occasional cherub.

Now she could see Antonia properly, Penelope could also see her look of exasperation, a slight frown marring the smooth brow.

"Why don't you wear them all the time? You got on well at school once they discovered you needed them. You look attractive in them. They add piquancy to your face. At least they would, if they were a better style."

Penelope forbore to tell her she had little choice. The heavy, tortoiseshell frames were the only ones available at the hurried consultation, which was all her mother had allowed her when she'd bought them five years before.

Penelope used one finger to push the offending spectacles further up her nose. "Aunt Cecilia feels the same way as my mother did. Neither of them allow me to wear my spectacles in public."

Antonia made a sound of annoyance. "Don't they realize how difficult it is for you? You can't even **see** to dance, for heaven's sake!"

It was true; if Penelope hadn't learned to dance at school, where the teachers had allowed her to wear her spectacles, she would have no confidence at all on the dance floor. As it was, she stumbled her way around unfamiliar rooms; the number of times she under or overestimated the distance between her hand and a doorknob was well into double figures. Taking due care of every movement she made paid its toll and Penelope often stumbled. Society labeled her clumsy, but her fortune and birth made her acceptable. Sometimes she wished it didn't.

"Aunt Cecilia feels that I wouldn't attract anyone wearing them, and people would label me a bluestocking."

Most people assumed she was "a little slow," but Penelope didn't mention that to Antonia. No sense her friend getting annoyed all over again. "I manage."

As it was, Antonia tsked. "Men are not always as stupid as women think them. What will you do about your spectacles once you're married?"

"My aunt says a marriage will be arranged in due course, and after that I may do as I please." She shrugged. "I don't suppose my husband will let me wear them either. But after I'm married I might decide to please myself."

"Well he is very foolish if he doesn't let you wear them." At first indignant, Antonia's eyes soon filled with speculation, a look Penelope knew well and one that had led her into trouble in the past. "Have they anyone in mind?"

Penelope shrugged. "Toby, of course. It would tie up the family's inheritance nicely."

Antonia shrugged. "It comes to us all."

Toby was pleasant, but uninspiring, and in the absence of anyone more exciting, Penelope considered him a much better choice than many others.

Antonia's brown eyes lit up. "Tell you what, Penny, shall I take you around the house tomorrow? *With* your spectacles?"

Penelope clapped her hands in a gesture she thought she'd forgotten at school. "That would be wonderful! I love this house, and I don't think I've *ever* seen it properly."

While many people guessed Penelope had a problem with her sight, no one except her family, her maid and her old school friends knew how bad it was. In fact, Penelope could barely see two feet in front of her face before her vision began to deteriorate into blurred into patches of color. It had worsened over the years, and Penelope had a secret fear she vouchsafed to no one; if it got any worse, would she go blind? There was no one she could ask, no one she knew who had any knowledge of the science of optics, so she kept her fears to herself.

Now she could see properly, she rose and went to the window to enjoy the view. Her room looked out over the clipped lawns of the South Front, leading to the great lake, a shimmer of blue in the summer sun. The occasional spark of brilliance showed where the breeze ruffled its surface. "I love this house," she breathed.

Antonia came to stand at her side. "It is a lovely house, but I daren't think about it too much. I'll have to move on soon, so I mustn't become too attached to it. How do *you* feel about your father's house?"

"The Abbey? The same way you do about Swithland House, I suppose. I don't think of it as a permanent residence. I will move on, unless I marry Toby."

"Is it worth it? Your portion is enough to attract a number of suitors, isn't it?"

Penelope shrugged. "I'm quite an heiress, otherwise people would be a lot ruder about me. I've had offers, but no one who took my fancy. Aunt Cecelia says I should take my time, not accept any offers until I'd thought about it and discussed it with her. She's probably right, there are any number of fortune hunters about and some of them can be quite charming."

Antonia put her hand on Penelope's sleeve. "I'm sorry I couldn't be there when your mother died. I was grateful to Severus for sending me to Italy when I asked him to, but I wanted to cut it short when I heard."

Penelope turned away from the view to touch her friend's hand, moved by Antonia's words "There was no need. You would have made me feel guilty. And I had your wonderful letters to look forward to. They cheered me up no end."

They stood for a while in silence, looking out at the glorious vista in front of them. This time next year there was no knowing where they would be, what they would be looking at. However, they would still be friends. Both knew that without a doubt.

Dinner that evening was a small affair. Penelope, her Aunt Cecilia, her cousin Toby and Antonia. They met in the Yellow Drawing room, which was one of the smaller rooms, but was still too large for the four people present. Toby was in his element, with three ladies to take care of. His gallantry was extreme, his condescension matching it.

"Of course, I must make the most of this opportunity to

15

enjoy the company of two such lovely young ladies. And Mama, of course." Neither lovely lady knew quite what to say, but Mrs. Makepiece smiled indulgently.

Antonia flicked her fan open with a slight air of irritation. "You're *too* kind, sir."

"A great pleasure. I understand I won't be enjoying this solitary delight for long, so I must make the most of it."

Antonia looked at him, one delicate brow upraised, but he addressed Penelope. "While you were upstairs, a message arrived for you. I happened to be passing through the hall at the time. Your father will be arriving, my dear, in company with his lordship, Lady Antonia's brother. And several other guests."

Not for the first time Penelope wondered at Toby's genius at being in the right place at the right time. His gossip was invariably of the superior kind. She had often suspected him of listening at doors. "Do you know who these guests might be?"

Toby smiled a secretive smile. "A bouquet of the most eligible ladies in London. Together with a raft of the most eligible young men. My guess is that your estimable brother, Lady Antonia, has decided to take a bride."

Penelope caught her breath and glanced at her friend, who smiled sweetly, not a whit abashed. "It's about time. Sev has been looking and flirting for far too long. Perhaps it will settle him."

Penelope suspected more than flirting. With his two particular friends, Severus had been cutting a deep swathe through the beauties of London for several years past.

How he could appear arch, Penelope didn't know, but Toby managed it. "Why Lady Antonia. Are you not the least bit disconcerted to hear the news?"

Antonia fanned herself with an elegant flick of her wrist. "Not at all. In fact, he mentioned it before he left for London. I've been his hostess since I came of age, Mr. Makepiece, but now I must look to my own future. Sev mentioned it some time past."

Toby quirked a light brown eyebrow and Antonia laughed. "Oh I have no one in particular in mind, sir, but I must consider the matter carefully. I have no one but my brother to look out for me, and he can hardly do so while he remains unwed."

Toby frowned a little. "I cannot fault your reasoning, although your manner may be thought a little forward in some circles. It seems a pity. Perhaps if Penelope was to marry she might help...?" He left the sentence unfinished, but from the significant glance he bestowed on his cousin, it was difficult to mistake his meaning.

Antonia covered Penelope's hand with her own. "I had no idea my dearest Penelope was considering the awful step." A lie, but a kind one. "I think no young man is courting her at present?"

"Well, not exactly," Toby admitted. Penelope relished his discomfiture. Toby frowned and chewed his bottom lip. He hadn't courted her, just took her acceptance for granted. He was her father's heir, and she was the possessor of a considerable portion, most of which had come from her mother's estate. Her father would welcome the match, but so far he had not pressured her to take it up, and Toby had not yet proposed.

Lord Wimbourne had often been away from home since his wife died. Penelope had spent more time with her aunt, who had offered to chaperone her until her marriage, but she soon learned that was an excuse to bring her and Toby together.

She had to consider her marriage imminent, or dwindle into an old maid. Toby might be prosy and stuffy, but Penelope believed he cared for her, and he had no serious defects of character like a tendency to gamble or debauchery.

Unlike Antonia's reprehensible brother, who had done his best to enjoy the treats a jaded world could offer a wealthy and titled reprobate. Sev's prowess in bed and at the gaming tables had been legendary, even though his activities had declined in recent years. Penelope had every intention of questioning Antonia about his activities, but she couldn't do it here.

Severus fascinated her. He'd always been kind to her in a big brother kind of way but never taken her seriously, or noticed her particularly. That summer ten years ago had ruined the casual friendliness between them, and it had been all her fault. She had conceived a passion for him, one that must have proved acutely embarrassing to a boy on the threshold of manhood, and he regarded her with caution now. She was sorry for it. Now it seemed he was to take the next big step in his life. She wondered what kind of woman would keep Severus Granville happy. No doubt she would find out soon.

Dinner was pleasant, and uneventful. Afterwards they played cards until bedtime, in a friendly atmosphere

Her maid had just left the room, having seen Penelope securely into her voluminous nightdress and robe, when Mrs. Makepiece, similarly attired, knocked, and without waiting for a reply, entered.

"I particularly wish to speak to you, Penelope." Penelope turned around on the stool before her dressing table where she had been polishing her nails. Her aunt sat herself on the daybed, feet firmly together on the floor, hands clasped in her lap. "I do not wish you to feel obliged in any way," she began.

Penelope saw the expression on her aunt's face and her stomach tightened. "Of course not, aunt."

"You have few people to look to for advice and I think I am one of the few who can venture to do so," her aunt said, fairly launched on what Penelope suspected to be a carefully constructed speech. "I trust you won't object to my advice?"

Mutely Penelope shook her head. She knew her aunt would give it anyway, so she reconciled herself to listening.

Mrs. Makepiece relaxed. Penelope saw her shoulders slump a little, and realized her aunt hadn't been at all sure of her welcome. "I know there is an unspoken connection between you and Toby," she said. Penelope loved that expression, and saved it up for future use, while being extremely doubtful about her response. "I also know he will make you an offer at some time this visit."

Penelope bridled. Why could her aunt not leave her son to make his own declaration?

Mrs. Makepiece's next words mollified her ruffled feelings. "I fully understand that your answer is none of my business, although I naturally have my opinions on the matter. What I want you to know is that if you should decide not to marry my son, I would still be willing to act as your chaperone until you find a suitable match. You must not let that concern affect your decision."

Mrs. Makepiece's chaperonage was every bit as strict as her mother's had been, and it irked Penelope considerably, but she couldn't help but be touched by her aunt's sentiments. If Aunt Cecilia left with her son, should Penelope refuse him, then she would have to cast around for a suitable poor relation or else take herself back to her home and remain there until she could find someone to lend her proper countenance. That was not a solution she would have readily accepted.

So, despite her aunt's constant strictures, Penelope said, "Thank you, Aunt Cecilia. That is very good of you. As for any match, I would value your opinion. I haven't come to any definite conclusions yet, but I know Toby is interested in making a match of it soon."

This wasn't quite true, but Penelope saw her aunt was chafing to have at it. At the mention of her only son, Mrs. Makepiece smiled, warming her usually stern features. Creases appeared at the corner of her mouth and spread over her dry cheeks. "It is the wish of my heart, my dear. I know Toby would make you a good and protective husband, and it would neatly tie the inheritance and the title together. He is a good son, and I wouldn't insult you by furthering the match if he wasn't. I hope you know that. Toby is of an age where he is ready to settle down, and you are a dutiful, obedient girl. I think you would make a successful union. You should know that he intends to ask you sometime during this visit, probably after your father's arrival."

She heard the last comment with a great deal of trepidation. Penelope hated upset, and would rather conform than make anyone unnecessarily angry, although she was quite capable of defending her corner if she needed to.

When she was young, she had chosen her acts of defiance badly and had invariably been forced to concede defeat, teaching her when it was better to concede a point. So now she left her spectacles off in company and kept her hobbies to herself, doing her best to conform to the image of the attractive young society lady. Not to do so might leave her a dried up old maid, never to find a full life and children of her own.

So Penelope chose her battles wisely. "I will not keep Toby waiting long, should he ask me and I'm glad you told me of his intentions." But Penelope knew, and from her complacent smile, her aunt knew, too, that if the combined might of Lord Wimbourne, Mrs. Makepiece and Toby Makepiece were set against her, Penelope would feel bound to conform. She had her secret dreams, but they could not form the basis for a successful life. She must put them aside and learn to face reality. It could be a lot worse.

After her aunt had left her, Penelope climbed wearily into bed. The day hadn't tired her out, but she felt tired. She would soon be an old married woman, no excitement, no adventure. Life wasn't like that. Not her life, anyway.

Chapter Two

Penelope felt less gloomy in the morning. The day was fine, with a slight breeze to cool the fevered brow, and the prospect from her window, once her maid had thrown back the shutters, was so enticing she decided to take a walk before breakfast. Stopping to tie on a simple straw bergère hat over her curls she escaped before anyone could stop her.

She felt freer out of doors, with the illusion that she could run away from the snares that were creeping their surreptitious threads around her. Soon she would be well and truly caught, probably by Toby and while the thought of marrying him had been tolerable when the wedding was a distant prospect, now it crept closer she wasn't sure she could accept it with equanimity.

She stopped to sniff a rose, narrowly missing a bee that decided to fly out of it just as she dipped her head. She would have spotted it earlier had she been wearing her spectacles, but someone might be watching from the house. It was foolish to deliberately court censure. But she had her spectacles in her pocket and every intention of wearing them once out of sight of the house.

Ruffled by the bee, she moved on, past the rose bushes and up a lavender-lined path. This garden was beautiful, a random gathering of plants in sumptuous colors, leading inexorably to the wide open spaces of the Home Park. The trees on the horizon were bought at great expense and planted there, instead of having grown naturally. If anything, Penelope's sight enhanced the vista of trees, as she could see the general shapes, the way they swept together and enhanced the skyline. In a hundred years, the saplings planted with the full-grown trees would flourish; in another hundred, the seeds planted in the ground would replace them. They would be as natural as anything else placed there, and as contrived as well.

Pondering the paradox gave Penelope some rest from the notions circling around in her head; should she accept Toby's offer when he made it or not? Sighing, she wished she had more choices.

Of course, there was no question; Toby would care for her and give her a family. Nobody else was in prospect, so it looked like Toby or a lifetime of tedious spinsterhood. Once she had dreamed of a strong man who would take her in his arms and declare his undying love. She must learn to do without dreams.

Penelope stopped her stroll across the shaved grass lawn and hugged herself... She wasn't unaware of the marital act; her mother had seen to that by informing her in a dry and factual manner when Penelope had reached eighteen, but try as she might she couldn't imagine Toby doing it.

Even though Toby was a healthy young male with no vices and would probably prove an adequate bed partner. But not hers. No lift of the spirits or anticipatory excitement urged her to consider it further. Penelope sighed, and started to walk again. She'd stopped dreaming of knights in armor years ago. Perhaps she should stop thinking about excitement, too.

An hour later Penelope returned to a bustling household. Even though she came in through the south entrance, there were signs of increased activity at the rear of the house, too. The activity at the front must be frantic. Maids and footmen crossed the hall towards the servants' entrance, all bearing pieces of luggage. Penelope made her way to the breakfast parlor, wondering who had arrived.

Several young ladies looked up when she came in and Penelope's heart sank. Three she recognized as the most vacuous young ladies of her acquaintance. Hastily, she whipped off her spectacles and restored them to her pocket. She'd seen enough, anyway.

She had made her come-out in the same year as two of them, and their constant simpering and fluttering irritated her. Even more irritating was the way their affected manners attracted young men.

Penelope had always told herself she didn't care, and after a while that became true. What surprised her was these three were still unwed. Penelope had decided to take her time, but these young ladies were the hopes of their respective families, expected to marry brilliantly. But dukes had come and gone, and they were resorting to vying for the affections of a mere earl, albeit one whose wealth vied with that of dukes and marquesses.

Penelope bade everyone good morning and after filling her plate at the buffet, headed for the seat next to her aunt. Toby stood and drew a chair back for her as she sat. She liked that.

"Did you have a good journey?" she asked Miss Caroline Trente in her best manner.

"Indeed, yes, thank you. We were only on the road for a short time today." From the petulant tone in her voice, Penelope could tell Miss Trente was pouting, although the subtleties of the lady's expression evaded her. "I expected dear Lord Swithland to arrive here before us, since he left on horseback two days ago."

"As far as I know he hasn't yet arrived. Perhaps he had an errand on the way." Penelope couldn't imagine Severus Granville delaying his arrival for long. A house full of diamonds of the first water, invited just to pay attention to him, must flatter his sensibilities. She was glad she wasn't considered a candidate, and wondered if he knew Antonia had invited her to stay.

A thread of melancholy wove its way through her, but Penelope ruthlessly pushed it back. Much as she liked Antonia, she wished Sev had invited her.

Mere self-pity. She had no time for that. "This will be a most interesting visit." She spread marmalade on a slice of toast, a task she could accomplish supremely well since it was within her field of clear vision.

"Indeed," said another of the young ladies, one gowned in blue. "My mama was glad to leave for her restorative month in Bath without me. Caro's dear mama offered to chaperone us both, so my own mama may rest and recover. She says I am too lively for her peace of mind, but I don't think I'm too vivacious, do you?"

Penelope replied with a polite, "I have never noticed it," unfortunately just at the same time as Caroline was replying, "Oh my dear, you are well known for your liveliness of spirit."

Penelope looked down and addressed her toast, feeling clumsy and stupid. She heard a titter. Penelope hated these moments. Some of them lodged in her mind like a bitter thorn to prick her when she felt too complaisant, like the time she had tumbled over on the dance floor in the middle of the Queensberry rout.

She tried to think of something else and felt the presence of Antonia, warm and friendly, next to her. Antonia leaned across and muttered; "See why I want to leave here soon? I don't think I want to be close to my sister-in-law, whoever she turns out to be." Penelope suppressed a chuckle. In her friend's place, she would feel the same.

A babble of male voices outside heralded the arrival of more breakfast guests. The room fell quiet before the door was flung open. In a cacophony of voices, several male guests came in and bowed in greeting.

Penelope wished she could see that far. All she could see was a blur of color, dark, country colors, not the gaudy kingfisher colors of town. But she would know Severus anywhere, with or without her spectacles. He was the tall, dark figure in the centre of the group. Next to him, the only slightly shorter figure must be his friend Peter Worsley. The gentlemen were rarely apart, and until his recent marriage, their friend Nicholas, Lord Cardington, had formed the third member of the notorious Triumvirate.

Smiling a vague welcome, Penelope returned to her meal. They weren't here for her.

"And how are you, Miss Makepiece?" one strong, rich voice asked. She hoped her sharp gasp of shock hadn't betrayed her. Severus sounded friendly, but his manners were always impeccable.

"I'm very well, sir. It was very kind of Antonia to invite me." She was pleased to note her voice didn't tremble at all.

"She takes great pleasure in your company," came the calm reply. He turned to the others present. "Such a delight!" he exclaimed, although from his formal tone Penelope had her doubts. "So many lovely ladies in one room."

Her old feelings for him revived, stronger than ever. Penelope picked up her tea dish to cover her discomfiture. She still liked him, as well as holding warmer, more sensual feelings for him. She told herself that was all, but his strong, handsome figure, more remembered than seen at this moment, would draw any red-blooded woman to him.

Having finished her meal, Penelope rose to leave with Antonia. She had something to do but she would relish a gossip with her friend. Unfortunately, Toby decided to join them. "A sad affair," he said, once they were clear of the breakfast parlor. Chatter and gossip followed them out, the animation of male voices vying with titters and feminine trills.

"It doesn't sound sad to me," Penelope commented.

"It seems a remarkably frivolous way of choosing a life partner." Toby would like that choice, Penelope felt sure.

"It's not as if Severus hasn't known the young ladies for years," Antonia protested. Her eyes sparked in a spirited defense of her brother.

Toby regarded her gravely. "I must admire your loyalty, but beg to differ. It is well known that his lordship intends to marry before the summer is out, but he has given no preference. The wagering at the London clubs is running very high on his choice."

This didn't deter Antonia. "Oh really? Who is favorite?"

"Really, Lady Antonia!" protested their staid companion. "I don't think it has any bearing on the situation. It seems his lordship has invited every beauty that has caught his fancy, with not a sensible mind amongst them. My own choice would be for a sensible, straightforward woman with no heirs."

Antonia glanced at Penelope, whose face was impassive. "Isn't beauty a pleasant thing to have in a woman you will be expected to start a family with?"

"Lady Antonia!" Toby seemed truly shocked, Penelope noted with delight. "A gently nurtured lady would not speak of such things." He pursed his thin lips and stared ahead, studiously

27

avoiding Antonia's perceptive glance.

"I may be a maiden, but I'm not entirely ignorant, sir."

"I suppose not." Toby turned to look at Penelope again, his sudden, snappish temper resolved. "Yes, it is pleasant to think of a good-looking woman as one's wife. But I would like a partner, someone to help me with life's vicissitudes."

"Is life that hard?" Penelope said.

"It can be." Toby had a new warmth in his eyes. "I would like to think that my wife had the resilience and hardihood to weather them at my side."

Despite his reassuring sentiments that he wanted a partner, not an ornament, Penelope was not convinced. "It sounds like a joyless existence."

"Not at all, dear lady. I do think it could be most pleasant—with the right woman." He glanced at Antonia. "Lady Antonia, I do not wish to be rude, but—"

Here it comes, thought Penelope, and she wanted nothing more than not to be alone with Toby. She would have to listen to his offer eventually, but she would much rather it was later. So she clapped her hand to her mouth, and exclaimed, "Goodness, Antonia, shouldn't we be making our way to—"

"Quite right." Antonia took Penelope's arm in a firm clasp. "I'm terribly sorry, sir, but my mantua maker is coming up from town, and I must not keep the poor woman waiting. Penelope has kindly offered to keep me company, and give me her opinion. And now she might need some new clothes of her own."

Toby was forced to bow, and release them. Antonia led Penelope away, wiping imaginary drops of sweat from her forehead. "That was close."

Penelope barely suppressed a giggle. "He intends to

propose, but I would rather he didn't do it quite so soon. I want to think about it." Or relish her last days as a single woman.

"Do you want him?"

Penelope shrugged. "I won't pretend to undying love, but I know Toby. He would be a kind husband, and not demand too much of me. I know he would allow me to continue with my present life. It seems that he will inherit, if my father doesn't remarry, but even if he doesn't inherit, he has a tidy property of his own. He inherited property from his godmother, who had no one else to leave it to."

Antonia raised an eyebrow. "All the same, it's hardly a brilliant match."

Penelope gripped her friend's arm in a hug. "I'm not expected to make a brilliant match. Half society thinks I'm stupid, because they don't know how nearsighted I am, and the other half doesn't care."

Because of Antonia's mendacious excuse they made their way to her room, where they disturbed a chambermaid busy putting the room to rights. The girl scurried out after a hasty curtsey. "I don't usually come back to my room after breakfast, so we've got the servants on the hop."

"Really, Antonia, such a whisker, the mantua maker indeed." Penelope finally gave way to her laughter.

"Well, she came last week, and it was the first thing I thought of. You didn't want to be alone with Mr. Makepiece, did you?"

Penelope shook her head. "No." She reached into her pocket and found her spectacles to perch on her nose. "That's better."

Antonia surveyed her friend critically, tilting her head to one side. "It's a pity your aunt won't let you wear them all the time," she commented. "It would mean fewer headaches, and people would know what you were really like."

29

Penelope sat up straighter, her improved vision giving her the confidence she lacked in company. "She has a point. I won't attract a husband like this, and I'd be labeled an oddity."

"If you chose a more flattering style it would be an improvement, Gold rims would suit you much better than those horn ones."

"Beggars can't be choosers." Penelope's acid tones revealed her true feelings.

Antonia's dark eyebrows went up. "Beggars? Your portion is as good as mine, my dear. Probably better. You could try for Sev if you'd a mind to it."

Penelope laughed. "Well if I did, I would look very foolish in that company. I can't flirt, nor can I say things like, 'la, sir, I declare!' with anything like a straight face." She rocked with laughter at the thought of it. "Severus probably thinks of me as a confounded nuisance."

"I think he likes you." Penelope disliked the speculative look that came into her friend's eyes. She crossed the room to one of the windows, aware of the ridiculousness of her friend's speculations and wanting to distance herself from them.

Two of the ladies and a man were chasing something, running around the garden laughing, but definitely in pursuit. A mouse, perhaps? Or would the ladies pretend to be afraid of such a tiny, harmless creature?

No. When she saw their quarry, anger filled her. A helpless creature cornered by people who had no thought except for their own enjoyment.

A flash of fur, a scurry and the flick of a tail and the creature hurried under a rosebush. One lady turned and said something, then picked up her skirts and hurried towards where the animal had run. Penelope saw it again: a tiny kitten, racing for its life.

The poor little thing was scared to death. Penelope ran across the room and hurtled out of it, not waiting to excuse herself with more than, "I'll be back in a minute."

Rattling down the backstairs took a matter of moments. Penelope blessed her good knowledge of this house, gained from spending a few weeks here most summers. She burst through a servant's door into the outside world, not pausing at all to acknowledge the startled stare of a couple of laundry maids, their hands full of wet linen. She sped out to the South Front.

She ran unhesitatingly to where she'd seen the trio. They were still there, laughing and calling out to each other. "Have you seen it?" and, "Goodness, it can run fast for a little thing!"

"Where did it go?" Penelope demanded. The three young people straightened and stared at her. "Well?" She propped her hands on her hips. "How could you torment the poor thing? If it gets lost without its mother, it could die. From what I saw it was hardly old enough to leave her."

One of the girls smiled, but there was no humor in it, only superiority and a kind of indulgent sneering. "Miss Makepiece, isn't it? I believe the creature went that way." Without looking back, Penelope plunged into the high-walled garden indicated by the girl.

Knowing better than to rush, Penelope stood still and listened. All she could hear was the chatter from behind the high hedge, combined with giggles as the gentleman made a sally she couldn't quite hear. "Puss," she tried in her gentlest, most coaxing tone.

Nothing. She made a soft noise between her teeth. There was a rustle at the base of a bush to her left. Wise in the ways of cats Penelope didn't go forward, but crouched down.

There it was. A fluffy tortoiseshell, its dappled markings well disguised by the colors under the bush. It peered at her.

Penelope smiled, and slowly extended her hand. She made the noise again.

Footsteps sounded behind her. "Whoever you are, be quiet, for heaven's sake. It might run off again."

To her relief the footsteps stilled. Penelope ventured to inch a little further towards the animal, crooning gently and making a clicking noise between her teeth that seemed to hold the creature steady.

After what seemed like an age, she eased near enough to touch it. Only lightly, and she had to lie on her stomach to do it. Her light hoops crushed beneath her and she bit her lip to still the involuntary protest as stomach met whalebone. Extending her hand she managed to stroke the kitten, and feel it tremble. A renewed flash of anger shot through her. She hated bullies, however attractive they were on the outside.

She closed her hand over the kitten and drew it from its place of safety. Before she could prevent it, the little creature had stuck out its claws and raked a scratch down the side of her arm. "Ouch!"

"Allow me." A male hand appeared before her, and without thinking, she grasped it with her spare hand and allowed him to haul her to her feet.

Just her luck. Severus.

Chapter Three

They stared at each other, his hand on her arm, the wriggling kitten in her other hand. An involuntary thrill went through Penelope.

She hadn't seen Severus clearly for a long time. She'd almost forgotten how handsome he was. At least, she had tried. Dark hair, almost black, was caught back from a pale complexion, out of which his eyes burned with a searing intensity. Now she looked at them she noticed they were actually dark blue. How could she have forgotten that?

He smiled down at her, and his face held a peculiarly arrested expression, as though looking at her for the first time.

Penelope stared back, lips parted, then she realized what he must be seeing. Even at a distance, she'd been able to see him clearly. She'd located the kitten, now clawing a path down her arm, with no problem at all. "Oh no!"

She lifted her free hand to her face, but he stopped her, one hand on her arm. "I didn't know you wore spectacles."

"You're not supposed to know. Please, promise not to tell my Aunt Cecilia you saw me."

"Why not?"

Was he stupid? Just male. She gave a resigned sigh. "Because young ladies on the marriage mart aren't so blind they have to wear spectacles all the time. My family thinks my prospects will be diminished if people knew I was as blind as a bat. Or if they knew I wore spectacles."

The kitten squealed. His attention caught, Severus looked at it and seeing the damage it had caused her, reached out and took it from her. He cradled it against his chest, and it cuddled closer, mewling. Absentmindedly, he stroked it with one long finger. Penelope felt a flash of jealousy. The thought of him holding her in his arms made her body heat.

She cut her thoughts short with a decided wrench. She couldn't start that again. "You mustn't tell about the spectacles. Please?"

He seemed not to hear her. "Is that why you bump into things, and trip? Why you don't always recognize people when they greet you?"

She hung her head. "Yes."

"How is it I never knew?"

"My mama only allowed me to keep my spectacles if no man saw me in them."

His voice hardened a trifle. "You should wear them. They shouldn't stop you. Do you get headaches?"

"Sometimes." His finger lodged under her chin, urging her to look up at him. She let him study her face and tried to keep her gaze steady. Acute embarrassment filled her, and at the same time resignation. It would have to be him, finding her squatting so ungracefully on the ground, wearing her spectacles.

"It's not too bad. Perhaps a different frame, and if you got rid of this—" He flipped the end of the string which held the spectacles together on one side. "Will Makepiece allow you to wear them?"

"Toby?" She pulled away, turned to one side, then looked back at him, annoyance streaking through her. "Does everyone know he's going to propose? Is it a done deed, even before he asks?"

"I saw your father in town. He seems to think it's arranged. Why? Don't you want to marry your cousin?"

She shrugged. "He's a pleasant man, I suppose. But—"

He watched her intently. "But he's a pompous bore."

She couldn't help it; she burst out laughing. "Really, sir, you shouldn't say it!"

The corner of his mouth quirked up in a grin. "As long as you don't repeat it, I think I'll be safe."

The little bundle of fur in his hand squeaked. He looked down as though he'd forgotten, and touched it again, gently, with the edge of one finger. "We'd better restore this scrap to his mother."

"Her," she corrected him.

He looked up with a small smile. "How can you know?"

"It's a tortoiseshell; they're usually female."

An instant connection sprang up between when they exchanged smiles. Penelope was reminded of girlhood behavior, brought back to it as though the years between had meant nothing. She flushed.

He noticed. "What is it?"

She looked away, gripping her hands into fists. "When I see you, it reminds me—"

"What?" He sounded puzzled, then his statement, a moment later, held relief. "Oh, that." He laughed, and Penelope hated him for it. "That was a long time ago, Miss Makepiece. I behaved very foolishly when you spoke to me, and I didn't know how to deal with the situation. I hope we're both a little more

35

adult than that, now."

She wouldn't look at him. "I hope so too." She couldn't leave, as she dearly wanted to. She felt she owed it to the kitten to see it safe. It seemed happy enough now, nestled in Severus's arm.

She ventured to look back at his face. He was right, of course he was. She had no idea why her foolish behavior of so long ago should come back so vividly now. "I hope you don't mind me intruding on your house party."

He frowned. "Intruding? No, of course not. You're Antonia's guest, and this is as much her house as it is mine. Besides, you're leaven to the dough." She thought she had heard wrong, but before she could protest, he continued, "I'm regretting this whole idea. The house party, choosing a bride like I'm some kind of Bluebeard. I was drunk and angry when I announced, in the middle of a ball, that I intended to marry this year. Not only that, but Peter egged me on to make a list. I don't know why I let him do these things to me." His grin became more pronounced. "Boredom and too much of a sense of mischief." He gazed at Penelope and lost the grin. "Now I have a house full of vacuous, beautiful females, and I don't know what to do with them all."

"Oh, I'm sure you'll think of something," she responded without thinking, but was rewarded by a rich laugh.

"I'm sure I will. It's my own mess, and I'll have to find some way to resolve it. I thought of inviting even more people, but the staff might rebel. It's an answer, though I won't make the mistake of confiding it to Peter when I'm in my cups again." His attention returned to the kitten, which seemed to have settled in, nestling against his waistcoat. "We'll have to have those scratches seen to as well."

Penelope thought he was talking about the kitten for a

moment, then she remembered her hand and arm, and saw his thoughtful regard on the thin red lines. "It's nothing. They'll be gone in a day or two."

"Still, I'd feel better if they were seen to. Cat scratches can fester."

She moved closer to him when he moved away, whipping her glasses off when they left the seclusion of the enclosed rose garden. It attracted his attention to them again, although she'd tried to be discreet. "How does Makepiece feel about your spectacles? Will he let you wear them when you marry?"

"No. He can't think why I should need them. I'm nearsighted, so I can see to do the household accounts, nurse a babe, or sew a fine seam. That's all I'll need to do as a wife."

He was close enough for her to see him properly; his expression was calm, but concentrated. "I always knew he was an unimaginative clod."

"You shouldn't say that, sir."

"Why not? I'm no hypocrite. I'll say it to his face, if you like. Oh Lord!"

The last remark made Penelope look at him, startled, for she heard genuine dismay in his tone. He glanced at her. "You haven't noticed, have you? Three of them, bearing down on us with the determination of well-trained hounds scenting the prey. Speed up, my dear, I'll make sure you don't bump into anything!"

"I'm not that bad." She chuckled, but quickened her pace. He took her to the servants' entrance, where his admirers wouldn't follow them. The laundry maids were gone, probably to drape the wet sheets over a bush. Laundry would dry well in this heat. They passed through the sheltered yard and into the narrow passage before the kitchen.

The width of the corridor meant Penelope had to move

closer to her host. She didn't dislike it. In this confined space, she became aware of his scent. His sharp, lemony perfume was laced with something spicy and exotic, making her stomach turn in an emotion she wasn't familiar with and couldn't put a name to. When she tried to move out of the way, she bumped her shoulder on the wall. It disturbed her being this close.

He appeared unaware of her discomfiture, only glancing at her once. "Put them on There are only servants here. They won't tell."

"My aunt's maid might be about. She'll tell."

He gave her a curious look, but didn't say anything, and didn't insist she put her spectacles back on. Penelope felt foolish, but then Sev often had that effect on her. "Y-you see, if I do insist on wearing them in public, my aunt, my cousin and my father will talk and nag me into oblivion. I hate that even more than not being able to see properly. That is the real dead bore."

He opened his mouth as if to speak but a maid started down the passage and Penelope dropped back to let her pass.

The kitchen was a bustle of hot activity. The fire burned brightly, despite the heat of the day. The two small boys scurrying about attending to it were bare to the waist, their skinny torsos gleaming with sweat. Penelope looked away hastily, towards the long table where the cooks and kitchen maids were already at work preparing the evening meal.

Lord Swithland grimaced. "I don't know how they manage in this heat."

"Perhaps they're used to it."

Although everyone stopped to stare at them and bow, there was little fluster at their arrival and the servants went back to their work. Penelope became aware of a suspicion forming in her mind. "This entrance isn't strange to you."

He flushed, and then laughed. "You've caught me out. I use this entrance as a bolt-hole. I've done it since I was small and no one has ever betrayed me. I trust. You will undertake not to tell anyone?"

His confidence delighted her. "So we have each others' secrets to keep."

He smiled, intimately friendly. "Precisely." Her last, bitter memories evaporated away. They could be friends now, she was sure of it.

At the first meow, they looked down. A very large, well-kept cat snaked around his legs and a tiny bundle of fur pranced in the cat's wake.

"This is yours, I believe, madam." He bent and carefully deposited the kitten at his feet. At once, the cat, after sniffing her offspring, took the creature up by the scruff of its neck and bore it away.

Lord Swithland examined his coat, now sprinkled with hairs of white, orange and black. Since his coat was brown, none of them quite matched. A maid approached and bobbed a timid curtsey. Severus bestowed one of his charming, practiced smiles on her. "A bowl of warm water, some cloths, and—some tea, please."

Penelope felt managed. He'd given her a few of those smiles since he'd found her in the rose garden. "I should go to my room and change." Grass stains marked the front of her skirt, and a curl straggled down her neck from the once neat bun at the back. She felt dowdy and uncomfortable.

"You certainly should," he agreed, "as should I. But allow me to see to your wounds first." Taking her arm he led her to a small table at the edge of the kitchen, mercifully as far away from the fire as anyone could get in this room. Seeing that he had no intention of letting her slink away, Penelope sat in the chair he held for her. He sat in a similar hard wooden chair opposite her. A maid followed them, with a brown pot of steaming tea, a milk jug and two dishes. Not the Chelsea and Bow china allotted to the Family Rooms, but plain white china. It spoke volumes about his lordship's familiarity with below stairs. The maid placed the bowl between them, and Lord Swithland took Penelope's hand in a firm grasp, forcing her to put it in the bowl. "I think, in the circumstances, I'll pour the tea." He proceeded to do so.

Penelope was rendered temporarily speechless. She hadn't considered that the suave, aristocratic Earl of Swithland would have such a practical bent. When she imagined him, which she tried not to do too often but for the most part failed, she saw him in an elegant drawing room surrounded by languishing maidens, all staggeringly beautiful, not sitting at a plain kitchen table prosaically drinking kitchen tea. She sipped her own brew and found it good.

"You don't take sugar?" he asked. "I'm sorry, I can get some at once."

"No, I got used to it without. At school, one of my dearest friends was a little—" she broke off, searching for words, but he didn't interrupt her, instead, giving her time "—large," she settled on. "We all gave up sugar in our tea to encourage her, and I grew to like it. My mother used to call it an affectation, but she didn't stop me."

Again, that shrewd glance, making Penelope feel he understood more than she'd meant to tell him. "Do I know the maiden?"

"It would be churlish for me to tell you, but I can't resist. It was Angela Childrin."

It was worth it to see his incredulous stare. "The Cit? The Beauteous Cit?"

Smiling in triumph, Penelope nodded. Angela Childrin was enormously wealthy, due to her father's successful banking and financial activities, and very beautiful. So much so that the ton was willing to forgive her plebeian background. The unattached male members of society vied to secure her hand, but from her letters Penelope knew that Angela was fussy. She was waiting for the Right Man, and while Penelope doubted that any such creature existed, she hoped her friend would have fun looking for him.

His lordship drew a deep breath of wonder. "You did the world a service there."

"Well, the male half, anyway."

They laughed in friendly accord, and he moved to take her hand out of soak, holding one of the cloths under it. He examined the scratches through narrowed eyes, and dabbed them dry. Penelope let her hand rest in his, enjoying the warmth, feeling a link with him while he concentrated on her wounds. "I think you're right. They're only light scratches. New, sharp claws, but not deep. They'll heal in a couple of days."

She let her hand lay on the cloth while he dried it for her. She loved feeling helpless, being cared for, but was honest enough to admit that she wouldn't be able to bear it for long. Sometimes it was pleasant. Did he mean to treat his wife that way? Or would he leave her moldering in the country with his children? She wouldn't mind that so much, if this was the house.

Who was she fooling? Certainly not herself. While Swithland House was her idea of the perfect country residence, Penelope knew that waiting here for Severus to return from town would instantly convert it into hell.

Foolish thoughts. She would marry her cousin and continue to live in her father's house, which would become hers and Toby's in due course. Severus had never showed a mite of interest in her as anything but Antonia's friend, even when she had let her emotions get the better of her. Now, finally, she could put her deep embarrassment in its proper place. A childish infatuation, easily forgotten.

Looking up, she met a stare that surprised her. Curiosity, and friendship. Interest, an expression she'd never seen before on Severus. Tentatively she smiled. He smiled back. Perhaps friendship was possible, if nothing else.

Severus didn't look away, and he didn't try to hide his expression. "It's good to have a friend in the house. I hope you'll look on me in that way, Penelope."

His use of her first name nearly undid all her good intentions. She swallowed. "Yes, I should like that—Severus."

His smile told her she had done the right thing, taken the simple offer of friendship in good spirit. She guessed that friends meant a great deal to Severus, and she felt privileged to be counted among them. It might be better to be his friend than his wife. Anyone as devastatingly male as Lord Swithland wouldn't stay faithful to one woman for long and Penelope looked for unfashionable fidelity in her mate.

After she finished her tea, Penelope thanked him and assured him she could find her own way to her room.

Severus watched Penelope's departure. He poured himself another dish of tea and leaned back, studying the bustling kitchen, now back at its proper duties. The staff here were used to him by now and apart from a few glances in his direction, took little notice of him. That was why he continued to come here when he wanted a few quiet moments without anyone finding him. The kitchen staff had never let him down.

He'd invited the young ladies, their chaperones and some of

his friends down in an impulsive moment, announced it at a tedious ball after spending the first part of the evening at White's, getting mildly drunk, a process he'd continued when he reached the ball. He was tired of being courted, sometimes so blatantly it took all his ingenuity to escape and at the time he'd thought the obvious solution was to find some willing, eligible damsel and tie the knot. Drinking through the night, then making a list with his friends and giving the orders to send the invitations before he'd gone to bed and slept off his drunk had to rank as one of the worst decisions he'd ever made.

However, here he was skulking in the kitchen regretting his decision. He'd been here less than a day, long enough to recognize this party as a disaster. Now the hounds were in full cry after him and he'd be lucky to escape parson's mousetrap. Having declared his intention of securing a bride, they were all after him.

It had been a relief to see a young lady who wasn't going to faint at him, lower her eyelashes or flutter her fan. He'd avoided Penelope since that disastrous summer several years ago, unwilling to cause either of them further embarrassment, but it had been a long time since then, and Penelope had grown into a charming young lady. Except for the clumsiness, which made many people, including himself, assume she was not very bright. Well, she had amply explained that this morning. Sev couldn't believe anyone would be foolish enough to deprive her of something she so obviously needed. Those dreadful horn-rimmed affairs did nothing for her appearance, it was true, but there were ways around that. And so close to her, he couldn't avoid noticing her trim, but alluring figure. At one point in that narrow corridor leading to the kitchen he'd had an unaccountable urge to pull her close and discover what she tasted like.

He shifted his feet uncomfortably. He shouldn't be thinking

about his sister's friend in that way. It seemed wrong, somehow. And with a house full of beauties, why should it be Penelope who intrigued him?

Because she did. Her lively smile, the way she responded to him and the edge of shy uncertainty drew his desire and his protective instincts, in a combination he'd never known before. If he didn't know better, he'd imagine he was falling for her. But that couldn't be true. Could it?

He knew he should have told her something he'd learned in London, but he didn't like being manipulated, and he knew that was what was happening this time. He was supposed to pave the way. Well he wouldn't. What was troubling him now was what it would mean to Penelope. He'd not thought of that aspect of the whole affair before. After rocking London, Lord Wimbourne was about to disturb his daughter's equilibrium. She might need a friend once she heard the news.

Chapter Four

Dinner that evening was not unalloyed pleasure for Antonia or Penelope. They had to watch a bevy of young ladies flirting and gossiping, and what was more, suffer them afterwards. Their main object of attention was Severus, but there were other candidates for their attention. He'd invited enough of his cronies to make up a balanced party, and avoid the crude connotations of what was the truth of the visit. Or had been.

Watching Severus, Penelope got the feeling his attention wasn't entirely on the party, and she wondered why, even after his confession to her that afternoon. Surely this would be any man's dream, to be the centre of attention for such lovely creatures. And rich. Not one of them was without a substantial dowry, so important for familial concerns.

During the third course, she met his gaze across the table in a strangely intimate moment. She couldn't make him out completely at that distance, but she could see when he raised his glass to her. Ten pairs of eyes followed the movement, and then their owners shrugged and continued. It was well known that Penelope Makepiece was here to make up the numbers, and she was all but contracted to marry her cousin. Perhaps she was a friend of Severus, no more than that. What could he see in a plain, only moderately dowered miss with nothing to recommend her?

The next few days passed in flirtation and gossip. Bored to tears by the retelling of old London stories and speculation about this man and that, Penelope and Antonia took to excusing themselves early, to go to Antonia's room, or the Old Library to read, play frivolous games of cards, and talk. Really talk, about things that mattered. When the next war would come, for instance, or what Mr. Fox thought he was doing, resigning at a time like this. Young girls weren't supposed to think of such things, at least in the presence of men. Why they were taught this passed Penelope's understanding, because if they married a man of affairs, they would be expected to act as political hostesses, assured and knowledgeable. How could they do that if they didn't discuss such things regularly?

The Old Library was where all the good books were kept, the ones that were for reading, not for show or display. Severus owned a precious medieval missal, but that was kept locked up in the Library with other books meant for display alone. Penelope loved the old books, but she couldn't curl up with one, and mistreat it by reading it.

Severus, Peter and the rest of the guests amused themselves in the salons and drawing rooms. Sometimes Penelope heard music coming from the drawing room, and once it was dance music and laughter. She told herself she didn't care. This party wasn't for her, and she would gain no pleasure from the ridicule aimed at her by the young ladies gathered here to snare the Earl of Swithland. She enjoyed dancing, or she did when she could see properly, but in company, it was another trial to be borne.

So it was that one night they were reading at the large table in the centre of the room, heads bent over the newspaper that had arrived earlier that day, when the door opened unexpectedly. Startled, both women looked towards the door to see Severus and Peter entering.

"Ha!" Peter turned to Severus in triumph. "I told you they'd be here."

Severus smiled. "So you did." He bowed to the ladies and showed them what he held in his hand, until now hidden behind his back. A decanter full of amber liquid. "I brought a peace offering, for Antonia anyway. I know she's fond of the occasional glass of brandy."

Antonia laughed. "Sometimes, but those cats in the drawing room are looking for anything to pick on. I'll have a glass after they've gone."

"You can have one now." Peter put the glasses he held onto the table. "Miss Makepiece?" He glanced at Penelope who smiled and accepted. She liked Peter, a clever man who never talked down to her. He had helped to make some of the London gatherings more bearable for her, looking on her frequent stumbles on the dance floor as a cause for shared amusement and not ridicule. He was an active member of Parliament, and quite willing to discuss current affairs with a *mere* woman. And, as a member of the notorious the Triumvirate, he was sinfully handsome, his lithe body seeming to ripple under his elaborately fashionable clothes. More slightly built and not as tall as Severus, but exuding an air of power and control, he had never intimidated Penelope. His presence helped her to steady her mood after the shock of seeing Severus standing in the doorway.

Peter was staring at Penelope rather strangely and it was a moment before she realized what he was staring at. "Oh!"

She put her hand up to her spectacles, but Peter put his hand over hers. "Don't. I never knew you wore them. It explains a lot."

She dropped her hand. "Yes. My family won't let me wear

them in public."

"Your family members are idiots," Peter said.

Penelope was inclined to agree, in this instance at least, but it wouldn't be proper to say it, so she stayed silent. She turned back to the paper and made a comment about the coming war. Peter leaned over to see the article she was referring to, and informed her, "I don't think it will come just yet. The lines aren't yet set up properly. Give it a year or two."

"I see. I thought as much myself, but it's good to have confirmation by someone in the thick of things."

Peter laughed. "In general I prefer to deal with domestic politics, but foreign affairs will keep intruding."

The prickling of the hairs on the nape of Penelope's neck told her Severus was close. She saw his hand, holding a glass with a generous tot of brandy in it. She took it, trying not to touch his fingers and turned to him with a smile. "Trying to get me tipsy, sir?"

He grinned back. "Not at all, ma'am. That's my sister's usual dose."

Antonia's voice came from the other side of Peter. "Penelope's not as used to it as I am. What brings you here, gentlemen?"

Penelope saw Peter's grimace. "Desperation." He lifted his head from contemplation of the newspaper and gave her a self-deprecating smile. "I'm sorry, I didn't mean it to sound like that. We needed to get away from the incessant flirting. I enjoy it as much as the next man, especially when the next man is Swithland, but not at this rate. Occasionally, rational conversation is at a premium."

That put her in her place. Good enough for conversation, but not for flirting. She would have liked to flirt, just occasionally, but it seemed she wasn't the type. Shrugging, trying not to care, she turned back to the paper.

By the time she had finished her drink, the current political situation had been discussed and she was feeling light-headed, though not, by any stretch of the imagination, tipsy. So she felt safe accepting another drink and agreeing to a game of cards.

They played silver loo, for astronomical imaginary stakes. It was the best card game Penelope could remember playing. It was just as well the Old Library was situated in the old part of the house, away from the usual reception rooms, as matters became raucous as the evening went on.

Severus watched his sister and her friend in amused detachment, cheating outrageously in order to allow them to win. The game involved building suits on base cards for points, in their case thousands of pounds, and more than once Severus ignored the cards in his own hand to allow his sister or Penelope to win.

Peter had a wonderful time; he had the politician's gift of fitting in with anyone, anywhere. He was very good at it. He relaxed them into his company, made them laugh, and Penelope became at ease with him, although his acquaintance with her was of the slightest until recently. It hadn't escaped Severus's notice that Peter had shown more interest in Penelope this season in London. He, too, had been thinking along fresh lines after their friend Nick Cardington had shown the way. They were of an age, all in their thirtieth year. While they could go on as they were, seeing Nick's happiness had given both Severus and Peter pause for thought. And sooner or later, Severus knew he had to marry to make an heir. Peter, being a second son, didn't have that extra pressure. So Severus would take the plunge. He didn't think marriage would necessarily change his way of life. His rakish tendencies had palled two or three years ago, and currently he was even without a mistress, having giving his last lady her congé six months ago.

Severus grimaced. He had no hopes of the kind of happiness Nick had achieved. All he hoped for was a suitable partner, someone he could share his responsibilities with, someone he didn't find repellent with whom he could make his heirs. It wasn't much to ask, so why had all the women he invited here failed his silent tests miserably? True, they were beautiful, without exception, but one was too vapid, one too fussy, and another too silly. What was more, they all bored him to tears after about half an hour in their company and Severus considered himself reasonably easygoing. If he could tolerate his prosy Aunt Julia for hours at a time, he could surely put up with one of the beauties on offer. Over the last few days he had singled each one out discreetly, to talk with them without any interference, and found them all wanting. It was his fault, he supposed.

Certainly, Peter hadn't stopped teasing him about it. "All the choice ones are picked off when they first enter society. But you wanted someone older. Did you never wonder why these ladies were passed over in favor of their less beautiful but more intelligent counterparts?"

With a sigh, he shook off his melancholy and his feeling that he had rarely made such a foolish mistake, and turned his mind to the present. Severus didn't dwell on what couldn't be for very long. His was aware that he was fortunate, and to dwell on imagined troubles struck him as idiotic beyond measure.

He laughed and pointed out that five didn't come after three. Penelope flushed and withdrew her card to crows of laughter from Antonia, but there was no doubt Penelope was enjoying herself. Severus decided she deserved better than Toby, especially in the light of the news he had learned just before he left London for Hertfordshire. She was unconsciously attractive, with a vivacity the other women here lacked—with the exception of his sister, of course. He suspected her of hidden depths, but since their re-acquaintance was of such recent date, he had no idea if he was right. Lord knew he had been wrong before.

He played a card. He knew Penelope had the five of spades, so he gave her the four to play on, with a chorus of groans from the other two. "Favoritism." his sister protested.

"I'm always considerate to our guests. Sev turned a bland gaze to his sister. "Your glass is empty. More brandy?"

Antonia smiled. "I might as well. I'm three parts cut as it is." She giggled when he sloshed the amber liquid into her glass, then he refilled Penelope's glass too. He handed the decanter to Peter for him to help himself, since his glass was too far away. Peter quirked an eyebrow at him. Severus had no idea what he meant and gave him a blinding smile in return. Peter blinked and turned back to the game.

Antonia frowned at the cards bunched in her hand. "Where did you tell them you were going, Sev?"

"To play billiards. Some of them wanted to join us, but the duennas were too comfortable to move, so they were unable to."

Peter grinned. "Just as well since we had no intention of staying there above five minutes."

"Just enough to put them off the scent," Severus agreed.

Penelope looked up at him, meeting his gaze with a direct one of her own. "You meant to come here?"

Severus flashed her a smile. "We wanted to know what you'd been doing with yourselves, and if it was more fun. It is."

Antonia clicked her tongue. "You invited the ladies, Sev. They're your guests. We have the manners to tolerate them, but they are dam—dashed unkind to Penelope."

That made Severus frown. "How so? Are they rude to you? I hope you appreciate that Penelope is as much a guest of mine as anyone and is entitled to the same courtesy." The use of her first name had come naturally to him as much as to Antonia. When he shot a glance at Penelope, he saw her heightened color, but she showed no other signs of noticing. He had an unaccountable urge to see how far the flush went.

"They tease her. You know her family doesn't allow her to wear her spectacles in public, and she trips and stumbles as a result, and ignores people who try to acknowledge her because she doesn't always recognize them immediately." She addressed Penelope next. "You should insist on wearing them."

Penelope smiled. "It would cause more trouble and give them more things to criticize. I am of the fondest hope that my husband, whoever he may be, will look on the situation a little more pragmatically and let me wear them. Toby doesn't like them, but he would come around if I put my mind to it, I'm sure."

"Is it a done thing, then?" Severus asked abruptly. "Are you to marry him?" For some reason the thought saddened him immeasurably.

Penelope shrugged. "No, but he will ask me soon, and there's no one else in prospect."

Severus looked up, catching her attention. "Don't accept him just yet."

"Why?"

Severus hesitated, unwilling to spoil the friendly atmosphere. "Just let's say I have a feeling. Fob him off, at least until your father gets here."

He changed the subject by putting a slew of cards on the table. "My game, I think."

While the others were exclaiming over his perfidy, Severus

caught Penelope's glance and winked. She smiled back at him and the exchange of that intimacy made him absurdly pleased with himself. The other young ladies teased Penelope, they spoke disparagingly of her to him, but he chose to ignore it. She deserved better than that. He should have warned them not to speak about her like that. He would see to it that her stay here was a little more pleasant. He owed her that at least, for his thoughtlessness. He hadn't considered her wants and needs when he planned this gathering, although he'd known she was coming, and she was as much his guest as the others in the house.

When they counted the tallies at the end of the evening, Severus, much to his surprise, found himself several thousand guineas to the good. He stretched, and rose from the table when the ladies stood, noticing Penelope's slight stagger. He held out his arm. "Will you trust me to see you to your chamber?"

In the sudden pause, Penelope caught hold of his arm. "Thank you, sir, I may need it." Her reaction was more natural than if she'd been sober, and Severus, far more used to strong drink, knew that if they had continued he might have been forced to carry her to the haven of her own room. He had called a halt just in time.

After dousing the candles the four left the room together in perfect accord and, in Antonia's case, yawning hugely. Peter elected to see her to her room and in some amusement Severus watched them sway up the corridor. He trusted his friend not to take advantage of his sister. Whatever his reputation, and it was a lot darker than Severus's own, Peter would never seduce an innocent, particularly one who had passed her personal capacity for strong drink.

He spared a glance for the woman leaning rather heavily on his own arm. He could trust himself, but only just. In his present state, she seemed very inviting, with or without the spectacles, which, he had to admit, were not at all becoming on her pale face. She needed something more delicate to enhance her elfin looks. Gold, perhaps.

They strolled to her room in perfect, amicable silence. Outside, Severus steadied her by holding her upper arms and looking into her face. Penelope stared back and Severus's sense of time ebbed away. She smiled slightly, her full mouth curving invitingly. Unaware of his movement, Severus bent his head and pressed his lips to hers in a hard, swift kiss. "Thank you for a wonderful evening. Good night, Penelope."

Her eyes snapped open, and the woozy look left them. Severus waited, and watched her smile.

"Thank you. Good night."

Before he could move, she had opened the door of her room and slipped inside. He stood, staring at the panels for a moment before turning and making his way to his own room.

Chapter Five

"Penelope! Penelope!"

Startled from sleep, Penelope sat bolt upright in bed. "Why, Antonia, whatever is the matter?"

Antonia, fully dressed, gasped, "Your papa is here!"

Penelope reached across to the nightstand and picked up the large pocket watch she kept there, then her spectacles. Eight o'clock. She usually woke earlier than that but they'd had another late evening, once they had retired to the privacy of Antonia's chamber. She had spent a quiet few days since that memorable evening in the library recovering from the effects of imbibing more than she was used to, and from her own tangled feelings.

She'd been prepared to pretend to forget the kiss, but she remembered it, relived it, as though it were new and fresh. Severus Granville was never, could never be a friend, because she wanted him. It wasn't a new realization, but older now, Penelope was confident she could cope with it better. He wasn't for her, any more than ten years ago. At least now, she could spare them both by keeping her guard up, pretending to mere friendship and retaining her dignity.

"Why shouldn't Papa be here?" she demanded of her friend. "What is there in that? Severus invited him, after all and he said he'd be here after attending to a few matters in town."

Antonia stopped, and gave her friend a strange look. "He wants to see you as soon as possible."

Penelope sighed, knowing her peace was at an end. "Then could you call for my maid, please?"

Penelope waited until her maid appeared then made her toilet. She didn't hasten, but neither did she linger and in half an hour she was ready, dressed in a light primrose silk which suited her dark coloring and was light enough for a warm summer day. Penelope studied her appearance in the mirror, then, with a grimace, took off her spectacles and slid them into her pocket.

It was a little early for breakfast, but fortified by a dish of chocolate and some bread and butter, Penelope sallied forth to meet her father. What could have startled Antonia so much in his arrival that she woke her? There was only one way to find out.

By dint of asking a maid, Penelope discovered that her father was in the Blue Drawing Room, awaiting the presence of his daughter. This was at the end of the corridor on the floor below her, so Penelope descended the marble staircase and continued on her way.

For the second time that day, she was startled, this time by Severus, who erupted from a door in front of her. "Miss Makepiece."

Despite the wild throb of her heart, caused in part by his sudden appearance, Penelope was able to command a smooth countenance. She hadn't seen him this close in days. "Good morning, sir." She bobbed a small curtsey of greeting. "I'm afraid I must go straight to my father."

To her surprise, he flushed. "Yes, I know." He hesitated, holding her attention with his arresting eyes. She waited, although he seemed unwilling to go on. "In London I discovered something your father is about to tell you. Please be assured I didn't keep the knowledge from you for any other reason than that I thought it was his place to tell you, not mine. If you wish, I'll discuss it with you afterwards." Abruptly he held out his arm, and with a surprised arch of her eyebrows, Penelope accepted his escort to the Blue Drawing Room. He left her there, and she went inside on her own.

The room was empty of servants. Only her father was within, accompanied by two people Penelope knew only slightly. By his side sat a dark lady, her hair smoothly drawn back from a broad, white forehead, her dark eyes expressionless at this distance. Behind the sofa they occupied stood a gentleman, similarly dark. It was the coloring that told Penelope they were the Spanish brother and sister occasionally viewed in London's ballrooms. Penelope wished she could see them properly to be sure of her identification.

Penelope made her curtsey. "Ah, my dear." Her father didn't rise to greet her, and neither did the lady. That meant she outranked Penelope. Strange, because she hadn't before. "I would like to introduce you to your new mama. My dear, this is my daughter Penelope. Penelope, this is Marcela, Lady Wimbourne, your new mama."

Penelope sank into another curtsey, her bowed head hiding her stunned expression. Her father introduced her to Don Alfonso Ortiz Escobedo, her new mama's brother. She'd met him before, but not in this capacity. He stared at her expressionlessly and she stared back, her mind racing but her face clear. All she could distinguish at this distance was the dark eyes, hair and long, pale face, but no nuances of expression. The poses of the brother and sister were still and informal, which made them more difficult to read. Many people betrayed themselves by gestures or poses she could interpret, when she wasn't wearing her spectacles and couldn't discern expressions at a distance. She'd put his air of intensity and his excessive formality down to his foreign bearing. Don Alfonso was above average height, taller than her father but not as tall as Lord Swithland. He stood unmoving. "How do I address you, sir?"

"Don Alfonso will do. I am *hidalgo*, like one of your barons or baronets, but my title is very ancient." His English was very good, with a hint of an accent added charm to whatever he said.

Penelope's mind reeled as though she had drunk too much. Trying to take everything in hurt.

"I thought Lord Swithland would have broken the news to you," her father said. Penelope knew he would be watching her closely, for any sign of dissent. Lord Wimbourne was a stickler for good manners. Penelope always had to stand in his presence until bidden to sit, although he never kept her waiting for long. Why had he done this, married this lady so precipitately?

"I think his lordship considered it your perquisite, sir." She didn't want to get Severus into trouble and knew as she was thinking it that her childish fear of her father had come to the fore. Her father's opinion couldn't matter to the earl.

The baron's lips tightened. "I had hoped to make my wishes clear to him but there is no harm done, after all. You may sit, my dear."

Penelope spread her skirts and sat, her attention all on her father, her mind spinning. What had caused him to do this? There was no clue in what she could see before her. It could be love, or the desire for an heir. Penelope thought of her cousin. Poor Toby. He might yet be supplanted, when he considered the inheritance all but settled.

"I am delighted to meet you, ma'am," she said to her father's new wife. "I hope you'll be happy with us."

At last the lady spoke. Her voice was low and musical, with

the same enchanting accent as her brother. "I am sure I will, Miss Makepiece."

"Penelope."

"Penelope." The word sounded strange in the accents of Spain.

Penelope desperately wanted to get away, to think this through, but she had no chance. Her father sounded formal, but kind. "I have desired my sister–in-law and her son to attend us here but I wanted to discuss another matter with you before they arrive."

Penelope folded her hands in her lap and bowed her head, the epitome of the submissive daughter. Inside she was starting to come to terms with the new situation.

"Has Mr. Makepiece proposed marriage to you yet?"

"No sir, although I believe he intends to do so."

Then her father said something most unexpected. "Before my marriage I most particularly desired you to accept his proposal. You were aware of this?"

"Yes sir." Though he had still left the final decision up to her.

"Now it is not so important. You may accept or reject him, as your fancy takes you now. Be assured I'll abide by your wishes. It is my desire to see you happy in your choice."

Penelope looked up, suppressing her desire to exclaim in relief. Until this moment, she hadn't realized how much the proposed marriage was depressing her. Family expectation had weighed heavily on her shoulders, and she knew, since no other better prospect offered, she would have accepted Toby. Now, with the weight taken away from her, she could freely admit to herself that she didn't want to marry Toby at all, even if it meant she lived for the rest of her days as a spinster.

Her father regarded her. "I think you may look higher for your husband, if you wish it. I still insist on being the primary instigator of your marriage, and that I believe it should take place soon because of your age." As if six and twenty put her in her dotage. "From the nature of the company here it would seem that you are in the ideal place."

Penelope disagreed, but she said nothing. She was a sparrow next to all the brightly colored finches on display here. None of the gentlemen paid her the kind of attention they bestowed on the female guests. Her relief at being unchained from Toby was replaced by a real fear of who else might enter the picture. Toby was kind and considerate, if prosy and affected by the male desire to control. There were many worse prospects than him on the market. "I will do my best to please you, sir. Be assured I won't choose anyone unsuitable."

"I know you will only choose someone appropriate." This wasn't said kindly, but with a complacent air.

Rebellious thoughts chased themselves around Penelope's head. So far, she had decided within herself that if she refused Toby nothing would force her to marry him, but she had nothing else to rebel against. Now he had taken even that from her. She felt foolish for even thinking it.

After a peremptory knock, the door opened to admit her aunt and cousin. Cecilia and Toby had no more idea of the reason behind the summons that Penelope had, but now she could sit back and watch their stunned amazement as they met the new member of the family. Don Alfonso watched, bowed when required but took no other part in the proceedings. Penelope had the feeling he was watching her. It made her uncomfortable.

Cecilia turned to sit next to her, and Penelope got a good look at her frozen, furious expression. This must be humiliating to her. She didn't dare imagine how Toby was feeling. He didn't depend on her for his security, he had a tidy little estate of his own but all his hopes of a title lay in the dust. She didn't look at him.

"I shall of course make arrangements to return home after our visit here," Mrs. Makepiece said. "You won't need my chaperonage for Penelope any more."

Lord Wimbourne smiled and inclined his head graciously. "Your help has been invaluable, madam, especially with Penelope. It is greatly appreciated."

The atmosphere had frozen so much Penelope shivered. She longed to leave so she could go somewhere quiet and think over what this would mean to her. Her new stepmother was young enough to have an heir. What Penelope's relationship with her would be remained to be seen.

She sat through polite enquiries of the new Lady Wimbourne's health, a discussion of the pleasures of Wimbourne Hall, and even a few comments on the weather. All the time the real issues were circumvented. Penelope sat, took part in the meaningless conversation by rote and watched, as much as she could. She would have loved to have worn her spectacles so she could see the expressions on the faces, instead of vague blurs. And she wanted to study her stepmother properly. Did she look kind? Penelope had no way of telling. But she would.

After discussing the weather a pause fell in the conversation, in which Penelope asked, "Did you see Mr. Grey in London, Papa?"

"Better than that," Lord Wimbourne said, "I brought him with me. He cannot stay for long, but I trust you will find his services useful while he is here."

For the first time since she'd entered the room, Penelope

was happy. At least she would have that. As soon as she could, she excused herself, saying she would bespeak tea for the company.

She received another shock when she stepped outside, and found that Severus was waiting for her.

"A word." He drew her into a small anteroom. She followed, curious to know what he wanted.

Severus went over to the window and stared out over the park for a moment before turning round, so swiftly that the full skirts of his coat followed the movement, curling around his legs before settling in well-ordered folds. "Miss Makepiece, you are aware I knew of this."

Penelope nodded. Severus bit his lip, and if Penelope had not known of his self- confidence, she could have sworn he was nervous. "Your father made me aware of the situation before I came down here, and I think he expected me to prepare you for it." He stared at a spot somewhere above her head, making Penelope want to turn and see what fascinated him. "I refused. Perhaps I was wrong." He looked at her then. "Put them on. No one will see you."

Penelope groped in her pocket and found her spectacles. Only when she had them on did she realize her sight was blurred with more than nearsightedness. She turned away, but felt his hand on her elbow. "No, it's all right. I won't tell anyone. It's bound to be a shock to you. I feel guilty now, seeing you like this. I should have told you, shouldn't I?"

She shook her head, blinking away the tears. "No, you're right, sir. My father would have liked me to know beforehand because he hates unpleasantness, but it was not your concern. It's a shock. I never thought he'd marry again, especially after—" The tears came then, but she fought them back.

"Your mother?" he murmured gently. "Come and sit down."

He drew her to a small sofa set at right angles to the window.

Unresisting, she allowed him to sit down with her. Severus and Antonia had a strong sense of honor, and they were enough alike for her to know she could trust him not to tell her story abroad, perhaps laugh at her. She had to tell someone. "Yes. My mother died just over two years ago. She and my father were never close, but I never dreamed—"

"Nor, I suspect, did he," Severus said dryly. "I think this is what is known as a *coup de foudre*. He's fallen for her, hook, line and sinker."

Penelope turned to him, a new fear clutching at her heart. "Do you think she ensnared him?"

Severus smiled, and shook his head. "I think there is only the brother, and he seems to have a great influence over her. I did a little investigation when I knew which way the wind blew. She is—or was—a wealthy Spanish lady, who appeared in town last season. She wasn't angling for a husband, at least not obviously, although she is lovely enough to have men scurrying for her."

"How old do you think she is?"

He considered, a small crease appearing between his brows. "No more than thirty-two or three, I think."

"I can't believe he's done this." The words left her involuntarily.

He laid a hand over hers, where it lay on her knee. She accepted it as a token of comfort, but she liked the warmth and sense of companionship it gave her. "I think you must learn to accept it."

"My father says he wants to see me married soon, although not necessarily to Toby. Before, he wanted the match because it would combine the heir and the fortune, but he must be considering making an heir, because he wants me out of his way."

"Well you can be thankful for that." His hand still rested on hers. She didn't attempt to move it, feeling the warmth of friendliness as a comfort. "I can think of few worse fates than being allied to that prosy bore Toby Makepiece."

She turned a startled face to him, to see a mischievous grin lighting his features. "There, that's better. You're beginning to see the advantages."

She shook her head. "I'm still very confused." She gazed at him, and his smile faded, as they stared at each other. Penelope became aware that he was moving closer to her, his head lowering, but then he closed his eyes and pressed his lips to her temple, and moved away again.

"I hope you'll think of yourself as our friend. Antonia and mine, that is." He got to his feet, stretching out his hand to help her up.

"I should like that."

He grinned. "Good. I have few close friends, you know, and none of the opposite sex. They all seem to want one thing from me. Perhaps I haven't the knack." He moved towards the door, and held it open for her to pass through. "I should like at least one female friend."

She wasn't at all sure he meant it, although she thought it very kind of him. "Thank you."

Before she left the room, he stretched a hand up to her face. Startled, Penelope moved back, but then realized what he was about. Gently he removed her spectacles and handed them to her. "Don't want you getting into trouble."

Penelope smiled, her heart lighter than when she stepped into the room. If friendship was all she could have with Severus, then she'd take it. Gladly. Well, almost gladly.

The first thing she did was to find a maid and ask for tea served to her father and her new stepmother. She asked the same maid where she could find Mr. Grey, and discovered he was in the Old Library. The geography of Swithland House still defeated her on occasion, with or without spectacles.

At the large central table—that table Penelope remembered from a memorable evening the week before—sat a middle-aged man of formidable appearance, who stood when Penelope entered, and held out his hand in welcome, his stern features breaking into a smile of genuine pleasure.

Unlike the gentlemen of fashion presently about the building, Mr. Grey didn't kiss Penelope's hand, but shook it warmly. Penelope bade him sit down again and took a seat close to him. "Mr. Grey, can you tell me something of what happened with my father?"

"He's in love," Mr. Grey told her without preamble. His craggy face seemed quite at ease, the light eyes calm.

"He wants an heir."

"Indeed he does, ma'am, but I believe that is secondary to his decision to remarry. He has nothing against Mr. Makepiece, you understand, but he would prefer the heir to be of his blood."

"Poor Toby." Penelope exclaimed, but her face was clear. She groped in her pocket for her spectacles.

"I venture to think that he will survive," Mr. Grey said. A suspicious twinkle in his eyes belied his stern appearance.

"Toby thought he was to marry me, you know. I'm sure he was waiting for Papa to arrive so that he could propose then arrange the match. He expected to be affianced, perhaps married by the time we left this house. Lord Swithland has a particularly fine chapel, and he probably thought to make use of it." She gave Mr. Grey a suspicious look. "Is that why Papa

65

brought you?"

Mr. Grey grinned, and the creases down both cheeks disappeared into the smile. "I think his lordship may have something else in mind. I agreed to come because it gave me a chance to review the portfolio with you."

Penelope clapped her hand to her mouth. "Oh Mr. Grey, pray forgive my appalling manners. I quite forgot to ask about your family."

"Perhaps because you knew I wouldn't come if there was anything amiss," he replied, still grinning. "They are all well, thank you, Miss Makepiece."

"I'm glad to hear it." Penelope turned to the papers that lay on the table before them. "I'm glad you brought this, as well. I've been pining for something to do. I can't spend all the time with frou-frou and flirting. Lord Swithland means to take a bride, you know, and the house is full of frivolous females. He just hasn't decided who it is to be yet."

Feeling much lighter at heart, despite the staggering news she'd received, Penelope prepared to absorb herself in work. Her nearsightedness was a blessing sometimes, as it facilitated close-up work like the columns of figures she perused now.

Lord Swithland was worried. He'd missed Penelope for most of the day, and he was concerned that she might be in some corner sobbing her heart out. While certain he wasn't in any way emotionally attached to the chit, he would feel much better if he knew she wasn't badly affected by the news of her father's remarriage. His brief interview with her earlier had shown him her self-control, but under it all, he had seen the bewilderment. He shouldn't have let her go off on her own. He wished the hand gripping his arm with such determination was Penelope's, but it was, instead, Miss Trente.

Miss Trente showed an irritating inclination to cling, but after all, he had invited her. She had accosted him while he was scouring the garden for Penelope, trying to appear as if he were taking a stroll in the bright sunshine, and he was obliged to squire her about for some time. Feeling an internal imp nudge him, he asked her, "Do you like my house, Miss Trente?"

She turned eyes of swimming blue up to him. Not one look at the house. "Oh above all things, sir! So magnificent an aspect! Such beautifully proportioned rooms!"

"It is, isn't it? What would you do to it? I ask because you and your mama are considered arbiters of taste by most of Society." He added the caveat hastily, unwilling to lead her too far into supposition.

"Perhaps the large salon may be refurbished. The furnishings are beautiful, but not quite in the current mode." She considered, while Sev wondered about the plight of the room called by a recent guidebook "the most beautiful in all England." Still, he had to concede to her that it was set up in the last century, so he supposed some people might consider it not modish. Miss Trente chattered on, and Sev realized her plans for his house were more developed than he liked. "Some of the bedrooms might benefit from some improvement. Not the one you have allotted to me, *dear* Lord Swithland, but one or two of the others might benefit from a woman's touch."

Sev contemplated the ruin of the house he loved. It was true he had plans for some of it, but the rooms Miss Trente considered worthy of refurbishment did not coincide with his. "The music room?"

"Ah yes, that room is exquisite."

Privately Sev considered it gloomy, and he couldn't help but notice that very little music was actually played there.

So much for taste. While Miss Trente no doubt had

excellent taste, it didn't coincide with his own. He studied her while she chattered on about his house. She was ethereally lovely with eyes that could take a man's breath away. Her figure was luscious, the skin soft and white. She caught him looking and smiled, before she took a deep breath so her breasts swelled above the tight lacing of her stays.

The movement was so deliberate it repelled Sev. She was enticing him to take hold, inciting him to take dalliance a step further. Normally he would be delighted to engage in a little saucy play with a young lady so beauteous, but he was not at all sure that was what he looked for in a wife and this time he would be playing for real. Who knew how long he would keep her away from the bucks? What existed beneath the soft, enticing exterior? Very little, he suspected, and he knew he wouldn't be satisfied with what this lady offered for long. Taking her to bed would be no hardship, but he knew, from his experiences with less respectable beauties, that it took more than physical loveliness to make a satisfactory bed partner. In fact, the lady with whom he'd had the longest connection was not considered a great beauty, but she was one of the most sought after courtesans in London. Intelligence, humor and a sense of the ridiculous easily compensated for any lack of pulchritude. Perhaps it was unfair, but it proved to Severus that he'd made a mistake in his requirements for a bride. He wanted more than beauty and breeding in a wife. He wanted intelligence and companionship too.

This thought startled Sev into stopping in his tracks, causing Miss Trente to stare up at him in wonder. For a moment, those amazing eyes drew him in and he moved closer, then, aware of where that would lead, he took a breath to steady his nerve and moved back again. He brought the easy smile to his face, and begged her pardon. "I must have stumbled."

His explanation mollified Miss Trente, but it gave Sev the opportunity to change direction and take her back to the house. He decided on a little flirtation, then he'd steer her back to the house, where he could find another person to keep them company. In short, lose her without losing his manners.

"Miss Trente, how do you feel about a man deliberately choosing his wife like some kind of latter-day Bluebeard?"

She laughed as if he'd made some kind of joke, whereas in reality he'd only spoken aloud his discomfort with this whole gathering. "Why, when one has as much to offer as you, dear Lord Swithland, it is not surprising that ladies vie for your hand! Nor surprising that you would wish to find the best candidate to help you in your life's work."

That sounded more interesting. If she understood the work involved in running this estate, there might be hope for her yet. However, she rattled on. "I do think, though, that some of your guests are a little less than you might expect. I collect that Miss Makepiece was invited to keep dear Lady Antonia company?"

Severus bit his lip and shame swept through him when he recollected he'd thought just that. He couldn't believe his stupidity and arrogance, in thinking he could go ahead with this misguided house party, and could only recall that he was well into his cups when he'd thought of it, and then plans had somehow been made around him. "She was invited because both my sister and I enjoy her company."

Miss Trente gave one of her tinkling laughs, making Severus yearn to hear someone laugh from real amusement. "As I thought. She can hardly be a serious contender for your hand." The last time Severus had heard the word contender, it had been in reference to an organized fist fight. Come to think of it, that wasn't entirely inappropriate here.

Miss Trente snuggled a bit closer to him, and tightened her

hold on his arm. "Miss Makepiece does not possess the level of refinement necessary for mistress of such a beautiful estate as yours, my lord. Nor the intelligence. Her social behavior borders on the unacceptable, certainly laughable. Let me tell you about an incident last season..." She recounted a series of incidents. Penelope going the wrong way in a dance, falling over her skirts, ignoring people she should have recognized. Severus tried to quicken his steps in his efforts to find someone else to turn the cozy twosome into three. Preferably more. Where was Peter hiding himself?

Her spiteful gossip about Miss Makepiece, ridiculing her and laughing at her shortcomings, made him even more determined to avoid her. And his sense of shame deepened when he realized he must have given her reason to assume he'd enjoy the stories she recounted. Or maybe she didn't understand the line between wit and cruelty. Many people didn't, in this age of excoriating satire and banter, but he would not have one of his guests traduced in such a way. His gentle reminder, "Miss Trente, Miss Makepiece is a guest in this house. Pray remember that," was met with a pretty blush and a quick apology, but he could accept neither of them as heartfelt.

He was satisfied that Miss Makepiece was not in the garden; he would search the house. Not in any definite way, of course, just a stroll through his house. Perfectly acceptable.

It took longer than he could have imagined to rid himself of Miss Trente. Although charming in a London ballroom, longer doses of her proved more difficult to abide. He needed to think. This revelation was new to him, something he had to ponder. He had been brought up with the notion that a wife was either a partner, to help him in the estate, or a beautiful decoration, but her main purpose was to provide heirs. While he still wanted this, he realized that he wanted more. More than friendship, more than a competent manager, more than a mother to his children. He wasn't just an earl, he was a man, and he wanted a wife who would truly be his other half. The revelation in the garden was his own road to Damascus.

An hour later, walking along the corridor above the main State Rooms, Peter accosted Sev. Peter wasn't an unwelcome companion, because Severus knew he could send his friend about his business if he wished without any fear of offence. "I'm looking for Miss Makepiece."

"So am I," Peter answered. "I've met Lord Wimbourne, and I know what's afoot. Whatever possessed the man?"

"Love," Severus said. "Have you seen the way he looks at his new wife? Penelope's aunt is convinced he did it to make an heir, but I doubt that."

Peter nodded, his brow creased in thought. "I hope it turns out better than his last marriage."

Severus glanced at him, eyebrow quirked, and then continued to stride along the corridor. "Was it the lack of an heir?"

"Most people assumed so. They spent a lot of their time apart. She became enceinte enough times, but couldn't carry to term, except for the one girl."

"Penelope."

"Yes, Penelope." They paused while Severus tried the door to a room. Empty.

"I saw you with Caroline Trente a little while ago."

Severus frowned. "I couldn't shake her off."

"Severus—" Severus turned to Peter when he heard the new, graver tone in his friend's voice. "I heard something at breakfast this morning. I was skulking and eavesdropping, I'm afraid. You might say that comes naturally to a politician." They shared a grin. "But in fact I was approaching the dining room when I heard some interesting snippets. There's a plot afoot."

"Good Lord!"

Peter continued. "A trap. The first one to get you alone is to try for you. You enjoy pretty women, Severus, you're an incorrigible flirt, but in this situation it could be fatal. They will take every word you say as gospel. You'll steal a kiss and you'll be caught. One of the others will always be nearby to witness the indiscretion and try to take it further. I'd like to wager that Annabelle Rivers was somewhere in the vicinity."

Severus remembered the way Caroline Trente had thrust her breasts at him and he shuddered. True, they looked most enticing, but not worth the price. He held out his hand, feeling a surge of gratitude. "Thank you, Peter. I owe you a favor."

Peter shook his hand heartily. "Never doubt I'll take you up on it, one day if I need it. Take care."

"You too," Severus reminded him. "You might be a younger son, but you're not a negligible prize."

Peter grimaced. "I'm keeping myself busy with Elizabeth Wisheart. She has no more wish for marriage than I do. I think, while we're here, that there's more safety in numbers for us both." Elizabeth Wisheart was a merry widow who had declared herself more than happy with her current situation. Peter had had an on-off relationship with her for years.

Severus pondered his problem. "I have no idea how to extricate myself from this particular problem. It's well known why this house party was arranged." So he could choose a bride. Only the willing and the hopeful had been invited. Sev made a moue of distaste. How vain of him.

"We all make mistakes, dear boy. We'll get out of this one as we've managed to get out of all of the others." Peter moved away. "I'll look for Penelope downstairs. I'll send word if I find her." Severus heard his brisk steps back up the corridor.

He stared out of the window, over the lovely prospect of the Home Park. Even at this elevated position, he owned the land as far as he could see. At least two of the young ladies present wanted *this* rather than him. They wouldn't be difficult to scare off. All he would have needed to do was make it clear that he was violently in love with them, and they would have fled back to London before the week was out, not wishing for the commitment involved in a relationship like that. Not possible now, with the plan they had concocted, but it would have been fun to try it.

With a careless shrug he turned away, and continued on his errand. For some reason it was some time before he thought of trying the Old Library, then the solution became obvious to him. How had he forgotten that evening they'd spent there?

Drawn to the room by the sound of laughter, he opened the door on a scene of merriment. Two heads bent over a sheet of paper, one male, and one female. Sev knew the female one, but to his knowledge, he'd never seen the male before.

The laughter stopped abruptly. They lifted their heads and stared at Severus who, although he owned the library, felt like an intruder.

Penelope got to her feet, and so did the man. She performed the introductions smilingly, and Sev met Mr. Thomas Grey, Lord Wimbourne's man of business. He regarded the tall, thin man with suspicion. What were they laughing at, and so soon after Penelope had heard the news about her father's marriage? He'd expected to find her tearful, huddled in a corner somewhere. He glared at Mr. Grey, who looked down at the jumble of papers littering the table.

"May I know what you are about?" It sounded intrusive, but he couldn't help that. He couldn't imagine what they were up to. It amounted to impropriety, a gently born lady entertaining a gentleman in private. It might be that the gentleman was older than the lady, but by the look of him, he wasn't in his dotage. Severus felt a jolt of something he was hard put to identify, but it felt suspiciously like jealousy.

However, Penelope didn't seem in the least put out by the request and sat down again, motioning to a chair by her side. Obediently Sev took it and Mr. Grey retook his seat on her other side.

"Papa agreed long ago that he had no head for business," Penelope explained, "and he agreed to let me take a turn at it. Only with spare money, you understand, money that would otherwise go into the bank and fester there." Her grimace showed what she thought of that. "Of course, I cannot undertake the investments myself, but as it happens Mr. Grey, although his profession is the law, takes quite an interest himself."

"Purely amateur, my lord," Mr. Grey hastened to add. "What Miss Makepiece is too modest to tell you is that she has quite a talent for speculation."

Sev stared at her, fascinated. "Hidden depths, Miss Makepiece?" He was also pleased that she had made no move to take off her spectacles when he'd entered the room. It showed she'd come to trust him, to that extent at least.

To his delight, Penelope blushed a pretty shade of pink. "It's just common sense." She picked up a piece of paper and studied it. "If we take the prices of the stock over time we can deduce quite a bit about future performance. Taken with the current state of the market and the general state of society we can refine our predictions and buy with reasonable confidence."

"Do you ever lose?" Sev was fascinated, not only with learning more about Penelope, but by the subject. He had investments, but his man of business in London took care of the details for him and had always given a satisfactory return on his money. It had never occurred to Sev to take more of an interest. But it seemed Penelope had.

Penelope kept her attention on the document she held. "Oh yes, we frequently lose, but we balance the losses with other stocks so the loss isn't so great. It's a fool who sinks his whole capital into one venture." She picked up a quill from an inkpot on the standish in front of them and made a note in the margin.

"Unless the fool is a visionary," Sev pointed out.

"It doesn't work in the stock market," Penelope said firmly.

Mr. Grey added his mite. "We do not venture our whole capital on risky stock, but some proportion of it is there, because that is where the greatest profits are found." He riffled through the stack of papers until he found the one he wanted, and then pushed it across to Severus. "This, for instance, is a diagram of how well the coconut stock is doing. There's a little South Sea island that seems to have coconut production down to a fine art. We sank some money into the trading company concerned, but only an amount we can afford to lose."

Sev studied the document. A red line of ink staggered like the path taken by a drunken ant across the paper from left to right. Penelope leaned over him, showing him the line. "This is time and this is price," she explained, pointing out the axes drawn along the side and bottom of the paper.

In a blinding flash, Sev understood. He saw the meaning of the graph. "My word!" He picked up another sheet and studied it. "What's this show?"

Penelope took the paper from his hands and turned it the right way around. "It's more moderate, you see. Cotton in the Americas."

"I see." Sev's hand went up to stroke his chin, his habit

when in deep thought. He looked up. Penelope's bespectacled countenance shone with intelligence. "This is fascinating. How long do you stay, Mr. Grey?"

"A few days only," Mr. Grey said. "I have matters to attend to in Town."

Sev nodded. "May I sit in on a few of these meetings? Please feel free to say no if I would be in the way. I don't want to stop any discussions."

"Please do." Penelope and Grey said at once, then looked at each other and laughed. Sev watched, and got the urge to be on the same terms with his sister's friend as Antonia was. It would be pleasant to have a female he could call friend. Particularly if it was Penelope.

This revelation rocked him. The realization that he wanted his wife to be more than ornament and beautiful breeding machine was so recent he was still pondering it. Then the thought that Penelope was in fact an attractive girl, and once her sight was corrected, no more clumsy, and more intelligent than anyone else was another shock. As was the desire to know her, understand her and what she liked.

How these two facts could be connected would take Sev a little time to work out. For now, he contentedly watched these two people discuss and decide what to do with their portfolio. From what he understood, Penelope held one that contained monies from her father and Mr. Grey held another one, but the holdings, although separate, resembled each other a great deal. His appreciation of Penelope's intelligence rose rapidly. Occasionally, she would break off a discussion to explain a point to him.

By the end of the session, Sev was hooked. "Of course we are careful," Penelope said. "If we were to risk more of our stock on risky ventures we would make more money, but we would also lose a lot more. Do you remember what happened in '22?"

"The South Sea Bubble?"

Penelope nodded. "The very same. It brought down the whole market and people panicked, selling everything. The thing to do in that market is to minimize your holdings then hang on, making sure they aren't just paper stocks. They do seem to come up a little after the initial panic is over."

"Has it ever happened since?"

"Not in such a bad way, no," said Grey, "but my guess is that it will happen again. Not soon, because we have the prospect of war."

"War is always good for the markets."

Sev was appalled and fascinated in equal measure by Penelope's words. He felt himself at the start of a fascinating new venture. He decided to try to learn more, and permission given, asked when they decided to meet again.

"If Miss Makepiece is willing, she may wish to give you some private tuition," said Grey, adding, with a deprecating grin, "She has far more patience than I do."

Penelope flushed, but accepted the compliment. "It would be an honor. And a pleasure." She wouldn't meet Sev's eyes, but stared down at the paper in front of her. Sighing, she took a sensible watch from her pocket. "I think we must stop before we're missed. I'm supposed to meet my new mother after lunch."

With a shock, Sev remembered why he had sought her out in the first place. "I thought you might be overset by the news, but this—" with a careful sweep of his arm he indicated the jumble of papers, "—took it out of my mind entirely."

Penelope began to pick up the sheets and put them into some semblance of order, sorting through them to see which belonged to which portfolio. "It does that to me, too."

They said no more until Mr. Grey had collected his pile of notes and left. Sev showed no inclination to follow him, but turned in his chair to face his guest. "I hope the news about your family hasn't distressed you any further? I shouldn't have left you so soon."

"Not really." She lifted her head to meet his gaze. "I didn't expect it, but now I think of it, it might be the best thing. Father wants a son to succeed him."

"Does he not have faith in your cousin?"

Penelope grinned. "It seems not." She bit the tip of the quill pen she still held. "It might be better for me, too."

"In what way?"

She slanted a quick look at him. "I won't have to marry Toby now. It was planned to give me a future and to keep the title and fortune together. My father has made me heir to most of the unentailed property, you see. It will be a disappointment to my Aunt Cecilia."

"You don't want to consider the match anyway?" He kept his expression merely interested, although he felt a glow of pleasure inside. She would no longer feel obliged to please anyone except herself.

Penelope sighed heavily, telling him exactly what she thought about the match. "Toby is considerate, and young enough to sire children, he won't insist his wife molders in the country all year. But he has very decided opinions on a woman's place, and—and—" She flushed.

"You don't want to see him in your bed?" he finished for her, intrigued to see her reaction.

As if forced to do it, she gave a sharp nod. "I'm sure he would be acceptable to any number of young ladies. I know I'm no prize, but I don't find any joy in the prospect." She gripped the pen, crushing the feathery quills, staring at the ruin of the pen.

"It's nothing to be ashamed of. And I can quite see why Toby wouldn't appeal to you. He's rather rotund, very pompous, and hasn't an eighth of your intelligence. And his breath smells."

She impulsively exclaimed, "Yes, doesn't it just!" and turned to look at Sev directly.

Sev sustained a severe shock. Those dark eyes, blazing with life and attention, appealed to him much more than the pair of dreamy blue ones. He could look at these for much longer, even if it was through a pair of unattractive spectacles. Not sure what that meant, he reached for her hand, taken with a sudden urge to touch her. She didn't seem averse to it.

"I-I shouldn't have said that," she whispered.

"I won't tell. And it's the truth."

She returned his smile shakily, and Sev came to himself. He dropped her hand and looked away, trying to regain his equilibrium. Behaving like a smitten schoolboy, he should know better, especially with one of his sister's oldest friends.

He stood up, refusing to look at her. "We shouldn't remain here alone. Whatever would your new mama say?"

Penelope stood and picked up her papers, rapping the edges on the table to straighten them. "I haven't the faintest idea. I suppose I'll find out soon."

"Spanish isn't she?" Sev said, relieved the tension had, for the moment, dissipated. "Sticklers for the proprieties."

"I know shamefully little about the Spanish. My Spanish is nonexistent."

He laughed. "I hope her English is good, otherwise

conversation at the dining table will be a little difficult."

Penelope laughed too and went to the door, allowing him to open it for her. As he did so, his arm brushed hers, and he felt a current go through it. Very unusual.

Chapter Six

Penelope entered the Blue Drawing Room, her nerves high, her throat tense. Inside, her new stepmother and her brother were the only occupants; the lady seated on a blue upholstered, carved wood sofa, the gentleman standing behind her. Penelope made her curtsey, and straightened, waiting to see what would happen. She'd expected her father to be present, but perhaps the lady wanted to meet her on her own. Why then was Don Alfonso here?

"Good afternoon," said the new Lady Wimbourne. "Please sit down." Her English sounded clipped, and she rolled her r's. "I am delighted to meet you. Your father thought it better if we met privately."

She leaned gracefully to a table at her elbow and poured tea. She did it very well. Penelope couldn't quite make out the expression on her stepmother's face, but she saw the shining, braided black hair, and the dark eyes. She was everything Penelope wasn't; graceful, assured and beautiful.

The familiar feeling of inadequacy swept over Penelope as she stepped forward to take the proffered dish of tea. Now she saw her stepmother's face. Smooth, porcelain fine with thin red lips. She realized she was staring. "I beg your pardon," she stammered, careful to find her seat. "My father may have told you I do not see very well."

81

Lady Wimbourne nodded. "It is a pity, but it can be managed."

"I can see most things," Penelope explained, "just not the detail."

"It should be enough," Lady Wimbourne said. "Do you wear—ah—" She leaned back, and her brother leaned down to her and murmured. "Spectacles!" the lady exclaimed. "You must forgive my English. It will improve. My brother went to school here, so his English is better than mine."

Don Alfonso bowed. "I hope I can be of service."

Tall, dark, with pools of black for eyes. Penelope ventured a smile. He smiled back, his lips, thin like his sister's, stretching very slightly. She remembered the question. "Yes, ma'am, I have spectacles." She hardly dared hope, but she could try. "I would be far less clumsy in public if I wore them."

No smiles now. "It is not suitable." Lady Wimbourne spoke with finality, and Penelope's hopes for an ally were dashed. "Young ladies should be obedient and beautiful. You cannot be beautiful in spectacles."

Penelope was not at all sure about this marriage, an opinion noisily repeated by her aunt very soon after Penelope's interview with her new stepmother. When she left the Blue Salon, after half an hour's dutiful conversation Toby was lying in wait for her. He bore her off to his mother's boudoir.

Mrs. Makepiece was as vociferous as her new sister-in-law had been reticent and serene. "How could he do this to us?" She took a turn around the small sitting room and returned to her chair.

Penelope pulled out her spectacles and put them on. Her aunt didn't comment, being in too much of a state about this news. "Sev—Lord Swithland said he knew, but it wasn't his business to tell us."

"What an invidious position he must have been put in!" cried Mrs. Makepiece. "What a thing to do to him."

Penelope agreed with her on this, at least. "It couldn't have been pleasant for him."

"Such a havey-cavey way of marrying. None of his family present. I cannot believe he would do this to me." Penelope couldn't remember seeing her aunt so agitated before. Mrs. Makepiece was used to being in control, and now someone—her father—had taken control away from her.

Penelope refrained from pointing out that his sister was the last thing on her father's mind at the time of his second marriage. Toby who, pale, but more collected, smiled at her. "We can still marry, Penelope. I intend to ask your father as soon as possible. You cannot stay under that woman's influence for too long."

"Why not?"

Mrs. Makepiece tutted with exasperation. "Because we don't know her, foolish girl. Who knows if she is telling the truth? Who knows where she came from?"

"I have sent to London to ask," Toby announced. He lifted his chin, the epitome of the bluff country squire.

Penelope remembered Sev saying he'd looked into the background of the couple, but she chose to keep the information to herself for now. Her aunt might well conclude that her association with Severus was becoming too particular, and decide to curtail it. She stared at Toby, his large, soft lips, his thinning brown hair caught back in a straggling queue and sighed. He was one person who looked better when she had her glasses off. She tried to imagine sharing his bed, however infrequently, and shuddered inside. It was no good. She couldn't. She would rather be single.

She didn't dare think of anything else. Or anyone.

Lord Wimbourne kept to his room for most of the day, but he made an appearance at dinner. He sat between two of the bevy of beauties invited as prospective wives for Swithland, and his round face beamed as he flattered them outrageously, but he remained avuncular, well within the bounds of propriety. That was more than the intended suitor did. He sat glumly at the head of the table, toying with his food, not impolite, but with his attention obviously elsewhere. Occasionally he glanced around, not seeming to see anyone in particular. After the first course, he seemed to pull himself together, and make an effort to entertain his guests. He leaned forward to listen to a sally from Miss Trente, inevitably sitting next to him, although there were other ladies of greater precedence who should be there. He said something and she rapped his knuckles with her fan. Very lightly.

Looking at them with their heads together, Penelope couldn't help but notice what a handsome couple they made. And she wasn't the only person to notice. Lady Carstaires, Miss Trente's mama, seated opposite Penelope, smiled in a proprietorial way. Toby leaned to Penelope and murmured; "If I were a betting man, I'd say the odds are shortening daily. Mark my words if she doesn't make a play for him before too many more days are out."

Penelope recoiled from the cloud of noxious air Toby released when he spoke, but sadly had to agree with her nearly intended. She liked Lord Swithland. It was one thing to idolize him, to imagine herself in love with him, as she had at fifteen, but quite another to see him as an adult, about to throw his life away on a tedious beauty. He could do so much better. There were women of impeccable birth, taste and intelligence who would make him a much better countess.

Unlike her host, Penelope made a good meal. Mr. Grey had been invited to dinner, and she was delighted to see him treated as a proper guest, as he deserved. She exchanged a small smile of greeting with him, but he sat further up the table, so she couldn't do more than that.

When one of the young ladies spoke to her, they were kind, sometimes condescending but friendly. She wasn't seen as a rival, whereas when they spoke to each other there always existed an edge of enmity. Penelope found the pursuit of Severus an amusing spectator sport, but Penelope could see that it riled Lord Swithland almost beyond bearing. He drank far too much during the course of the meal, although his fiercest critic couldn't accuse him of intoxication.

When the ladies retired to the drawing room Penelope took a seat at the side of the room and picked up a book she had no intention of reading.

Miss Wilcox, a gorgeous brunette, began the offensive. "I always understood Lord Swithland preferred brunettes."

Not surprisingly, Lady Annabelle Rivers, a glorious blonde, objected. "He seems to have distributed his favors evenly so far."

"You've taken note of his *chéres amies*?" Miss Trente joined the fray, her affected drawl distinctively low and alluring.

Lady Annabelle shrugged. The diamonds around her neck glittered, drawing attention to her fine, long throat, reminding everyone present of her nickname of *The Swan of Berkshire*. "One can't help but notice the women he prefers to consort with."

"If he proposes to me I shall ensure he gives them up. At least for a while," Miss Trente announced.

"You'll let him resume his connections?" Lady Annabelle gave her a sideways look.

"Girls!" came the half-hearted admonition from one of the duennas who sat in a group a little way from them. They ignored her.

"It suits me." Miss Trente's white shoulders shook with an exaggerated shudder. "The marriage bed is not my preferred choice of recreational activity."

A chorus of agreement and a fluttering of fans followed. "Oh no."

Penelope wondered why they would object to it. From the little she had heard some of the intimacies a husband expected of his wife sounded interesting, to say the least. She was willing to wait and try it before she gave her verdict.

With a rustle of expensive silk, Penelope's stepmother swept across the room to sit next to her. "It is not the conversation I am accustomed to," she remarked in a low voice. "If it continues in this way I would like you to withdraw."

Penelope thought about protesting, but she didn't want to get off on the wrong foot with her father's new wife, and in any case she had no objection to retiring early. She could study her portfolio, or read her book. She bowed her head in acquiescence.

The girls didn't desist. "Have you seen his latest flirt?"

The others leaned forward, but there was no consequent lowering of voices. "I don't know her name, but I saw her at the opera. Full of jewels. Trophies, I wouldn't wonder."

Every mouth formed a pretty "o" of wonder. "How can they bear it?"

"Women of that class aren't as sensitive as we are," Miss Trente assured them. "It's why they're useful to us. They keep the men's baser instincts at bay for us. Let them have their jewels, as long as we have the estates and the titles."

General merriment ensued, but Lady Wimbourne's frown deepened, creasing her smooth forehead. Penelope glanced at her and she shook her head. "I shall retire," Penelope assured her. She had no desire to listen to any more in any case.

Putting the book down unread, Penelope curtseyed to the dowagers and left the room. No one noticed her go.

Outside she paused for a moment to get her bearings, and heard the sound of raucous laughter from the dining room. It sounded as if the gentlemen had settled in for the night. The ladies would be disappointed.

If she had been more concerned with her bearings than with the behavior of the society beauties, Penelope wouldn't have turned and walked slap into Lord Swithland. His immediate reaction was to catch her, but he didn't release her, and she didn't ask him to. He was close enough for her to see him properly. "I'm sorry," she mumbled, but he still didn't let her go. Instead, he held her and stared at her.

Penelope was unsure what to do. Was he drunk? She didn't think so, though his eyes seemed a little unfocussed. "Are you going to bed?" he asked abruptly.

"I thought I might go upstairs, sir."

He sighed gustily. "I wish I could go with you." When her eyes widened and her jaw dropped, he laughed. "Oh I didn't mean it to come out like that, I do beg your pardon."

Penelope closed her mouth and sighed in relief. At least, she thought it was relief.

"I just meant I would give a monkey to get away and have a decent conversation. That's all."

"Of course."

He still held her; she felt his hands heating her skin through the material of her thin gown. He smiled down at her, turning her heart over. She couldn't help smiling back.

The communication was instant and more than friendly. From the arrested expression on his face, Penelope guessed he knew it too. Then he grinned. With a small jerk of his head, he indicated the noise coming from the dining room. "They've set up a book. All the girls have the names of fillies, to disguise their identities. Miss Trente is odds-on favorite." He grimaced.

"And they're discussing your *chéres amies* in the drawing room," Penelope told him.

"Oh God, are they? I thought I was discreet."

Penelope giggled. "They seem to know all about it." She paused. "Them."

He regarded her closely. "Well I sent a congé to the latest six months past." Something the women in the drawing room didn't know. Penelope smiled to think she knew more than they did. It certainly made a change, Miss Trente and her intimates usually had the marriage mart gossip first. "Greedy little madam, that one."

Penelope gave the women the benefit of the doubt. "Well they have to make the most of things, the ladies of the night. They hardly bring a portion with them."

"Ha!" It was as well the noise from both rooms was increasing, or someone would have heard his crack of laughter. "True enough, but the requests for carriage horses, a house, jewelry seem to overwhelm everything else. The worst part came when—" He glanced away. "Never mind. I shouldn't be talking to you like this. Trouble is, you make it so damnably easy to do so."

Penelope laughed at his discomfiture. "I don't mind."

He sighed gustily. "How pleasant." Releasing her, he crooked his arm in the approved manner. "Come on."

Penelope stared at him in bewilderment. "Where?" for he was facing away from the drawing room.

"I want to show you something. Don't worry, it's all harmless." He stared down at her, his eyes expectant.

There was nothing more Penelope could do but go with him. She laid her hand on his arm and let him take her, at quite a pace, upstairs. Her heart thudded, not just from the brisk pace he set. He led her past the bedrooms and up another, smaller staircase, at the end of the corridor. It was an old wooden stair that looked like part of the original Jacobean house, black with age and polish, sporting elaborately carved balusters. They didn't pause at the next floor but continued up, where the stairs became less elaborate and narrower.

Throwing caution aside, Penelope let him take her where he willed. She knew he was a little drunk, but not how much, and he had an air of recklessness she'd never seen in the drawing room. Day by day Sev was becoming less Antonia's big brother and more her friend.

At the very top of the house, he opened a plain deal door. Once inside Penelope gasped.

It led into a large, whitewashed room that Penelope guessed had once been a storage attic. The windows had been enlarged, until one wall was nearly all glass, open to the night sky. Reminded by a gentle hand in the small of her back, Penelope stepped in the room and he closed the door.

This situation was now beyond propriety, particularly for an unmarried lady, but Penelope's thoughts strayed far from proper behavior. Awed, she stared out at the night sky. In the clear sky, stars shone brightly. She dipped her hand into her pocket and retrieved her spectacles, propping them on her nose. Vanity left far behind, she walked to the window and gazed her fill.

Sev came up behind her and laid a gentle hand on her shoulder. "Lovely, isn't it? Welcome to my obsession."

Turning, she saw a collection of gleaming brass instruments. "Telescopes!"

He grinned. "As you say. Telescopes. Didn't you know?"

"Yes of course, but I didn't know—" She stopped, flustered. She'd heard of Severus's interest in astronomy, but hadn't seen much evidence of it and supposed it a passing fancy. Well the way this room was set out didn't indicate anything of the kind and she would be insulting him if she voiced it.

"Come here." He took her to the largest instrument, taking up much of the floor space in the middle of the room. "Sit down." A stool was set before it, something like a three legged milking stool. Casting her skirts over it Penelope sat.

Sev went to the side of the instrument. "Look through here." She bent her head and looked through the little eyepiece he indicated. She bent once more and peered through the eyepiece.

The stars resolved into dazzling lights, traced by specks she couldn't see when she leaned back and looked at the view without the telescope. She bent to the instrument again. Everything fell away except her sense of awe, and the feeling that she was about to discover something new. "It's wonderful."

She saw his smile when she drew back. It gleamed in the moonlight through the broad windows, the only illumination they were currently using. "I'm glad you like it."

"Do you just look?" She peered through the eyepiece again, feasting on the new world Severus had introduced her to.

"Mostly. I started when I was a boy, just after my parents died."

He sounded more relaxed and friendly than she had ever

heard him before. Penelope suspected he found it easier to confide in her when she didn't look at him. She wondered if he would be so forthcoming if he were entirely sober. She guessed not.

"I'd never felt so alone. God knows there were few other people to talk to. No one wanted to listen to me, so I stopped telling them how I felt and what I wanted. I learned my lessons, did my duty and worked hard at my studies. Then I discovered the stars. I started to talk to them. I know it sounds odd, but I needed something." Not to another lonely child. Penelope knew what he meant, though in her case she found solace in books and taking control of her father's investment portfolio. "I found friends when I went to school, but I never left the stars behind." It sounded as if they had much more in common than she'd ever suspected. Both feeling out of place, but for different reasons, with dreams they shouldn't be thinking of, and both of them found outlets for themselves. "So you created this place?"

"Yes. Only Antonia has seen it before." Shocked by this admission Penelope drew back. She had never seen him so open, so confiding. There was nothing of the haughty, worldly earl in the man who watched her with simple friendliness. She'd always known that Severus kept part of himself separate, regarded the world coolly and dispassionately but tonight she felt no barriers between them. Sev trusted her enough to show her himself, the caring man behind the cool, aristocratic exterior. She glowed.

"I don't let the maids in here. They might break something, so Antonia occasionally takes pity on me and dusts around a bit. I wouldn't trust anyone else to do it."

"I knew you were interested, but I didn't realize what it meant. Or how beautiful it is. The night sky, I mean." Although Severus looked handsome, too.

"I'm glad you can see that."

"Have the others seen it? Have you shown them anything of this?"

"Who?" He sounded puzzled.

"Miss Trente and the rest."

"Good Lord, no!" He got to his feet in an economically athletic move and went to a table pushed against the wall. He fiddled with some papers. She heard the rustle. "You let me into your secret obsession, so I thought it was fair that I show you mine."

"I won't tell." She needed to say it, so he knew for sure. "And thank you for showing me." She took a breath. She needed to put a little space between them before her hopes and wishes overwhelmed her once more. Sev was showing her friendship here. Nothing else. She couldn't afford to lose that perspective. "You've spoken to the Royal Society, haven't you? Antonia told me."

His hands stilled, and his head bowed over the papers. "Yes, but on an amateur basis. I'm an enthusiast, not a Newton."

Rising, she went over to him, and looked at the papers. It was difficult to make anything out in the dusky light but she could make out symbols and colored diagrams, as meaningless to her as her graphs had been to him earlier. "I'm trying to map Venus," he told her. "I don't think I'll be able to, but it gives me a reason to come up here and look."

"I have every confidence in you." With one finger, she gently traced the curves of a gleaming brass instrument lying in a case on the table. "A sextant," he told her. "They use them at sea to calculate their position."

"It's lovely." The gleaming curves fascinated her. She looked up at him and realized he was watching her, not the sextant, in what she could only describe as a noticing way. He seemed to be looking at her with a new awareness. She felt the same. "They do have a—a beauty of their own, don't they?" Suddenly shy, she looked down.

He reached out, put a finger under her chin and guided it up, so she met his intent gaze. "It seems appropriate."

"At least you don't look right through me."

All humor gone, he glared at her. "Who does that?"

She tried to smile, but failed and settled for a shrug. "Most people do. Women don't see me as a rival in their matrimonial aspirations."

"Why not?"

She was astonished by his response. That should have been obvious, she thought. "Look at me. Add that to my clumsiness, and social ineptitude and you can see why they do that. They think I'm slow, they laugh at me. I don't mind, really I don't, but I don't court their company, either."

He looked at her, studying her until she felt uncomfortably warm. Then he lifted a hand from her arm and caressed her cheek. She didn't mean to, but she leant into his hand, loving the feeling of being cherished, however false.

Because she'd closed her eyes for a moment she missed his bending his head to hers, but she felt the soft pressure of his lips. He slid his hand around her neck, and when she didn't withdraw, touched her lips with his tongue. She shuddered, and heat spread through her. When she opened her mouth slightly, he took advantage of it, sliding his tongue just between them to taste her.

Toby had kissed her once, about three years ago, a kiss stolen in the orchard one summer. She'd allowed it, but escaped soon afterwards and felt no inclination to repeat the experience. Sev's kiss wasn't like that. It felt wonderful, as

93

unlike Toby's wet, messy embrace as possible. Penelope responded instinctively, reaching up to hold on to him. His response was to draw her closer and deepen the kiss.

Penelope tasted the brandy on his lips and knew that if he wasn't drunk, he was well-to-go. She didn't care. If he hadn't been, he would not be kissing her like this, in this hot, demanding way that drove tingles to the tips of her toes. He broke the kiss, took a quick breath and returned to the fray. He caressed the back of her neck, his fingers moving slowly over the small curls clustered there. He seemed to be enjoying himself. Or perhaps, Penelope thought cynically, he wanted flirting without any expectations. If he'd done this with any one of the other young ladies in the house, taken her up to a private room and then kissed her, she would have expected a proposal of marriage in the morning. Penelope wouldn't insist, wouldn't tell anyone or demand anything from him that he wasn't willing to give.

With one small touch of his lips against hers, he drew back, and gazed at her, his eyes dark in the gloom. They were both breathing quicker, and Penelope followed his gaze to see her breasts rising and falling above her tight-laced, low-cut evening gown. "Sir?"

"Sev. Penelope, I'm sorry, I don't know what came over me—"

Was he apologizing because he remembered, rather belatedly, that he was a gentleman, or because he didn't find the kiss interesting? "Sev, I—no, I'm sorry. I don't expect—well, I'm not officially—" She stopped, floundering.

"It makes me wish you were," he murmured, still too close to her for comfort. He rested his forehead against hers before drawing back. His gaze remained intent on hers as he withdrew his hand from her neck and touched her face, drawing his fingers down her cheek and tracing the line of her lips.

She stared up at him, the dim starlight softening his face. She wasn't averse to another kiss, but she was unsure what to do. Should she behave like a lady, and deny all pleasure, or invite further caresses and perhaps the sobriquet of wanton?

Her experience didn't extend this far. Nobody had looked at her in such a caressing way, or shown any inclination to kiss her. She'd assumed her lot in life was to be taken for granted and perhaps laughed at for her clumsiness. Now she was rapidly reassessing that. If such a connoisseur of women as Severus Granville took notice of her, she must have something worth looking at.

He bent to kiss her once more, this time briefly. "I didn't mean this to happen. I wanted to reciprocate—show you my obsession. Believe me, this isn't an attempt at seduction. It's just that I haven't—noticed you before this visit and I like what I see. Very much. I'm sorry."

"Don't be." The words were out before she could suppress them. "I'm glad you wanted to show me this. And it was only a kiss."

"Yes." His mouth twisted up at one corner. "Only a kiss." He paused. "Penelope, I would like to share this obsession of mine with you, if you're interested. Have I blotted my copybook completely?"

She smiled. *Only a kiss.* "No, of course not. This is an enchanting room. I would love to learn more about the stars." *Especially with you,* she thought, but she didn't speak it aloud.

His answering smile was intimate, but friendly. He turned and held out his arm. "May I escort you to your bedchamber, ma'am?"

Penelope felt the flush spread from her feet to the top of her head, warming her body. His smile broadened. "Not that, foolish

95

girl! The bedchamber door. You won't know your way from here, you've never been to this part of the house before."

"Oh!" Now she felt foolish, but she reached out and tucked her hand into the crook of his arm.

They reached the brief journey to her bedchamber at a brisk pace, and then he turned to look at her, friend once again, the more intimate expression gone. "I shall bid you goodnight, Miss Makepiece. I hope this doesn't mean I won't be welcome in the library tomorrow?"

"Oh, no—no," she stammered. She would have to ensure that Mr. Grey stayed there, that was all because she knew she could no longer trust herself alone with Severus.

He leaned forward and kissed her cheek. "Good. Goodnight then."

Taking it as dismissal, Penelope turned the knob and went into her room.

Sev hurried back to the dining room, so no one would note his disappearance. He'd been excluded from the book someone had started, as he was one of the participants. They wouldn't even give him a look, but later Peter murmured to him that Miss Trente was still odds-on to become the new Countess of Swithland before this visit was over.

Sev had his doubts, but didn't tell Peter about them. He wasn't sure of anything any more.

Chapter Seven

Penelope went to the library early the next day. She almost hoped that Sev wouldn't make an appearance, but just when she and Mr. Grey were involved in some difficult calculations, he made an appearance.

He didn't demand immediate attention but drew up a chair and sat by Penelope, waiting until they had leisure to attend to him. Penelope appreciated that and wondered how many other men of power and fashion would have the consideration to do such a thing.

His proximity unnerved her. Before last night, she could have accepted his presence with the ease of long, if distant, acquaintance, but now she became vividly aware of his sleeve close to hers. Her skin tingled. Desperately, she pulled her quivering senses together and attended to her work.

After covering a sheet of paper with sums, some of them superfluous, she came to the same conclusion as Mr. Grey. She pushed away the diagram. "We have to sell these stocks."

"Agreed," he replied, making a mark on the diagram and putting it aside. Penelope glanced round and gave Sev a small, shy smile. He smiled back, in a way that seemed more intimate than ever before. Penelope gave herself a mental shake. Severus Granville's appeal and personal charm were legendary. She had never been the recipient of them before, that was all. He'd most likely forgotten the kiss as soon as he'd said good-bye to her at her door.

"Sleep well?"

"Yes, thank you." Her reply sounding trite and forced even to her ears.

"I slept like the dead," he answered. "Your company must agree with me."

Penelope glanced at Mr. Grey who was watching the exchange with amused interest. "Se—Lord Swithland is a little tired of the mating game. Since I'm not involved, I think he finds me more restful."

"Not the word that sprang immediately to mind," Sev murmured, increasing Penelope's confusion.

Mr. Grey turned his gaze to Severus, his expression sharpened. It gave Penelope a chance to draw another sheet of paper towards her, but to her disappointment, the share represented on the diagram was not an exciting one.

Instead, she found her list, trying desperately to change the subject to something more impersonal. "That's all the shares in my portfolio. Or I should say, my father's. Although I have increased my portion by some use of the markets."

"Really? Perhaps it's the best use for it." Sev, teasing forgotten in his new interest. Penelope breathed a sigh of relief.

Mr. Grey was only too happy to explain what the investments meant. "A lady's dowry is usually invested for her potential widowhood or for her daughter's portions. While a certain amount of capital should be available for immediate use in the unfortunate occurrence of the demise of the husband, a proportion of it can be set to work. Lord Wimbourne has given us permission to use Penelope's inheritance in this way. We've turned it into a separate portfolio, so see how its investments perform against our other investments."

Severus leaned further in and Penelope felt his attention withdraw from her. She breathed a quiet sigh of relief.

They spent the rest of the morning, and part of the afternoon studying and explaining the mechanics of their system to Swithland, who seemed to absorb it like a sponge. "This is much better than cards at White's. Though it still doesn't compare with astronomy." He exchanged a quick, intimate look with Penelope and plunged her right back in to the maelstrom she wanted to avoid.

Penelope excused herself early, planning to find something to eat before escaping to the gardens with a book, but she was doomed to failure. On entering the dining room, where a cold luncheon was set out on the buffet, she encountered her stepmother's brother, Don Alfonso. The Don was surrounded by beautiful women, but he excused himself and came over to where she sat. Penelope would have had to be a saint not to feel gratified by his pointed attention. Don Alfonso was a very handsome man.

His white teeth flashed in a smile. "Would you like to take a walk after lunch? It would be my pleasure to accompany you."

In all honesty, Penelope couldn't refuse, since that had been her plan. It would perhaps give her the opportunity to get to know this man better, and since he was now family, of a sort, she should make the effort. And the event she had dreaded and anticipated, being alone with Swithland again, would be averted.

She needed time to think, to let her ruffled sensibilities calm down, and Don Alfonso looked like a sensible man.

After finding her best straw bergère hat, she tied it on over her curls and went down to the back hall, where Don Alfonso waited for her. His smile transformed his features into something far more welcoming, but it was brief, and his face settled back into its customary grave expression.

Penelope found the Don a pleasant companion. He expounded on the beauties of Spain, until she longed to see the country for herself, but he paused occasionally to give her time to question him. Despite her earlier misgivings, Penelope found herself enjoying her walk with Don Alfonso.

"You must tell me if I bore you," he told her. "I can get a little carried away when I speak of my country."

"Not at all, sir, it sounds like a beautiful country. Have you estates there?"

"Oh yes. My main estate is about thirty miles north of Madrid, quite close to Toledo. Some people do not think this country is as beautiful as that in the south, but it is my home and I love it." His dark face took on an inner glow as he remembered. "My parents died when I was at school in England, but I have an excellent steward and a land manager who took excellent care of it for me. But I look forward to the day when I may go home and oversee it for myself."

That was one query answered, then. They were not destitute, Don Alfonso and his sister. "Does your sister share your love of the land?"

He glanced away, then back at her. "No. How did you guess?"

"I didn't. I don't know her very well."

"She has a different father. We share a mother. Marcela's father was wellborn but poor. My lands come from my father, who gave her a dowry, but she has never seen the estate as hers, so she does not love it as I do."

So perhaps the lady was poor, if not the Don. Perhaps she married Penelope's father for money. She still wanted to know precisely why her new stepmother had married her father when, by what Mr. Grey told her, she could have married even higher, had she wished. And why had they come to England? Don Alfonso watched her closely, so Penelope schooled her features to polite interest. They passed through an arbor into an enclosed rose garden. The atmosphere was thick with the scent of the roses, although they were not all in bloom yet. The high hedges enclosing the garden kept the scent in the small space, concentrating the sweet, rich scent so associated with the English summer. She loved it. Penelope bent to smell a pink rose and the petals fell softly over her hand. She dropped the blossom and a few petals drifted to the ground.

"I love the scent of roses," she said, and moved away a trifle, uncomfortable with his proximity.

Don Alfonso must have noticed, because he drew back, allowing her to smooth her skirts and shake them into place in a gesture more nervous than needful. Penelope was glad of her hoops. The day was close, and the hoops held the fabric away from her body, stopping it from clinging hotly. Today she wore pink, and had chosen the gown with more than her usual care, but not for Don Alfonso. Nevertheless, he seemed to be enjoying the sight of her in it. When she glanced at him she saw his dark eyes warm with appreciation. She wasn't entirely sure she liked it, but perhaps that was because gentlemen didn't usually look at her in such a way.

"You know I wear spectacles?" she said abruptly.

"Yes, but only when you are private. Ladies do not need to see clearly."

That kind of nonsense irritated Penelope. She had to endure it from her father, but there was no reason she should endure it from him. "I would like to see properly, once in a while."

"It would mar your beauty," he said, "and it would not be

dignified."

"It's hardly dignified to trip over a carpet because one hasn't seen the ruck in it," she snapped, reminded of the several times she had done so, and felt foolish doing it.

"Your escort should take more care. Be assured, when you are with me, you will not trip over any carpets."

She didn't like the proprietorial tone of that remark, but she let it pass. His English was good, but not perfect, so perhaps the phrasing of the sentence had not been what he intended.

Stealing a look at the Don, Penelope wondered if he had meant it, after all. He was regarding her with an intent expression that made her feel distinctly nervous. Perhaps it was because he had such dark eyes, that he seemed so intense. Penelope hoped so. She hardly knew the man.

He turned to look at the rose bushes. "I have vineyards. Perhaps I may be fortunate enough to show them to you one day."

Penelope murmured that she would be overjoyed to see his vineyards. "Will you go home to Spain soon?"

He shrugged. "I spend at least half the year there, but I do not like the Court in Madrid. I go when I am summoned, or when I need a favor, but the English society is more to my taste. I know more people here; I went to school with many of them. And it is too hot to stay in Spain in summer. The air is stifling at this time of year. So I come here every year, usually for the Season and return home when the weather is more acceptable."

When she thought about it, she had seen the Don at several affairs in London in recent years, but he'd never sought her out, only danced with her a time or two, and that, she'd always thought, was because of his impeccable manners, not any wish of his to do so. Penelope usually found herself by the wall at these affairs and had come to regard them as a dead bore and a waste of her time.

If Spain was hotter than this, she didn't want to visit it. If the day became any hotter she would find it most unpleasant. Moisture trickled down her back. Although she'd desired her maid not to lace her tightly that day, it was unthinkable to go without stays altogether. The ones she had on were of fine linen, but still boned and stitched and two layers thick. Still far too tight and far too hot.

When she turned her head she had to force a smile, and Don Alfonso must have noticed, for he said, "I think we should go in now. It is getting very warm, is it not?"

She agreed, and accepted the support of his arm. She was not usually so feeble, but the heat had proved too much for her.

When they went inside, Don Alfonso made her sit in the breakfast room, which was cool at this time of day, and went to fetch her a cold drink. He came back with cold white wine. Penelope would rather have had lemonade, but she accepted the wine and sipped it gratefully.

It didn't do any good. Pretty soon, she was feeling even more faint, and a headache was developing, the pressure increasing behind one eye and that side of her head. She knew what was coming and she desperately needed to get to her room. "I'm dreadfully sorry, sir," she managed, fumbling to put her glass down safely, "but I think I must go upstairs for a while."

Don Alfonso got to his feet. "Let me help you."

"No, no, I'm sure I'll be fine," she protested, rising too.

Whether she stood too quickly or the burgeoning headache was more developed than she'd thought, Penelope didn't know. Whatever the reason, the room swam before her hazed eyes, and she staggered, reaching for the chair for support.

Strong arms went under her and swept her off her feet. She knew no more.

Chapter Eight

When Penelope recovered her senses, she was lying down with something cold over her forehead. Moving to one side, she moaned when pain shot through her head. A soft voice said, "Stay still."

She obeyed, because it was easiest. Now properly conscious she murmured, "There's nothing to worry about. I get these headaches sometimes. I'll be fine in no time."

"Do you want some laudanum?"

"No thank you." She hated the woozy feeling laudanum left her with, although she would resort to it if the pain got too bad. It wasn't too bad now.

Belatedly, she recognized the owner of the voice. She opened her eyes wide with shock. "Oh!"

"Lie still," said Severus, pushing her back down. "Does this happen often?"

"It's nothing," she protested, subsiding. "If I could just go to my room, I'll be fine. It's only a headache. Yes, I get them quite a lot. Eyestrain."

He nodded. "I suspected something of that nature. From what I've seen of you, you're not the kind of person to repine on a twinge." He grimaced in disapproval. "They should let you wear your spectacles more often."

"And be called a bluestocking?" Penelope felt foolish lying on the sofa like an invalid, but when she tried to sit up, potential nausea made her head swim. With her experience of headaches, she knew a few hours lying down would put paid to it, and if she drank the wine at dinner only sparingly, or found a substitute for it, she would be fine.

She opened her mouth tell him, but he interrupted her. "Where are your spectacles?"

"In my pocket."

"Can you reach them? You might feel better you put them on."

She was forced to agree, and she fished them out. They hadn't been squashed so she perched them on her nose. She had to admit that it was an improvement. On her pain, anyway, though it did nothing for her looks.

She looked around. She was still in the breakfast room, on the sofa that had been pulled away from its usual spot under the window, where the light would have been brighter. "Where's the Don?"

"Gone to get some lemonade."

"Thank you. He gave me some wine but lemonade would be much more the thing."

He gave her that boyish grin she was learning to love, the one that reduced the distance between them and gave her thoughts she shouldn't under any circumstances be having. That it should pierce through one of her headaches surprised her. "My mama used to have terrible headaches, and she could never abide alcohol in any form while she was suffering."

So that was how he understood. His mother had died when he was young, but he probably remembered her better than Antonia could. Penelope closed her eyes, and felt him remove the cloth. She hadn't noticed a basin but she heard the trickle of water when he wrung out the cloth then felt the renewed coolness on her forehead. It felt like heaven. "When you feel better, I'll take you up to your room."

Despite her misery, Penelope couldn't resist. "You've done that once before." She opened one eye and peered at him.

"So I have, but this time I'll ask Antonia to come with us and we'll send for your maid." He frowned, biting his lip and Penelope wondered what was wrong. As if he had heard her unspoken question, he answered her. "Your family should allow you to wear your spectacles more often. Bluestocking or no. You shouldn't go through this kind of suffering."

She hastened to reassure him. "It doesn't happen too often. Not more than once every few weeks."

"Once is too much, if it can be prevented."

The door opened and the Don come in bearing a tray, on which reposed a jug covered by a beaded cloth and a large goblet. His dark gaze passed over Penelope's face. "How do you feel?"

"Pampered." She managed a wan smile.

"Did you find my sister?" Sev demanded.

Don Alfonso set the tray down on the large table in the centre of the room. "She is coming down directly. She was resting in her room."

Immediately, Penelope felt guilty. "Oh, I wouldn't have had you disturb her."

"I'm sure she won't mind," Sev assured her.

It seemed not, because the door opened and Antonia came in, a frown of concern between her brows. "A headache? She didn't get as many at school, Sev, because they allowed her to wear her spectacles."

His lips firmed into a straight line. "I knew it was that." He glanced down at Penelope. "I'll take her up to her room, if you'll come with us."

"Then if you'll leave for a moment, I'll help her off with her side hoops."

Penelope offered to walk, but no one would allow that, so, sighing, she allowed them to have their way.

The gentlemen left the room while Antonia lifted her friend's skirts and undid the tapes that fastened the hoops at the waist so Penelope could slip them off. They were collapsible, but would have provided an uncomfortable and undignified whalebone barrier had Severus carried her while she still wore them. Antonia folded the cages and held them bunched in one hand, while she called out to her brother that Penelope was decent again.

Penelope half hoped that the Don would carry her, but Sev overrode him. "You must allow me the privilege," he said, bending to slip his arms under her, so he gave her little choice but to loop her arms around his neck when he requested her to.

It felt wonderful. Penelope wished she were in a state to thoroughly enjoy it, but her head throbbed when Severus lifted her so she concentrated on fighting down the rising nausea the movement caused. They were out of the room before she felt safe opening her eyes again. "You can put me down, I'll be fine, I promise."

"It pleases me to do this for you." His voice sounded like a low caress. "Would you deny me the pleasure?"

Penelope wondered what he meant by that. From the look in his eyes, he meant a great deal, but she knew he was kind, and it had to be friendship. Resolutely she pushed the thought aside and concentrated on fighting down the waves of nausea. She closed her eyes, so she wouldn't meet the gaze of anyone who met them, and only opened them when they reached her room.

She met Sev's gaze, and he smiled at her reassuringly. Warmly. Penelope wasn't used to being pampered like this. When she had a headache, she usually crept off to her room where no one came near her for a few hours, not even to bring her a pot of tea. Except for her maid, who attended to her with a kindly efficiency she appreciated. But not like this, not with this level of—concern.

Sev laid Penelope on the bed, then stepped back so that Antonia could arrange her skirts. "I'll help you with your stays," she said. "Your maid will be here directly to help you with anything you need."

Sev left quietly, and Antonia soon followed, leaving her friend to rest with the jug of lemonade and a little hand bell nearby, to ring when she wanted help.

Penelope lay still for a long time and eventually slipped into slumber, praying the pain would be gone when she woke.

Back in the morning room, Sev turned on his sister angrily. "How can anyone do that to her?"

Antonia shrugged. "No one gives her the headaches." She flopped into a chair in a most unladylike manner. Antonia decided her brother needed a push, and she was the only one to do it. She saw the way the wind was blowing, even if he couldn't. And she would far rather welcome Penelope into her family than any of the vapid females Severus had invited as candidates for his hand.

She prayed neither of them discovered that she'd invited Penelope specifically to push her together with Sev. She'd have to be blind to ignore the occasional longing gazes Penelope allowed herself, and the way her friend's eyes lit up when she spoke of her brother, though she shrewdly suspected Penelope had no idea that she knew. Still, it was time the matter came to a head and Penelope either attracted Sev, or learned to move on. While Antonia hadn't expected the company of a bevy of society beauties, they would help to resolve the matter. One way or the other.

Sev sat in a chair opposite his sister, long legs sprawled before him. "Yes they do. If she was allowed to wear those damned spectacles, she might not get the headaches."

"It's possible. She didn't have many headaches at school."

"Where she was allowed to wear them," Sev said grimly.

Antonia busied herself pouring tea from the tray she'd ordered on their way back downstairs. "Why should you care?" She carried his tea dish across to him. He took the dish from her by the saucer, and stared at her, an arrested expression on his face.

"Because she's your friend, and because I like her," he replied, but Antonia could tell he was still thinking about her question. She·sat down, congratulating herself on her tactics. Sev couldn't avoid the issue any longer. He'd have to make a decision about his life, and if Penelope belonged in it or not.

"Oh." Antonia sipped her tea, letting her brother have some quiet time to think, but Sev caught her watching him over the rim of her tea dish.

He gave her a reluctant grin. "What is it?"

"Have you decided on your countess yet?" Antonia asked, in a seeming change of subject. "It's getting very tiring, having all these young ladies about. Like living in an aviary. They're all doing their best to attract you. You'll exhaust them all before you make your decision."

"And trap me," Sev told her, exasperation writ large on his features. "I feel like a fugitive in my own house."

"Well, it's your own fault. You shouldn't have invited them. Why did you invite them if you weren't making a decision on your future life?"

Sev groaned. "I got beastly drunk one night at White's, and caught sight of the book running on me. Almost every bachelor member has one, but interest in mine has heated up since Nick took the marital plunge." He swallowed more tea. "I'm tired of it, Antonia, so I decided to put an end to it. The young ladies in this house are the front runners in the book. Foolishly I thought White's had the right of it."

"Once you make your mind up they'll leave you alone."

"No they won't. They'll get married then come back to try to become my mistress." Sev sipped his tea.

Antonia's peal of laughter was not ladylike, or softly trilling. "Oh, Sev, what a coxcomb you are." He wasn't usually so foolish, but he had never found himself in this position before. Trapped. He'd never allowed it.

If he decided to marry one of the feather-brained, spoiled misses in the house, Antonia would do her best to move out of his presence and his house. Perhaps go to stay with her Aunt Julia for a while, until she met her own future. If she ever did. Penelope and Severus were made for each other. Severus had that protective nature that Penelope needed, but not the severity that would cow and subdue her. While Penelope had a lot of personal courage, she lacked the kind of bravery that would make her go her own way, without considering the wishes of people who genuinely cared for her, however misguided their opinions. Like her aunt, and her cousin Toby. Toby would be kind to her, but oh, what a prosy bore.

Sev was forced to join in Antonia's laughter, shaking his head at his own foolishness. "I had the invitations sent out the next day, before I had a chance to reflect on the idea. They want to marry me for the title, Antonia, not for myself. But yes, that was a trifle swollen headed of me. I apologize. All I can say in my defense is that they do pursue me."

Still smiling, Antonia put down her cup. "Well you invited them here, so it's your fault."

"I thought it was time I forced myself to make a decision. The trouble is, Antonia, I can't see myself spending any amount of time with any of 'em. They're spoiled, and silly—"

"And beautiful." She arched her eyebrows.

"Yes, all right, and beautiful. Serves me right for thinking those fools at White's knew what they were talking about. If this disaster has persuaded me of anything, it is that I need a proper countess. One who will share the burdens with me, as well as the pleasures. I want a wife who will help me run the estates, be intelligent enough to be a political hostess when needed, and—" he paused, sheepishly, before he glanced at Antonia and continued, "—be a friend." He put his cup down. "God that sounds mawkish."

Antonia didn't laugh. "I think your decision shows great good sense. After all, you might have to spend a very long time with your wife—whoever she is." She finished her tea and put her cup down on the small table by her side. "So what will you do now, Sev? You've caused expectations in many hearts, and they'll all be offended if you don't live up to them. You should think about offering for somebody before this party is over."

He shrugged. "Let them be disappointed. I made a mistake when I asked the wrong kind of woman here. Perhaps I should try with a more sensible batch."

Antonia couldn't help but burst out laughing once more. "Really, Sev! They'll be calling you Bluebeard."

Sev grinned and stood up, shoving his hands in his pockets. "I know. It's just that I'm in a damned hole of my own making and I can't see myself clear." He spun around and stared out of the window. "What am I to do, Antonia?"

She gave him her best advice, but kept a little knowledge back. He would have to work the last part out for himself. "Be brave and send them back to London. They'll hate you, but what does that matter?" She lifted the teapot and poured more tea.

"I don't want to humiliate them like that. They're all expecting me to choose—preferably Miss Trente." He turned round, his face a picture of gloom. "She's the reigning queen of the unmarried set but she won't be for much longer. Getting too long in the tooth, her friends inform me. But I don't like her, Antonia. I can't bear the thought of being leg-shackled to a beautiful idiot."

"You've only just realized you couldn't stand that idea?"

"Yes. And she is cruel. To Penelope, to you, to anyone not of her set who she considers beneath her. She takes wit and turns it into spite."

They gazed at each other. Antonia knew she was the only person he would talk to in this way. He wouldn't talk to a woman with the same frankness as he used with his sister. Perhaps one other woman, one day. She could still hope.

Antonia stared at him, and let Sev see anticipation, but she said nothing. He frowned. "I'm a complete idiot, aren't I?"

She smiled then. "No, you didn't think properly, that's all."

"No, I didn't, did I?"

Antonia nodded. She picked up her cup, feeling much less cool than she appeared to be. Finishing her second dish quickly, she stood. "Sev, it's up to you. I won't push you, unlike the women you've taken such a dislike to, but you have to decide something. If you send them all away and remain unmarried, you'll gain a reputation, maybe for fussiness, or bad temper, or vacillation, or something. They'll settle on something to save face. But you still have that decision to make. So for your own sake, think hard and make up your mind."

Her work was done. While Antonia would love Sev to settle for Penelope, she was wise enough to realize her brother and her friend deserved to be happy, together or apart. They must make their own decisions.

Sev knew if he didn't finalize his wedding plans soon, he would be forced into it. The hounds were closing in, and even if he left on a long trip abroad, word would spread and it was likely he would end up with a French or Italian bride. He felt hunted, not without reason.

He went up to his observatory and locked the door behind him, trying to find solace in his charts. He opened the case and stared at the sextant, reaching out one finger to touch it, just as Penelope had done. Stroking the softly gleaming metal he forgot the charts, forgot everything except his current dilemma.

Except, suddenly, it didn't seem like a dilemma any more. It was an opportunity. He'd always yearned for someone close to share his life with, especially now Antonia had grown up. He couldn't expect his sister to dance attendance on him for the rest of her days; she'd want to marry soon, and he'd be alone again.

All his cogitation that afternoon converged on one person. Once he'd settled on his decision he tried it out in his mind, let himself think of life ten, twenty years from now. Then he tried to pick holes in it. He couldn't. Cursing himself for his blindness, Severus made the decision he knew was right. While he didn't know if he loved Penelope or not, he knew he liked her much more than anyone else at this damned house party, more than any other eligible lady in society, come to that. The night after he'd shown her his observatory he'd awoken with her taste on his lips, and he wanted more. That she should evoke such passion in him when everyone else left him cold made him wonder, but he didn't question it. He wanted her in his bed and in his life. Her intelligence, humor and her delectable curves could only enhance his life. Severus wanted Penelope.

Resolved on his course, Severus left the room without a backward glance. He had things to arrange, and he had to move fast.

Dinner that evening passed with a tedium Sev found hard to bear. He spent it being charming to his guests and their guardians, but he could do that without thinking. Inside, he made plans. Several times Miss Trente, who had again contrived to sit on his left, called him to order and forced him to pay attention.

"I said, my lord, that there are enough of us here to get up a makeshift ball. If you should like it I could help to make the arrangements." She looked at him hopefully, her blue eyes large and glistening with hopeful pleading.

Sev glanced across to where Lady Carstaires sat, a little further down the table. She had evidently heard the request, and was smiling beatifically at him. Sev wondered when they had hatched this scheme, too wise to assume it was the spontaneous request it seemed. Perhaps this afternoon, as a counter to his withdrawal from the feminine society on offer.

An irritation with the constant machinations of his guests was countered by the new tranquility engendered by his recent decision. Perhaps he'd have something to celebrate, after all. "Why not?"

Miss Trente clapped her hands together in delight, careful not to make too much noise or upset her wineglass. Her social dexterity was remarkable, Sev realized, and grinned, struck by an impulse to provoke them a little more. "It had better be soon," he added, allowing his voice to lower to a caressing softness, "who knows what news there may be?"

He kept Miss Trente's attention just longer than necessary, and then looked away into the disapproving eyes of his sister, acting as his hostess at the other end of the table. His soft smile turned into a wicked grin, but she didn't grin back. She gave her best imitation of a vacuous society beauty. Beautiful Antonia might be, vacuous she was not. "Oh that would be marvelous! We haven't held a ball for far too long."

"I think we can muster a fair show, even at short notice," Lady Carstaires said thoughtfully. "It is most kind of you to consider this, my lord. It will be a pleasure to lend my assistance to the scheme." Sev saw Lord Carstaires, sitting at the other side of the table, try to catch his wife's attention, but he was unsuccessful, partly because of the large flower arrangement that stood between them, but also because she seemed to be avoiding looking in his direction.

After dinner, with the gentlemen left alone in the dining room, Lord Carstaires approached him. "It's kind of you to allow my wife her head, but you're likely to find yourself sadly dipped, if you don't keep a tight rein on the expenses."

"It's very kind of Lady Carstaires and her daughter to take it on," Sev said. "My sister would be fatigued to make all the arrangements herself, and she wouldn't enjoy the occasion. I wish her to enjoy this gathering."

"Oho!" said Peter, who rarely missed anything. "Have we been looking in the wrong direction then? Is it your charming sister who will deliver some Interesting News in the near future?"

"Not to my knowledge." Sev took a moderate amount of port

and passed the decanter on. Lord Carstaires became engrossed in conversation with a man sitting on his other side. "Are you suggesting that I may have some news?"

Peter snorted. "Possibly. At least you've left us dangling on a string while you make up your mind. I've a monkey riding on this, Sev—won't you tell us?"

"Before I've asked her parents?" Sev said mildly.

"Ha!" Peter clapped his hands. "So I'll be collecting my winnings soon?"

The tutting noise indicated the displeasure of an older male further up the table, but crows of delight instantly drowned this out. "The race draws to a close," someone cried. "When should we close the book, Swithland?"

"Tomorrow," Sev said firmly. "I'll do the necessary tomorrow."

Chapter Nine

Penelope was disappointed at Sev's absence from the breakfast table the next morning, but she bore it well. She felt much better this morning, the headache gone, and she made a hearty breakfast. Mr. Grey would have to return to London soon so she needed to make the most of him while he was here. She planned to spend most of the day in the library, finalizing their decisions about their investments. If Lord Swithland chose to join them, who was she to deny him access to the library in his own house?

Her plans were doomed to be thwarted. When she had taken the edge off her appetite with a dish of eggs, chops and crisp, hot bacon, Penelope leaned back with her dish of tea in her hand, prepared to watch the latest installment of the show that had been going on since this house party began.

There was heightened excitement today, heightened levels of gossip mingling with the scents of bacon and coffee. The young ladies discussed the forthcoming ball in great excitement. It meant the prolonging of the house party and increased hopes that Sev would come up to scratch very soon now.

Her new stepmother was present, as was Don Alfonso, but not her father. Penelope was a little concerned by his absence. "Is Papa well?"

"Yes, perfectly well," replied Lady Wimbourne in her slightly accented, too perfect English. "I believe he has some business to settle with Mr. Grey before he returns to London, that is all."

Satisfied, Penelope returned her attention to the pack of beauties who were at their usual occupation of giggling and gossiping. "He said today," Miss Trente, a vision in pink, announced, and turned to Peter. "Isn't that so my lord?"

"He said we could—ah—leave off our speculations today, certainly," said Peter, glancing at one of his companions. "I'm not sure what that means."

A sharp rap from Miss Wilcox's fan and a sultry look from under her dark lashes rewarded him. "Indeed, sir, I think you do. His lordship has made up his mind."

"You could be right," Peter acknowledged, "but he might not let it be known today. He must consult the guardians of the unfortunate girl he has settled his heart on. And she might not have him, you know."

General laughter ensued at the foolish idea that anyone might consider rejecting a proposal from such a good-looking, well set up peer.

Miss Trente laid down her fork, although she had eaten very little. "My parents are here. They don't take breakfast. He could be with them now for all we know." She gave a triumphant smile. "I had better concentrate on planning that ball, don't you think? Should you like to help me, Annabelle?"

Lady Annabelle smilingly agreed to Miss Trente's proposition, and two other girls, including Miss Rivers, offered to help.

"Could I do anything?" Penelope asked.

Miss Trente's stare could have frozen water into ice. "I hardly think so. Your social prowess doesn't give me the confidence I need to ensure this ball is the best we can produce.

Miss Makepiece, we should have the sense to know when we are out of our depth."

Penelope would not show how much Miss Trente's words stung; she absolutely refused to care, even though tears of hurt pricked at her eyes.

She stood and excused herself, leaving the room for the library. Before she could do so, the door of the breakfast parlor closed and her cousin left the room. After a smile of greeting, she would have been on her way except he stopped her. "A word, cousin, if you please."

Folding her hands in front of her like a schoolgirl waiting for a lecture she prepared for boredom. "Of course, Toby. What can I do for you?"

Toby looked around. "Is there a place near here we can be private?"

Penelope thought rapidly and remembered a little-used parlor close by. She took him to it, a feeling of apprehension growing inside her. She hoped he hadn't finally made his mind up to it, but she was afraid that this was the day.

She wasn't wrong. She let Toby open the door for her and went into the room, trying to keep her head high. It was a small room, for which she was sorry. She would have preferred to keep her distance.

Toby closed the door and walked closer to her. Penelope tried very hard not to back away. She folded her hands in front of her again. She didn't want him too close.

Taking a few deep breaths, Penelope tried to concentrate on what her cousin was saying to her. His round face was earnest, and sweat beaded his forehead. It was going to be a hot day, but Penelope knew the weather hadn't caused his perspiration. She was surprised to find herself remarkably cool. She smiled a little, feeling she should give him some encouragement. It was only fair.

"I—I think what I am about to say cannot be a complete surprise to you," he began.

Penelope said nothing, though he clearly expected her to. Toby licked his lips. Not for the first time Penelope noticed how his lower lip hung down a little, and remembered how wet his kiss was, that one time she'd allowed it. She repressed a shudder.

"It has been an expected thing for some time," Toby continued. "I know that circumstances have changed, but my regard for you has not. You are a sensible woman, not at all like the fashionable fribbles we have just left."

Penelope irritation rose. She felt an unreasoning dislike for being described as "sensible." For once, she wanted to be a fashionable fribble.

Toby was into his stride now. "I know you are fond of the womanly pursuits of embroidery, and your father has made me aware of your other interest. I cannot say I approve of your dealings in stocks. Women's minds were not made for such calculations, and I would not condone it if you were to—ah—but I get past myself."

"Have you spoken to my father?" Penelope asked abruptly.

He looked surprised, his sandy eyebrows rising. "Yes, naturally I spoke to him."

"What did he say?" Her new resolve gave her strength. She didn't want this and she would not accept it.

"He—er—he gave us his blessing, but I should inform you that he left the decision up to you."

Then her rejection wouldn't come as too much of a shock.

Toby stared at his hands, then back up at Penelope. His pale eyes studied her face, but Penelope had no idea what he was thinking. "I have much to offer you, Penelope. I have a fair estate, and I might still inherit from your father one day. I can provide a companion for you in my mother. She would love to have you for a daughter, I am sure of that." Penelope imagined a life with Toby's mother. No, she wouldn't bear that. "If you accept my offer, I can give you a full and interesting life."

"How do you feel about me?" Penelope demanded.

"Why—why I am very fond of you, of course," Toby blinked rapidly. "I have always thought of you as my future bride. I know I cannot attract the most desirable women in society, but they haven't your sense and your gravity."

Penelope didn't want gravity. With every word, he pushed her further away and while she had entered the room with every intention of giving him a fair hearing, with every word he spoke, Toby only strengthened her resolve. However, this was much harder than she'd thought it would be. They had spent so long assuming that they would eventually marry, it would be difficult to tell him of her change of heart.

Searching for the right words, Penelope took his hand, wanting to establish a friendly communication. He lifted her hand and pressed his lips to it. The cold dampness felt as though a snail had crawled over her skin.

She repressed a shudder, her second since she'd entered the room. "Toby, I'm very flattered by your offer. It's more than I deserve. I'm fond of you, too, and if you'd asked me six months ago—" She saw the light in his eyes fade a little, and was sorry for it. But she wouldn't make him happy only to make herself miserable. She opened her mouth to continue, but before she could, the door to the parlor opened with some force, banging against the small table that stood too close to it.

Released from the intensity of emotion that swirled around them Penelope looked towards the precipitate entrance of the small, dapper man.

Her father's valet seemed flustered; most unlike his usual self. "I regret the intrusion, Miss Makepiece." He gasped, panting to recover his breath. He must have hurried here.

Apprehension gripped Penelope. "My father?" She looked at Toby.

What she saw there killed any tender feelings she might have harbored for him. The same thought had occurred to her cousin; that Lord Wimbourne had been taken ill. Before he masked it, Penelope saw hope in Toby's eyes. Hope that her father would die before siring a son of his own. Hope that Toby would be the next Lord Wimbourne. He'd lived on that hope for years, and now it returned. Penelope knew she could never live with that hope.

She turned to Flannery. The little Irishman seemed most agitated, his wig slightly askew, and his breath coming in sharp pants. "I'll come at once."

The valet didn't hesitate, but led the way at a brisk pace, only glancing behind him once to ensure she was following him. Her tension increasing, Penelope followed into her father's rooms.

Only to confront him seated on a large sofa in front of a dead fire. He wasn't yet dressed for the day, but wore a colorful banyan and matching cap over his shaved head. He was alone. The valet showed her in and closed the door, leaving Penelope with her father. When she entered, he turned an anxious countenance to her. "Have you accepted him?"

"Who, Papa? What is this? I thought you were unwell."

He waved her concerns away with a casual gesture. "I do feel a little under the weather this morning. Stomach playing up, you know, but it's nothing to signify. In fact, it's been a lot better since I married Marcela. She has a receipt for a tisane;

she's gone to make it now." His warm smile revealed that he was thinking about his new wife. Despite her anxiety, and now her irritation that she had been rudely interrupted for very little reason, Penelope was glad of it.

She forced a frown. "That's nothing to the point, Papa, although I'm glad you're finding some respite from the gout. However, Cousin Toby was very upset to be interrupted at that point. You've done him no service by making Flannery force his way in like that." She knew the manservant wouldn't have dreamed of doing such a thing on his own; he had to have been ordered to do so.

Recalled to the present, Lord Wimbourne glanced at his daughter sharply. "Did you accept him?"

"Did you know Toby was planning to propose this morning?"

His lordship frowned. "Yes, he asked me last night. I said he could try, though I'm no longer as set on the match as I used to be. I hope you realized I left the decision up to you? At least," he added, reflectively, rubbing his freshly shaven chin with one hand, "at least I thought I did. So did you accept him?"

Penelope sighed. "No, Papa." She didn't want to tell her father she'd been about to refuse Toby until she knew what was going on. Why was he so keen that she not accept her cousin's hand? It would still be a neat solution to her father's dilemma of what to do with her. She hoped that it was not to remain at home with him and minister to his needs, but with a new wife, she'd thought he'd have his hands busy, and be glad to see the back of her.

"You'd better sit."

Penelope sat on a chair opposite her father. Her father regarded her silently. "Damned if I can see it."

Penelope folded her hands demurely in her lap and waited

for an explanation.

It wasn't long in coming. "It's been a strange kind of morning. First, Toby Makepiece, then—but I'm getting ahead of myself."

"Papa?"

He cleared his throat. "Thing is, I've received two requests to address you this morning. Better than Makepiece, so I didn't want you engaging yourself before you'd heard 'em. Don Alfonso was the first one."

"Don Alfonso?" Penelope was amazed. She hardly knew the man.

"Says he's fallen in love with you. Don't know if he has or not, but the marriage would be a damn fine one." Lord Wimbourne fixed his daughter with a steely look which, spectacles or no, she couldn't escape. "I had the family investigated when I married Marcela. Didn't want any hangers-on, you know, however I felt about—well, never mind." He cleared his throat with a harrumph.

"The Don is Marcela's half brother—they share a mother. So he has land and a title, all thriving. His title isn't a great one, it's more or less the equivalent of a baronetcy but his family has held it for generations and with it, the estate. He owns a great deal of land in Spain. What's more, he won't expect you to live there all the time. Says Spain can get very hot in the summer, and he comes to England. He has a very tidy estate in Herefordshire. I've been there—we stayed there a night or two before we came here. Very snug." Dazed, Penelope stared at her father. "He's a good prospect and damn me if I'm not proud of you for snagging him from under the eyes of all those females running around here."

Penelope found her voice. "They—their attention is somewhere else. Though I daresay they have him in their sights."

"Don't doubt it for a minute."

Penelope wondered. Toby and Don Alfonso? She was going up a peg. The Don was handsome, charming and young, and it sounded as though he was very comfortably off. She could imagine life with him; long evenings spent wandering in his vineyard—Penelope had a hazy idea of what such a thing might look like, but she imagined lines of lush plants, from which she could pluck a grape or two. Attendance at the Spanish court, perhaps, the English one certainly. A place in society.

"I should like to know him better," she ventured. "I met him recently."

"It was enough for him. For what it's worth, my girl, I think he'll look after you. He seems most sincere."

"How well do you know him?"

"I told you, I had him investigated. He's very well to do."

Penelope looked at her father; saw nothing but sincerity there. While she hadn't been close to her sire, they had a fondness for each other, and she knew he wouldn't force her into anything she might not like. He might force her "for her own good," though.

"Will he ask me soon?"

"Bound to; he says he burns for you."

Penelope wasn't sure she liked the sound of that. If it had been someone else...she mentally shook herself. Two offers for her hand were two more than anyone else had received in this visit. "Who would you like me to take, Papa?" If she hadn't been sure she would take whom she pleased, she wouldn't have asked this, but it showed a good spirit, and she didn't want to fall out with her father unless she had to. He'd pulled her out of her meeting with Toby to inform her of Don Alfonso's offer, so surely he wanted her to accept him? The new life offered was much more to her taste, and the Don a much more attractive prospect than Toby. So why wasn't she more elated by the prospect?

"You haven't heard everything yet," her father said. "There's someone else."

Penelope heart raced; she stopped herself thinking forward. Instead, she concentrated on listening to her father, an expression of polite interest fixed to her face.

"Swithland wants you."

Chapter Ten

Penelope stopped breathing. Then she thought she had misheard, so she opened her mouth, took a very deep breath and asked, with a slight quaver in her voice, "What does he want me for?"

She didn't dare believe what she so wanted to believe, but what else was there? Perhaps he wanted her advice on financial matters, or on something else. Firmly, she stopped her speculations.

"Foolish girl! He's offered for your hand."

"Why would he do that?" Why would he look twice at her, especially now he had seen her in her execrable but necessary spectacles? Surely, he didn't want to encumber himself with a short-sighted spouse, one forever falling over carpets and blanking important visitors because she couldn't see them properly? Penelope couldn't believe anyone would want that. She didn't want it herself.

"He says he has a great respect for you. He wants a wife who will take her responsibilities as countess seriously, not a frivolous girl." He regarded his daughter for a moment. "You will be a credit to him, I'm sure."

Penelope was trembling; she clasped her hands together to still them. "I need to think about this," she managed.

"Nothing to think about. I've accepted Swithland for you. If the Don approaches you, you may blame me."

"Papa!"

"I wouldn't be doing my duty if I didn't snap up the offer. If you wish to reject him, you'll have to do it yourself."

"There must be some mistake." Penelope couldn't believe this. "He invited all those women so he could make his choice. He is expected to propose to Miss Trente." She had to stop to draw breath. She pulled it into her lungs in a great cool stream.

Her father watched her with a satisfied smile. "He's anxious to make it soon; he's had enough of waiting, he says."

"Never say he has a tendre for me. I've known him since I met Antonia at school, and he's never shown any sign of such a thing." The more she considered it, the more Penelope became convinced that it was some kind of joke; perhaps a cruel jest by the young ladies, or an attempt to hurry Sev into making his mind up. Her father was convinced; Penelope was not so sure.

"He's realized that a wife is a very different thing to a—a passing fancy."

Penelope refrained from making a comment about a breeding machine when she remembered why her father had married. "I am to accept his lordship's offer, then?" She had regained some control; she now felt steely with anger.

"You are, my dear." Her father leaned forward. "Penelope, you think I haven't noticed how you shake like a newborn filly every time he comes near you? I've seen you look at him, child, when you thought no one watched you. And no, I don't think you've been looking at him like a mooncalf. The others are too taken up with their own concerns to notice you, but you're my daughter and I made it my business to notice. So I did the hard work for you. If you want him, he's yours."

The door opened to admit Lady Wimbourne, bearing a small tray with a steaming cup set upon it. His lordship's smile was all welcome. "Ah, my dear."

It was the first time Penelope had seen Marcela smile. She tried a tentative smile and was rewarded by a slight movement of the coral lips and a warming of the dark eyes.

Penelope felt superfluous, and uncomfortable, and she longed to go to her chamber to think. She stood, forgetting to be graceful and elegant, and received a raised eyebrow for her pains.

"He will no doubt come and find you shortly," her father informed her. "Be sure you can be found. I know your skill for losing yourself, pray don't do it this time."

With a brief promise to obey, Penelope fled.

In her bedchamber, she threw herself on the bed, and let thoughts wash over her. Did she want this? It seemed it was a *fait accompli* or a jest, and she still didn't know which. She decided that wherever he came to see her, it would be in a place of her own choosing. That way there wouldn't be any listeners— and gigglers—at the doors and windows.

After an hour Penelope still wasn't any the wiser, but she felt calmer. Anger simmered beneath the surface, but she had control of it now. She tidied herself at the mirror; pinned her hair up and smoothed the creases from her light blue striped gown of summer silk. Time to face the world, and accept her fate. Or rail against it. Either way, she couldn't stay here forever.

Venturing downstairs, she headed for the small parlor at the end of the state rooms. The newspapers were left there, and she was too shaken to join Mr. Grey just yet. She would spend a little time calming herself then go to him. He'd waited too long already.

The murmur of voices startled her, and she was on them

before she could take a detour.

The State Rooms ran in enfilade along the first floor in double file. There was a service corridor and a few anterooms in a hidden corridor in between, but Penelope was too late to dart through the nearest jib door. In her agitation, she'd forgotten what her maid had divulged to her that morning when she was dressing; it was a Public Day.

On certain days, the public were allowed to tour the state rooms in the company of the housekeeper, Mrs. Yeovil. It didn't usually happen with the family in residence, but this time the visitors were some kind of relatives of the housekeeper, so Severus had allowed it. He'd mentioned it at dinner the previous evening, to forewarn his guests.

Penelope's first thought on reluctantly entering the Music Room was that the housekeeper had a lot of relatives. There must be ten people there, listening intently to the lady informing them of the room's history. Penelope paused to listen and shook her head at Mrs. Yeovil as a sign that she didn't want her presence acknowledged. She wanted to hear more about this beautiful house.

She hadn't realized the Music Room had been created for Charles II's visit. Penelope was a glutton for history. Catching the housekeeper's glance, she shook her head slightly, and moved to the outskirts of the group. She wasn't dressed extravagantly so she fitted in.

They passed through to the Gold Salon and everyone drew breath at the sight of the gilded magnificence within. It was a large room, the centre of this side of the building, with an elaborately painted ceiling and gilded furniture. Everything was arranged with precision, even the Sevres ornaments on the mantelpiece. An earl from past ages gazed benevolently down, not a long hair out of place, his lace collar exquisitely rendered.

His lady hung on the other side of the room, forever separated from her lord, her satin gown gleaming seductively.

An arm slid about her waist and pressed against her stomach. Penelope, about to shriek in shock, turned to see her nemesis by her side. Severus released her. His touch had been a warning to her. She looked up and saw his small signal to Mrs. Yeovil that he didn't want to be recognized.

Dressed in a country frock coat over his plain waistcoat and breeches, he shouldn't have stood out from the stolidly dressed citizenry clustered around the housekeeper, but he did. His height, his air of authority and his animal grace all marked him out to Penelope's biased gaze. He leant close to her to murmur, "That's my great grandfather. He and my great grandmother hated each other. They produced the heir and parted, never to share the same roof again."

Before she could stop herself Penelope replied, "Arranged marriages. They don't always work."

"Then it's as well ours has been arranged by ourselves."

She turned her head to look at him. "By you and my father, you mean."

He frowned, and when she would have moved away, took her hand. Mortified, Penelope watched Mrs. Yeovil's gaze go sharply to the joined hands, then back to her face. She masked her look of astonishment almost instantly but not soon enough. Penelope flushed and turned away.

To meet the concerned expression in the eyes of her betrothed. Her betrothed. Penelope didn't know where to turn, so she went inside herself. She schooled her face to obedience and forced a bland, interested look on it, so when she turned back, her hand still clasped in his, she could have been another tourist. So her mother's training in acceptable social behavior counted for something, after all.

His fingers felt warm and firm, a physical joining made deeper by the circumstances. Embarrassed and thrilled in equal measure, Penelope felt a deep connection, more than just the two of them. Surrounded by the great house, a shell to hold its precious contents, Penelope knew she belonged. For the first time in her life, she knew that, if she willed it, this could be hers. A real home.

If she willed it. She still had one power. Her father wouldn't compel her to the marriage, if she objected violently especially if, as now it seemed, she had alternatives. Sev's intimate friendliness had broken through all her resistance, and now she stood with him, listening to Mrs. Yeovil intone the beauties of the Gold Salon. "If you will pass this way..." She led her flock to the next room.

This was the Blue anteroom, although there was little blue to be seen these days, after a refurbishing in mahogany and the adornment of more recent forefathers. Startled, Penelope gazed up into the blue eyes of her betrothed—her beloved.

Painted life-size he bestrode the wall above the mantelpiece, staring forever out of the large windows opposite. Penelope recoiled, only to be gripped and steadied by Sev's free hand. Only then, she noticed the full-bottomed wig, the excessively full skirts of the silver-laced coat, out of fashion these last ten years or more. Sev wore his own hair neatly tied back, and his coats were less flamboyant. "Your father?" she murmured.

Sev, who had taken refuge behind her whispered, "Yes." If one of the visitors cared to compare Sev to the portrait, he had no chance of hiding his identity.

"A remarkable resemblance." She studied the strong features, the mobile, elegant hands and saw where Sev's had originated.

"Not when I was a boy. I grew into the looks. I was more like my mother when I was younger."

"Was it hard, growing up without them?"

"Yes." The single word was imbued with sadness, melancholy, and Penelope, who had more than once wished her remaining parent at the devil, realized how lucky she was. Sev didn't customarily show this side of himself to the world, and his admission brought them closer together, that he should trust her with such a confidence. "I had nurses, devoted attendants, but only Antonia was a constant."

She turned to look at him, and he smiled reassuringly. "But I'm here now," he murmured.

"Yes."

Fortunately, the visitors were listening to Mrs. Yeovil, who was recounting an intricate story about a Greek statue in the corner, how it had been brought to England after years of neglect on a tiny Greek island. Penelope felt Sev's breath tickle her ear. "I think my father bought it from a dealer in Rome. The story probably increased its value."

Then Mrs. Yeovil described the previous earl and his achievements, introducing his mother as the story went on. She was very good, able to hold her audience effortlessly, and no one took much notice of the young man who had belatedly joined them. It was clear that if some of the crowd were Mrs. Yeovil's relatives, others were paying customers. They were all respectably dressed, and remarkably docile under the patronage of the housekeeper.

Penelope was by now fascinated by the way Mrs. Yeovil drew the visitors through the house's story. They were almost up to date now, and after the next room on this side, she would lead them through the treasure chamber at the end and into the ballroom on the other side.

The next room was the State Bedroom. Penelope gazed with awe at the faded, embroidered hangings, surmounted by Prince of Wales feathers at each corner. She turned impulsively to Sev, and heard his rich chuckle. "No one has ever slept in that bed. Isn't that so, Mrs. Yeovil?"

The housekeeper turned to him, uncertainty in her eyes. "Yes," she replied, then after a short struggle added, "Sir."

"Have you been here before?" A stout, well set up lady faced him, together with a younger lady who, from her similarity of feature, was probably her daughter.

"I have," Sev replied. "It's my favorite house bar none."

"It is very fine," the lady admitted. "Though the Music Room at Chatsworth is a marvel, and I've seen nothing like that here."

"There's a Gibbons room the other side of the Great Hall," Sev informed her, referring to the great woodcarver who had visited Chatsworth and Swithland House in his time.

"That would be most interesting," the lady replied. "I shall look forward to seeing it."

Sev nodded in response to Mrs. Yeovil's unspoken question, giving her permission to take the visitors to the Gibbons Parlor.

The Treasure Room was exclaimed over with its collections of fine porcelain and glass in locked cabinets, then they passed on to the ballroom. "His lordship is to hold a ball here shortly," Mrs. Yeovil informed them. "His guests are making arrangements for it now."

"Who will come?"

"Everyone," came the simple reply.

Sev, standing next to Penelope, his fingers still entwined with hers, gazed around the white and gold expanse blandly. Penelope remarkably felt her nerves steady. His warmth, his presence reassured her even though he was the cause of her agitation.

"It is expected that his lordship will make an interesting announcement at the ball." The housekeeper glanced guiltily at Sev. He met her gaze with a lifted brow.

"Ha!" the same lady who had spoken before said. "You can't get away from the gossip in the papers about it. The smart money is on Miss Trente, or so I read this morning."

"Really?" Sev's expression of polite interest held an undertone so carefully masked that only Penelope was aware of it. "I must put some money down on that outcome."

"She is a beautiful girl," murmured another lady, younger than the first speaker. "She would make a lovely countess."

"I daresay." Sev seemed to lose interest. He gazed at the gilded and painted ceiling.

"A society wedding," breathed the girl, eyes wide.

Penelope regarded her with misgiving. "They're usually private affairs, aren't they?"

"This one will be," Sev muttered under his breath.

Penelope gripped his hand tighter in reproval. "If there is one."

"I'm convinced there will be," Sev said. "And soon."

The others stilled their chatter, and watched with interest. An edge had entered the conversation, and the magnificent ballroom temporarily forgotten, everyone watched the gentleman and his lady, overtly or otherwise.

The older lady tilted her head to one side. "You sound as if you know more than we do, sir."

"I'm not at liberty to say."

Sev's enigmatic comment only served to garner more interest. Penelope couldn't work out what Sev was trying to do here. It seemed a spirit of mischief had entered, to deposit a frivolity she hadn't noticed before.

Sev released her hand. "The earl and the lady of his choice will be asked to begin the ball with the minuet. Madam?"

He bowed low, with a courtly flourish, taking the hand of the older lady. Bemused, she laughed, but accepted his hold. When Penelope realized what he was doing, she caught the spirit of mischief, light-hearted by his proximity and her sudden surge of hope, and she hurried to the harpsichord at the end of the large room. Lifting the lid, she picked out the notes of a minuet.

Sev led the lady forward, and into the dance. He led superbly, and even though the lady stumbled once or twice, he waited for her to catch up and carried on, with a genuine smile, one his guests had rarely seen recently.

Penelope warmed to him, and wondered how many other haughty aristocrats would bother to entertain people in their homes in this way. At the end of the dance he gallantly led the lady off the floor, bowing over her hand with another courtly flourish. The smiles wreathing the dame's face showed how much she had enjoyed the exercise.

Sev gave her a mischievous grin. "Now you've led out a ball at Swithland House."

"I enjoyed it very much," she replied, turning to her husband wreathed in smiles, not at all the strict dame she had appeared at first.

Sev crossed the room to where Penelope sat at the harpsichord, and offered his hand to raise her. She stood, trying to be as graceful as possible and was rewarded by a warm smile. "Mrs. Yeovil," he said softly, without turning around.

A new note had entered his voice. A note of command to

which the housekeeper responded. "Yes, my lord?"

"We'll have the ball in a week. I don't intend to wait any longer."

"Yes, my lord."

The little group fell silent, as, with Penelope resting her fingers on one arm, he walked to the group and bowed. "It was a pleasure to meet you all." He added, with a smile, "I wouldn't put any money on Miss Trente, if I were you."

The looks on their faces ranged from dawning comprehension to blank astonishment.

Penelope had no choice but to allow him to lead her from the room.

Chapter Eleven

Severus didn't speak again until they were safely behind a closed door in a small room overlooking the back of the house. The windows lay open, allowing a light summer breeze to circulate, but Penelope still felt hot. She knew what was coming, and she'd have no choice but to listen.

He stayed by the windows, and Penelope stood in the middle of the room, waiting. She didn't know what to say. She almost recoiled when he came closer, but he stopped about a foot away. "I want you to see me properly," he said softly.

Penelope nodded, relieved and disappointed at the same time. "That's—considerate of you."

"Your father told me he'd informed you of the contract—believe me, Penelope, that's not what I wanted. I didn't realize he'd be so quick off the mark."

She swallowed. "How did you want it to be?"

"I wanted you to think about spending your life with me—not with the Earl of Swithland. I wanted to ask you myself."

"I-I'm sorry, I don't understand. You *are* the Earl of Swithland."

He shook his head, not losing the eye contact he'd established between them. "I'm Severus Granville. You're the only woman in this benighted house party who recognized that.

The others want to marry the earl, but not you. Or am I wrong?"

She swallowed. Yes, it was Severus she wanted, not the earl. "No-o. I see what you mean, but I've known you a long time. I can see past the earl part because I knew you when I was a child."

"So has Caroline Trente. Her mother's had hopes of hooking me for some time. We've been thrown together since we were children." He wouldn't let her look away, holding her eyes with his transfixing gaze. "But every time she looks at me, it's as though she's looking through me. To the family jewels, the house, and all the other things. She doesn't see me, she never has."

"So you want me as compensation?" Her tone was dry. What he said was just fuelling her anger. It made her feel like second best.

"No. What I see in you is a regard for me—Severus—not for the station I was born to. You're not compensation, Penelope. Far from it."

He moved forward, and Penelope folded her arms in front of her. He stopped.

"And you're telling me that out of all the beauties you've invited here for your pleasure, you've chosen *me*? Clumsy, dowdy, stupid Penelope Makepiece? My lord, you can have the pick of the crop. You don't want me." She turned away, so he couldn't see her bitterness. "Who in their right mind would choose me over beautiful Caroline Trente or sultry Annabelle Rivers?"

"Many people. Including me."

Having regained control over her wayward emotions, Penelope turned back to face him. He hadn't moved, but still watched her. Her heart ached; she knew she wanted him, but she wouldn't let herself be used or disregarded. "Do you want a complacent wife, one who will let you go about your affairs unhindered? If so, you won't want me, my lord. I couldn't live like that. I'd rather buy myself a small house somewhere and become a local eccentric. Better that than—" Face twisting, despite her best efforts to keep it clear, she turned away again.

His arms came around her waist from behind. She felt his breath on her neck, his warmth against the thin silk of her gown and she shivered with want. If only—

"No, no, Penelope, I don't want that. I want a partner, a companion and a friend. And a clever businesswoman, a lovely woman. For you are all those things too, Penelope, not the person you seem to think you are."

She pulled away, but he wouldn't let her, drawing her close, the heat from his chest burning into her back. It was torture. It was exquisite. "I'm not lovely," she managed, sounding, even to her own ears like a child.

"Oh you are. Your beauty isn't the dazzling kind, but it will last longer. And if you hold your head up and stare the world in the face, they'll all see it. I want to be the man by your side when you do that."

Penelope listened, astonished. Never in her life had anyone said anything like that to her. He must want her to think these things.

"Turn around, Penelope. Look at me."

The intimacy tempted her and filled her with the desire to turn around to face him, but nerves rose to fret at her. She was afraid it wasn't real, that it was all a trick, but he sounded sincere, and he had never given her any reason to suspect him of duplicity. Once before, at school, someone had tricked her like that, a brother of one of her school friends and the results had devastated her. He'd sworn his undying love, and then trumpeted his triumph to everyone who would listen when she'd believed him.

Then she had fallen for Severus and ever since she'd denied her feelings for him, trying to see him only as a friend. She had failed.

Penelope turned her mind away from the remembrance, as she had so many times before. It hurt too much and she couldn't change it. Time to deal with the here and now. "What will happen if I accept you?"

He laid his cheek on her hair. It was the sweetest caress she could ever remember. "I'll go to London, get a special license and have the contract drawn up. I'd like you and your parents to come too, just to do some shopping, if you wish, and to sign the contract. Only a few days. Then we'll be married on the day of that damned ball, and give it a purpose."

"Miss Trente thinks she's arranging her own betrothal ball."

"Then we won't tell her until her plans are well under way or she'll make an attempt at sabotage." That was cruel, Penelope thought, and opened her mouth to protest, but he forestalled her words.

He lifted his head. "Please turn around, Penelope. Let me show you what made my mind up for me."

Trembling, she did as he bid her, and turned within the circle of his arms. He looked down at her for a moment before he bent his head and put his mouth to hers.

When he'd kissed her before he'd been tipsy, if not drunk, but now, in the light of day, with no trace of alcohol, it was even better.

His lips warmed hers, inviting her response. She reached her arms up and tentatively placed them on his shoulders for support. He pulled her closer. He broke the kiss, but temporarily, to open his eyes and look at her, then he kissed her again.

He opened his lips against hers, urging them apart, then took advantage and slipped his tongue between them, tasting her in a series of flickering licks which ravished her senses. She could argue with him, but she couldn't resist this. She responded, opening her mouth wider to take him in.

With a small groan deep in his throat, he pressed against her, crushing her to his body from head to foot. Everything concentrated where they joined, and she felt the caress of his hands on her whalebone-encased body. She put her arms around him, under his coat. To her mind, the discussion was far from over, though she would be mad to refuse this. She couldn't have pushed him away if her life depended on it.

He possessed her totally, took her will and thought with his kisses. She gasped when he released her mouth to drop small kisses on her upturned face. "You taste like no one else. I want to make love to you, every bone in my body is urging me to. I can't remember when I last felt this way."

"Just before you gave your last mistress her congé?" she asked, smiling, although the thought of anyone else having this pierced her to the heart.

Smiling back, he shook his head. "No one. I want to possess you, Penelope. It's a primitive urge, something beyond rationality."

Penelope thought of the other girls trying to attract his attention. "Why me?"

"God knows." He regarded her for a moment, his gaze frankly possessive. "I'm being honest, Penny."

She giggled. "No one's called me that since school."

"It suits you." He kissed the tip of her nose. "I don't know why you. I can intellectualize, say it's your intelligence, your friendliness, your inviting figure." He drew his hands from her waist up to her armpits, caressed her shoulders with his thumbs, then curved them around her back. "All these things attracted me to you, but that's not it. I first noticed you, really noticed you, when I saw how you behaved, compared to the other women here. I began to seek you out and I discovered that I enjoyed your company. And the feeling has grown. I *need* to hold you, to care for you. It would make me very happy to see you happy. That's more than I hoped for in a wife, and I'm still coming to terms with it. Can you care for me, even if just a little?"

His wistful tone crept through the warmth darkening his voice. Penelope couldn't resist. She studied his face, wondering how he couldn't see how she felt about him. It must be in her eyes; she was no more capable of hiding it now than she was of flying. "Yes, Sev. I can care for you. I do care for you."

She could say no more because he bent to kiss her again, fiercely. She felt his longing for her, his need, and she responded, trying to show him her acceptance and her love for him. Because she could deny her feelings no longer. Ten years ago, she'd had an unthinking passion for him. Now, as a grown woman, she knew the difference and she loved him. She saw the real man and loved him for it, not some ideal paper figure she'd created for herself.

The kisses deepened, the caresses became more intimate. When he laid his hand on the swell of her breast then slipped it under her fichu to touch bare skin, she pressed closer. His fingers moved closer to the top of her bodice, stroked the line and eased underneath. Penelope welcomed the caress. With anyone else, she would have felt cheapened, but with Sev, she was flattered that he would want to touch her. He could have done anything, and she'd welcome it. She arched, wanting more. His kiss consumed her and she gave it back to him. His other hand fisted in her skirts and she felt the cooler air when he dragged them up. But his hand on her outer thigh felt like fire against her skin. And suddenly, Penelope wanted to burn. His hand curved around her buttock, pulled her against him with a force that crushed her side-hoops between their bodies and forced her to feel the heat of his erection, pushing against the fabric of his breeches. Penelope pushed back, unable to resist his forceful loving.

With shocking suddenness, he pulled away, removed his hands and placed them lightly, harmlessly, on her waist. Panting, wide-eyed, he stared at her. "My God." His voice shook. "Penny, no one, *no one* has affected me like that before, made me forget everything in her arms. I've wanted women, of course I have, and set out to seduce them but you draw me in, make me yours. I'm as untutored in this as you are. Please let me teach you the little I know so we can go on together. We can't do that without marrying. Not in this life." Then he smiled, the crooked smile she loved.

Penelope stared at him, and knew she couldn't refuse. "Yes. I want it too."

This kiss was a soft caress; the whisper of his fingers on her chin a reverence. "Let's sit down before we fall down, and discuss this like civilized people."

He took her hand and led her to the sofa, putting his arm around her shoulders when she sat and drawing her close. One side of her full skirts, held out by small side hoops, lay across his lap in startling intimacy. He pressed his lips to her temple, and she relaxed and laid her head on his shoulder. "We must tell Antonia, of course."

"Did she tell you?"

"She told me nothing. She did suggest you would make a better wife than the others, but since she is your friend, I would have expected that. What should she tell me?"

Penelope felt bashful. "I—that I—wouldn't object to you

145

addressing me."

He laughed, no shadows in it, but pure amusement. "Is that what it is? Addressing you?" He pressed another kiss to her forehead. "No, Antonia said nothing to me. Should she have?"

"No. I thought you wanted one of the others. I didn't want you to know." She looked up at him, her head resting against his shoulder. "I'm still not wholly convinced. I keep thinking that the whole party will burst in and laugh at me for being so well gulled."

His appalled expression convinced her. "You thought I would do that?"

"Someone did it to me once. You've always been kind to me, but I know you have a sense of humor which has driven you to pranks in the past."

"That wouldn't be a prank. More like a cruel trick. My sense of humor wouldn't find it in the least funny." He studied her face, his eyes seeming to seek out her innermost thoughts. "I don't think this is about me. It's you, your doubts about yourself. Why shouldn't you be as good as anyone else?"

"Because I can't see properly. I don't recognize people except close up, I trip over things. I don't dance with any confidence. I can't help it, and I do my best, but—" She bit her lower lip, overcome by the emotions sweeping through her.

He pulled her closer, to rest on his chest, both arms around her. "I won't let you feel that way again. You'll do nothing you don't wish to do, and in the dance, I'll hold you so carefully you won't stumble once." He chuckled. "I never realized you were so badly nearsighted until recently, but I never thought of you as clumsy. You make the occasional stumble, and some people think you're arrogant, not shy, when you take no notice of them. We'll make it better."

She buried her head in the sweet smelling folds of his soft woolen waistcoat. "I'll cope. There are many people worse off than I am. But I don't want to let you down, or embarrass you. I want to do the best I can."

"You will, you will," he murmured, rocking her against him. "I'll be there, by your side. I can tell you when someone wants to approach you, help you all I can—" When she looked up, he had an arrested expression on his face.

"What is it?"

He smiled down at her, so soft, she could swear he loved her. That was something he hadn't said, and something she daren't ask for. What he was prepared to give her was enough, more than she'd ever hoped would come her way. "Nothing. Or rather—there might be something, but you must trust me for now. I have to make a few enquiries first."

Too full to think of anything else, she agreed, though she couldn't see how he could do anything about something no one could help. "Will you tell them at dinner?"

"No, unless you wish it. Instead, I suggest we accompany Mr. Grey to London tomorrow, with your stepmother and father. Your father is very keen to arrange matters as soon as we can. Then we can get the business of the contract over with, and purchase a special license. We can't marry in fourteen days without one."

"You meant it?"

He bent his head and gave her a soft kiss. "Assuredly I meant it. I want you, Penny, and as soon as I can have you. You'll need some new clothes, other things, so come and shop in London while we see to our business."

She wouldn't be going home for some time. "I want my other things from my father's house."

"Send for them. I'll put a traveling carriage at your disposal and you may send someone for them this afternoon." It seemed so easy. "I don't think we should tell the other guests until we get back, because if we do Miss Trente will stop her preparations for the ball and spread what rumors she can. I don't want your happiness compromised in any way."

"Isn't that a bit hard on Miss Trente? She wanted you to marry her."

He frowned. "For the past week, she's constantly denigrated you in my hearing. She found out that we've been spending more time together, even if it has been in study and business."

A pang shot through Penelope. She had no idea anything like that had been going on. They had taken very little notice of her when she'd been present. The thought that they had been gossiping without her made her miserable.

His frown deepened. "It seems like small revenge. I don't like anyone hurt in that way. It's only worsened because it's you they attacked. I have to admit that around that time I began to actively ignore them and try to think of an excuse to clear the house. But all I could think of were reasons that would make you leave, too, and I didn't want that. Gossip is one thing, but this was sheer spite, and it was aimed at you."

She sighed. "I shouldn't care, really. Why should what they say make any difference?"

"You're not a saint, and sometimes these things are hurtful." He bent and kissed her, a gentle touch of his lips to hers. "Do you still feel sad?"

She smiled up at him. "No. I feel wonderful."

"Hopefully, you'll feel even better before too long."

Penelope went straight to Antonia and found her friend delighted by her news. Penelope stared at her hands while making her confession and was almost bowled over by the ferocity of Antonia's response.

They were in Antonia's boudoir. As soon as Penelope imparted her news, Antonia was on her, hugging her with a thoroughness that left both of them breathless.

Antonia soon recovered her breath. "Oh I can't tell you how pleased I am! You shall live here, and we shall be sisters, and we need never be apart again."

Penelope gasped, her ribs squeezed tight. "Between you and your brother, I'll be bruised all over by this evening."

Antonia leaned back, her face creased with concern. "Why? What has he been doing to you?" Penelope flushed red, and Antonia laughed to see it. "Oh! He hugged you."

"You could say that."

Antonia released her, so that she nearly fell backwards. "Yes, yes," she muttered in confusion. "Did he kiss you?"

"Of course he did!" Penelope laughed, felt light-headed, ready to find anything amusing.

"Yes, yes, of course." Antonia turned away, then back to her friend. "I've always thought of you as a sister, you see, and if you kiss my brother, it just seems a bit odd." She grinned, so reminiscent of Sev at his most mischievous. "I'm sure I'll get accustomed to it." Her grin widened. "Better than I would if it were one of the others."

With one interview successfully behind her, Penelope had others to face, but she decided on a turn in the gardens first, to try to calm herself down a little, a task she was beginning to believe was impossible.

Dreaming of what was to come, Penelope didn't notice the brooding presence of Don Alfonso until he stepped out of the

149

door to the breakfast parlor to confront her. "Is this true, what your father has told me?

His face was dark with displeasure and Penelope didn't want to risk confronting him in the house, where raised voices might be heard by anyone. "Come outside. We can walk in the gardens."

She led the way to the entrance to the South Front. The Don followed in silence, stalking her like some jungle cat. Outside he walked next to her, not touching, until they were on the terrace, the formal gardens at the back of the house. "Your father informs me that you have accepted an offer of marriage from Lord Swithland." He kept his voice low, but Penelope heard the tension in it.

"It was very sudden," she ventured.

"Did your father not tell you? You were promised to me!" His voice rose towards the end of the sentence.

Penelope stopped walking and turned to face him, her face a mask of astonishment. "My father told me of your offer, Don Alfonso, but in the end it was my decision."

"The decision was not yours to make. A daughter does as her father instructs her."

This was difficult. He was wrong, but Penelope didn't think the arrogant Don Alfonso would accept that and now that she didn't have to think about facing him every day, she didn't wish to provoke him any further than she had to. "My father instructed me to make the decision. He strongly advised me to accept Lord Swithland." The sun blazed down on his dark head, intensifying the paleness of his face, the startling, exotic black eyes, now lit with an inner fire that had nothing to do with the sunny day.

"That was not wise," he said, his voice low and purringly menacing. "When he married my sister, part of the agreement was my marriage to you."

This shook Penelope. "I'll talk to him about it but the decision is made. My father would not compel my marriage to someone not of my choosing. I didn't accept you, Don Alfonso. My father informed me of your flattering offer but I wished to accept Lord Swithland."

"It was agreed." His mouth firmed in a hard line.

A cold hand clutched at her stomach. "Was there a contract, an agreement in writing?" That could be awkward. It still wouldn't be legal, to force her to marry against her wishes, not in this enlightened age, but there would be repercussions. A lawsuit, probably a very expensive one, certainly a scandalous one

"It was understood," the Don admitted, drawing himself up to his full, not inconsiderable height. "I understood your father gave his word."

She had to stand firm. She would not be bullied into marrying this man. "You must talk to him about that, but I should tell you that I have no intention of changing my mind. I have accepted Lord Swithland." She glanced away at a rose dropping its petals on to the green grass beneath it; shadowed by the rose bush it seemed greener than the grass bleached by the sun. "I should tell you that it is my own preference also. I want to marry Severus."

She swallowed, and looked back to see how the Don was taking her confession. If she'd hoped to sway him by her confession, she was to be disappointed.

"A woman should marry where her family wills it. My sister is your mother now, and she must favor my suit."

"She didn't seem to object to my acceptance of Severus's offer."

"She was most likely ordered to it by her husband. My

sister is an obedient woman, she knows her duty."

To Penelope this sounded ominous. Was it Marcela's choice to marry Lord Wimbourne, or had her preferences lain elsewhere? She would have to tell Severus in case the Don decided to make good on his veiled threats of legal action. She shivered, despite the heat of the day. "Did you order your sister to marry my father?"

"I did not need to. She wished for the match." Penelope didn't trust this assertion. If the new Lady Wimbourne saw it as her duty she might well accede to it. "In truth I cannot blame you for this now I have heard that your father ordered you to it. I am disappointed in him. I will speak to him of the matter."

That, too, sounded ominous to Penelope. "I'm afraid there is nothing you can do. I am to marry Lord Swithland."

Silence fell between them. Penelope heard birds singing in the woods beyond. A swift soared high above, a blue flash against the celestial sky. He stared at her, and his hand went out to her, and then dropped to his side with a heavy slap. "I wanted you," he said softly, the intensity of his gaze burning her more than the hot sun. "That is why I asked."

"How could you?" she said without thought. "We never really knew each other before this."

"I saw you. At a ball in London last year. I asked who you were. You looked helpless, in need of a protector. And beautiful. You try to hide your beauty. You should not." His gaze raked her from head to foot.

Penelope nearly laughed. Where had these men who thought her beautiful been before this? Devoting themselves to Miss Trente's eyes, or Lady Annabelle's hair, that was where. When she had felt alone and vulnerable there had been no one except, perhaps, Toby, and his proprietary attitude had always irked her. "You didn't approach me."

"No," he said. "I approached your father."

The unspoken words seared her mind. *And offered him your sister?* She knew she was right; Don Alfonso's had been offered in return for her, and now her father had reneged on the agreement. Thank goodness none of this had been written down, agreed upon. She might have listened to Don Alfonso's suit had it not been for Sev, might have made what she was coming to acknowledge would have been a serious mistake.

"Penelope!" The voice behind her made her shriek.

She turned to see Sev approaching quickly, something in his hands. "You forgot this. You'll get another headache if you don't put it on."

Penelope laughed; released from the ring of intensity the Don had erected around them. "Not ruin my complexion? Get freckles?"

Sev put the hat on her head and tied the broad ribbon under her chin, rather like Penelope's old nurse had done when she had heedlessly run into the sunny garden when she was a child. Severus twitched the bow into place and smiled at her. "I think a freckle or two might suit you, but headaches don't."

She laughed with him; turned and saw Don Alfonso staring at them both. What had he seen? With eyes so dark, it was difficult to read him, to understand what he was thinking. He showed very little outwardly; that was why Penelope was so taken aback by his passionate avowal of a moment ago. She had known he was interested. Just not how much.

"I understand congratulations are in order."

Sev stared at him, startled. "I would appreciate it if you kept the information to yourself for now. We haven't yet told the company and I wish to formalize the union with a marriage contract before we make it public."

The Don bowed and let his searing gaze take in the couple.

"I hope you are both happy with the decision."

Sev bowed in return. "Indeed we are, sir."

Abruptly the Don bowed once more and turned to stride back to the house, the skirts of his heavy, formal coat billowing behind him.

Penelope watched him, then turned to see Sev's serious gaze on her. "What is it? What's wrong?"

She bit her lip. "It seems the Don thought I was going to marry him."

"Well, you're not." Leaning closer, he murmured, "In case you've forgotten, you're mine."

She blushed rosily. "I could never forget that, Sev." She tucked her hand into the crook of his arm and they strolled on together, leaving the shelter of the rose garden and taking one of the walks away from the house. "He thinks he gave his sister to my father in return for me."

"Whatever gave him such a foolish idea?"

She paused, staring at the lush grass at her feet. "I think my father did. I don't know if he meant to, or if there was a misunderstanding. Knowing my father, he probably promised to put in a word for Don Alfonso. Which he did, you know, but he made it clear he preferred your suit."

"And you chose me," Sev said. "For which I can only be grateful. And grateful too, that I got to you before Don Alfonso." Penelope laughed, her mood lightened by his presence and the way he was taking the news. "As far as I see it, it's your father's problem, not yours."

"I'm sorry the Don thought that. He seems to regard women as property."

Sev frowned. "Well they are in law. When you marry me, you'll become my chattel. It offends me; I've never thought of women in that way. I hope you don't either."

They had reached the edge of the formal gardens, but they carried on walking, up a small path towards a Greek temple. "I've never considered it. I try to avoid it when I can. It irks me that I have to ask my father to sign my stock dealings, and after Saturday, I suppose I'll have to ask you. I've seen women traded like playing cards though, and I'm glad my father never thought of me in that way."

He lifted her hand to his lips then settled it back on his arm. "I've seen that too. I've told Antonia that she must make her own decisions for her future life. I've also warned her that if I consider a man unsuitable, I'll do all in my power to prevent the match."

"She hasn't told me of anyone. I think she would if she felt a particular tendre."

"Long may that continue." He glanced around. "I think that's far enough."

"For what?"

He stopped walking and turned her into his arms. "I want to kiss you, but I don't want an audience. They can't see us from the house here."

"Oh." Firmly deciding on not allowing anything to spoil this marvelous day, Penelope settled in his arms and turned her face up. "Kiss away."

Chapter Twelve

Back at the house, they found two footmen hauling a trunk across the black-and-white tiled floor. At Sev's questioning look, they stood up, and bowed. The tallest informed them, "Don Alfonso has left a note for you with Mr. Hutton, my lord."

Sev let them get on with their work, leading Penelope across the hall to find the butler. The note Hutton handed him was a formal note of regret that urgent business called the Don away. He sent them his best wishes for their future happiness. Sev glanced down at Penelope, one dark eyebrow raised. "One less complication."

"I want to ask my father what he meant," she told him. "I don't think he meant to give his word to Don Alfonso, but I want to be sure."

"I'll come with you," he said, brooking no disagreement. He put a gentle finger to her lips, hushing any protest she might want to make. "It's as much my business as it is yours."

She let him have his way, relieved that she wouldn't have to face her father on her own.

They found Lord Wimbourne laid out on a large daybed in the private sitting room adjoining his bedroom. Penelope made an exclamation of concern and hurried forward to lay her hand on his forehead for any signs of temperature. He felt cool enough, and knocked off her hand irritably. "Just bellyache, my dear. It's nothing."

From his pale face, Penelope doubted it. "We can leave you to rest, Papa."

"I'd appreciate it," he said briefly. "Was there something in particular you wanted? You don't look as happy as you did when I spoke to you earlier. Is there something wrong?"

"Yes, Papa. I would like some clarification."

Sitting down in a comfortable chair close to him, she recounted to her father what had happened between Don Alfonso and her in the garden. "And now he is leaving suddenly. Papa—did you give your word to him? Did you promise me to him? If you did, he can claim a pre-contract, and contest my marriage to Sev."

His lordship frowned, his thin mouth turned down at the corners. "No. Not officially." His frown deepened. "Let me think."

They waited in silence, Sev standing behind Penelope's chair, his hand gripping the back of it just next to her head.

His lordship's face cleared. "I remember very well. When I decided to propose to Marcela, she asked me to apply to her brother, more for form's sake than anything else. After all, she's older than he is and a widow, so she could do as she wished. I didn't mind; the Don introduced us in the first place, and encouraged me to think Marcela might be interested in me." His frown lifted completely. "He wasn't wrong. When I talked to him, he asked me for your hand. I didn't see why not, but I explained that he might have rivals, although at that time I only meant Toby Makepiece. But he was a better prospect than Toby, so I decided to allow him to ask. I suggested that he should come with us here to court you." He lifted his head and regarded Penelope gravely. "At no time did I promise him your hand. I swear it, Penelope. I did say I would put in a word for him with you."

Sev's hand, the only part of him she could see, relaxed. "That's it then. He said you gave your word." He moved his hand to rest on Penelope's shoulder, and she warmed to this acknowledgement that they were now a couple.

She leaned back into the contact. "So you said you would put a word in for him, and he thought you were giving your word?"

"That must have been it," his lordship said. He leaned back against the cushions behind his head with a sigh. "I'm sorry anyone was hurt, and I'll talk to him when I feel better, try to explain the difference in what I said and what he thought I said. I don't want him upset; it will upset Marcela."

"You'll have to write to him," said Sev. "He's leaving."

"Probably just as well," his lordship agreed.

The door opened to admit Lady Wimbourne, who bore a tray on which reposed a large dish of steaming brew. "Oh!"

Sev went and took the tray from her, and placed it on a small table at his lordship's side. He helped Marcela to a chair. "We came to talk to your husband about your brother. He seemed to be under the illusion that Penelope was promised to him."

Lady Wimbourne let a Spanish word pass her lips, a word Penelope hadn't come across before. "What a fool! I told him he must take his chances."

"Have you seen him, ma'am?" Sev asked.

"Yes; he came to see me just now, after telling his man to pack. We are to say he has been called away on urgent business, but it is your refusal which has sent him away." She turned dark eyes on Penelope, but she couldn't detect reproach there. "You are not to worry. He takes violent fancies to people. He has done it before. If he had not left, I would have sent him away. He will not spoil your wedding day and he will recover

158

soon enough."

"He's done it before?" Penelope queried. She put her hand up, and Sev took it in his. She felt the need of contact.

"Oh yes." Her ladyship shrugged. "There was a girl in Madrid. He followed her around all summer but she was promised to a great man. He asked her to run away with him, but she refused. It was just as well. There would have been great trouble if she had accepted him."

Severus informed them of his plans to visit London. "I would rather take Penelope with me, and you, sir, so we can sign the contract then and there, but if you wish, I'll go alone."

Lord Wimbourne smiled. "No, I think your original idea is a good one. My man of business is there too, and if we call them in for a meeting, we can get the matter formalized much quicker than making them dash about the country. Should you have any objection to a few days in London, my dear?"

Penelope tried not to look surprised—after watching her parents move further and further away from each other, this new fondness of her father's to remain close to his new wife surprised her.

And Lady Wimbourne seemed surprised, too. Penelope found it difficult to read any expression in her dark, fathomless eyes, but she thought she saw relief. Or maybe pleasure. "I would like that. I need to replenish my stock of herbs."

At dinner, they behaved as if nothing had changed. At Severus's request, they were to keep the matter private until the contracts were signed. If the guests here got even an inkling of the news, it would be all over the country in days. Not that Penelope or Severus minded that. What they wanted to avoid, Severus in particular, was any unpleasantness coming Penelope's way because of her new status. The cats would descend, claws out, and rend her limb from limb.

On the surface, everything was as it always had been, with Penelope sitting far away from her host, and not able to talk to him. She was glad of that, afraid that too close a contact would lead to detection. She still wasn't sure that she wanted to conceal the news, Severus had persuaded her into temporary secrecy, but matters arose that convinced her.

Miss Trente wore a dazzling gown of rich green, embroidered with a pattern of rosebuds, and a petticoat of white and silver. The neckline was cut low, so the tops of her white breasts rose precariously above it, threatening every moment to escape the tight lacing beneath them. The saucy frill of lace, ostensibly for modesty, served to frame and enhance. Penelope saw Sev glance at them and blink.

Miss Trente noticed his glance, and leaned forward, offering him a better view, as she whispered something to him behind her fan. Sev's response was to arch an eyebrow, and reply, in low tones that nevertheless could be heard right down the table, "Temptation indeed! But if I repeat it to your mama, I fear she wouldn't quite like it."

He reached for a bowl of roast parsnip, taking him away from her and towards the sultry Lady Annabelle, smiling her welcome. At least her gown wasn't quite so precariously cut, although it was a close run thing. It reminded Penelope of the Judgment of Paris. Who would have thought that she was playing the part of Aphrodite?

Despite his cool demeanor, Severus was finding it difficult to fend off the attentions of the front-runners. He felt like a marked man, which indeed he was. Had he not been aware that he was merely a means to an end—wealth, a position in society—he might have been flattered. Trapped between two palpitating bosoms, he hoped Penelope wasn't getting the wrong idea. The flirting grew ever more blatant. Miss Trente had just suggested to him that they might find somewhere a little more secluded after dinner, as she had something particular she wished to say to him. She was dressed to kill tonight, and he was the prey. He'd promised to announce his decision tonight, and he couldn't get out of it now, but he'd never felt so trapped in his life as he did between the society ladies vying for his title and fortune.

"I fear I find myself in an awkward situation," he announced, in a lull in the conversation. "I have to go up to town and I cannot give you the decision I promised until I return." Or they might take their spite out on Penelope, one of his reasons for asking her to accompany him. Even with her accompanying him, they would plot and criticize her for having the effrontery to win him from under their noses. He wouldn't leave Penelope at the mercy of these harpies. Better he sprang his decision on them once they had dispersed to their various estates. His protectiveness towards her astounded him with its ferocity and forced him to reconsider many of his preconceptions about how his marriage would affect his life. "It is most reprehensible of me to creep away at such a time, especially since I have committed you to the ball, but there is no way out of it. Urgent business calls."

There was a general pouting and coos of disappointment. "I'll only be a few days. I'll be back well in time for the ball. Have you a theme for it?"

Miss Trente smiled. "Roses, since there are so abundant. And they are the flower of romance, don't you think, sir?"

"Certainly," he agreed blandly, desperate to make contact with his betrothed, to see what she thought. He kept his gaze rigidly away from her, knowing he would betray himself if he looked at her now.

Miss Trente gazed at him through her lashes and Sev wondered how many times she had practiced that particular expression in the mirror. It would be seductive if it wasn't so calculated. "I shall wear pink. It's as well I brought it with me."

"You'll be the centre of attention, my love," her mother purred.

Miss Trente smiled at her parent complacently. For the first time Sev felt a little sorry for the girl, and resolved to let her down lightly. He would tell her before the ball so she wouldn't expect too much. Perhaps he would put Peter in her way. He seemed to admire her and while a younger son, he was in possession of a considerable fortune of his own and was making a fine political career for himself.

"I've brought the date forward a little. I trust that will cause you no inconvenience?"

The rising excitement in her eyes easily overcame her confusion. "No problem at all, my lord. I look forward to it—immensely."

The announcement that the Wimbournes were also taking the opportunity to go to Town, and the barely heard concurrence from Mr. Grey passed almost without comment. Nobody asked them if they intended to return for the ball. Penelope wasn't surprised. They would be sent an invitation, but not urged to attend.

Miss Trente could hardly wait for the conclusion of the meal to escape to the drawing room and discuss this turn of events. Despite a few odd looks from the others, Penelope joined the eager group by the fire, a book resting unread in her hands. Two of the young ladies had to move aside so she could draw a chair up. They gave her a cool stare, but she didn't care.

Miss Trente smiled beatifically at her. Everyone was

welcome tonight. Her eyes shone with joy at the prospect of a speedy conclusion to her campaign. "When do you think he will ask?" one asked.

"And who?" said Lady Annabelle, pointedly. "It's not a foregone conclusion."

Miss Wilcox shrugged her plump shoulders. "By no means."

"Oh, I think it is," said Miss Trente. She stared at Miss Wilcox until that lady looked away. Her carelessness fooled no one. Penelope couldn't fault her, as Miss Trente's calm assumption of authority was beginning to wear her down. It was true that the lady was a front-runner, but horses had fallen before, and this one had fallen badly.

Not that she knew that yet. The more they discussed Sev, the less possible it seemed that he had actually asked her to marry him. His desire to keep the betrothal secret played into her feeling of unreality. It meant she could conceal the secret with more assurance, not quite believing in it.

Miss Trente clapped her hands. "I'm sure I know why he's going to London. To buy a ring, and perhaps even a special license." This was so near the truth Penelope winced. "However, I've no mind to be married in haste. I want to be able to arrange things far more suitably than that!"

"Do you think he will ask before he leaves?"

Yes, thought Penelope.

"I don't think he will have the time. I must consider the matter and consult with my parents." She glanced at her new stepmother, who was shamelessly eavesdropping from a comfortable couch in the corner.

Penelope spoke. "Don't you burn to have him in your arms?" She chose the most lurid description she could think of, a wicked impulse urging her to see how far she could push Miss Trente.

163

Miss Trente's lip turned up at the corner in an unbecoming sneer. "Not at all." She smoothed her shining skirts. "I cannot imagine that particular activity is anything but boring and uncomfortable. There is no dignity in it, and the Countess of Swithland must always remember her dignity. Even in private."

General murmurs of agreement followed the statement, and Penelope was the recipient of several pitying looks.

"The sentiments expressed in the popular novel are not at all what we look for in real life," said Lady Annabelle, Miss Trente's shadow.

"You won't mind his *chéres amies*?" Penelope continued.

"I shall welcome them. I can think of few things worse than being the centre of a man's life, to be his sole means of—" Even Miss Trente had the grace to blush. She looked down.

Penelope felt Antonia's hand on her shoulder. It was shaking, and Penelope guessed that her friend was angry. She wouldn't tell Sev, but Antonia might. "So you want him for the position?" Antonia asked. "You want to be countess?"

Miss Trente was clearly surprised. "Why, of course. And he is the most delightful gentleman. Who could wish for a better escort? I am supposed to be worthy of a duke, but Swithland's estate is equal to anything most dukes can offer, and I must admit I like him better than any of them."

"You're not in love with him."

Miss Trente's laughter was clear and tinkling, an oft-practiced sound. "How plebeian! I feel nothing stronger than respect, or liking, on principle. The stronger emotions play havoc with one's complexion, you know." She cast a pitying look at Antonia. "I am glad we are to be sisters. I can put you in the way of so much."

"Indeed." Antonia's frosty tone showed Penelope how much she disliked the notion. For the first time Penelope thought that

Miss Trente deserved the setdown Sev had threatened to give her. It might even do her good, if it forced her to think again about the meaning of marriage. She pitied the man Miss Trente managed to snag. At least Miss Wilcox, with her sultry glances and expanse of delicious flesh, promised more. Penelope wondered why she hadn't appealed to his lordship. Or was Sev just tired of being pursued, and had decided upon the one who seemed least trouble?

Remembering his kisses earlier that day Penelope sincerely hoped not, but she knew she was too inexperienced to know for sure. Her feelings for him were now certain. She was lost.

Realizing she couldn't face him any more that night without everyone knowing the truth, Penelope took her book and went to her room, only to be disturbed an hour later by a soft knock. She put the book down, still unread, and opened the door.

She smiled stupidly at him. He smiled back before stepping inside and closing the door. She moved enough to let him in, not sure what he wanted. Nervous.

"I just wanted to bid you goodnight," he said. "A stipulation of our marriage."

"Yes?"

"That whenever possible I kiss you good night."

"Just kiss?"

He laughed, hearing the mild disappointment in her voice. "Oh more than that, much more. But not tonight. We're making an early start in the morning, and you'll need your rest. Good night, sleep well."

She went to him gladly, filled his arms, held her face up for his kiss. It was sweet and thorough, but with passion held well in check.

Penelope slept very well that night.

Chapter Thirteen

They left in the morning before the rest of the household rose and arrived in London early the following day after an overnight stop at an inn. They could have reached London in a day, but Lady Wimbourne didn't wish to hurry.

Severus's London house was in a quiet street near Grosvenor Square. There weren't many knockers on the doors, this being the season for country house living and sojourns at fashionable spas and they agreed that it would be foolish to open more than one house for a few days' stay.

The stately pace of their travel allowed for the servants at the town house to be forewarned, so the house was dusted, clean linens on the beds, and the covers off the furniture. It was modern, but the earl had leased the property for a number of years, so it had, to Penelope's prejudiced eyes, his stamp about it. A few books on a table, some walking canes in the hall, that was all, but it was enough. She wondered what his bedroom was like then stopped herself following that dangerous path. She would know that soon enough. She was fascinated and afraid, in equal measure, of the physical feelings he evoked in her. Nothing like Toby. This man could possess her, as he said he wanted to. But on the journey, he'd behaved like the perfect suitor, at least perfect in Lady Wimbourne's eyes. Penelope was disappointed, hoping for more passionate kisses and caresses, but apart from a brief goodnight kiss, he remained polite and a little distant.

It was too early to visit Mr. Grey's office that morning, as he had traveled up with them. However, Severus promised to talk to the Swithland's man of business and have a contract ready for them to discuss and sign the day after tomorrow.

Lady Wimbourne was delighted to have the opportunity to visit a mantua maker out of season. "She will be glad of the business and we may choose in peace. It will be a pleasure to shop."

"I love the season." Penelope said.

Sev's attention was caught. "I thought you would dislike the crush. My sister does."

Penelope smiled. "I like being a person in a crowd. I love to overhear them, little parts of their lives, and I like to be part of it all."

"Not a country girl then?" He quirked an eyebrow.

"There's a time for that as well."

"Are you tired, do you need to rest?" he asked abruptly. "There's an establishment I must visit, and I would appreciate it if you came with me."

"Oh?"

"The man who makes my instruments for me. I have a new telescope on order; and he sometimes keeps things for me he knows I like. Would you like to come?"

"Yes, above all things."

"Oh, I hope not above everything."

Chuckling, he got to his feet. So did Lady Wimbourne. "I will accompany you. Lord Wimbourne is feeling a little unwell, and once he is safely resting now, I will be free to go where you wish."

Penelope was concerned. Her father had been ill more than usual lately. "What is it? Is it serious?"

"No, or I would not be going out. His stomach troubles him. I have given him a draught and I will leave him to rest. He will be well by dinnertime."

She stood, smoothing non-existing creases from her dark gown. The new Lady Wimbourne seemed to favor dark colors. Her dark hair shone with energetic brushing, never a hair out of place. Penelope, standing before the mirror smoothing her own more errant chestnut locks, felt envy rise within her. Her hair always took so much taming. It was as well her maid was so efficient; otherwise she might well resemble a haystack.

Collins came up behind her and, clucking in disapproval, took the brush. "I have to ask you, ma'am, if you will require my services after your marriage."

Penelope was startled into saying, "Why should I not?"

"You may require someone else, ma'am, as befits your new station in life. If you wish to do this, I would appreciate you telling me when we're in London, so I can consult a register office."

Penelope met her eyes in the mirror. "Are you happy with me, Collins?"

"Oh yes, miss!" Occasionally Collins would forget Penelope was now "ma'am," but Penelope liked the reminder. Generally a young lady became "ma'am" when she entered society, but old habits died hard and although Penelope had been moving in society for eight years now, Collins occasionally forgot. The maid had been her mother's assistant, then her own maid. Discreet and clever, Penelope felt lucky to have her. She had no desire to acquire a fashionable French maid.

"Then there's no reason to change. You might need someone to help you though, especially when I have to dress for

168

more formal occasions. I'll have to have a laundry maid, and someone to help you at other times, like when I'm in Town. I look to you to advise me. Tell me when you need someone, if you would."

"Yes, ma'am." Back to "ma'am" again, Penelope noted. She wondered how Collins would manage with "my lady" and decided she'd probably cope excellently.

Attired becomingly in a fresh gown of white, printed with primroses, a pretty beribboned straw bergère on her head and the inevitable fan in her gloved hands, Penelope was ready. Sev and Lady Wimbourne were waiting for her, and they climbed into the traveling carriage and set off.

Penelope was aware of an atmosphere, a tension between the other two, as though they shared a secret. Sev gave a boyish grin, but she assumed that was pleasurable anticipation at visiting a favorite place.

The shop was ordinary looking, in a narrow street close to Bond Street. The window held a telescope in a shagreen case, several pairs of opera glasses and a complicated looking brass instrument, the likes of which Penelope had never seen before.

It seemed they were expected, being greeted by the proprietor himself. Sev's handshake was extremely warm, clasping Mr. Brough's arm at the elbow with his free hand in the way gentlemen who knew and respected each other tended to do. "I'm afraid your new telescope isn't quite ready, my lord."

Penelope expected Sev to be disappointed. Instead, he smiled and turned to Penelope. "It's of no matter. I daresay I'll be busy enough with other things for the foreseeable future. This is the young lady I wrote to you about, and this is her—ah—"

"Mother," said Penelope firmly.

Mr. Brough bowed. He must be about sixty, with dark

clothes and gold-rimmed spectacles. Instinctively she liked him, but there was something that confused her, the way he stared at her in a distinctly speculative way.

"Sev?" she asked, turning to him.

"Something I promised myself I would do for you. Come and sit down."

He led her to a large, high chair, upholstered in brown velvet. Feeling apprehensive now, Penelope let him hand her into it. Her stepmother sat in a smaller chair across the room. It was a large room, the shop area, but Mr. Brough went to the door and locked it. "You have my undivided attention, Miss Makepiece."

Penelope jerked her head around to find Severus smiling reassuringly. "Those headaches of yours. I don't want you to suffer them any more. My guess is that you don't wear your spectacles enough and you've never been tested properly. Have you ever had your eyesight assessed?"

"I don't understand."

He took her hand. "I mean with near sight as severe as yours, you should have someone look at it. Will you do it?"

"What does it mean?"

"It means you'll be able to see properly for once. And for further than a foot or two."

"But—"

"Will you?"

She gave in. "Why didn't you tell me?"

He grinned. "I didn't know if you'd agree. And I wanted it to be a surprise. I suppose I shouldn't have done it, but I apprised Brough here of your problem and he said he might be able to help."

She grinned back. "Very well."

Penelope didn't like the idea of anyone touching or meddling with her eyes in any way, but it seemed there was nothing of the kind involved. Mr. Brough proceeded to put a contraption on her face, like a pair of spectacles with open tops, but made out of iron and much heavier. "Ma'am, you say you are nearsighted?"

"Yes."

"Then could you please focus your attention on the shelves on the far side of the shop, if you please?"

Penelope squinted. "I can't see much."

"Good. If you will excuse me, ma'am." He slid something into the groove on the left side of the spectacles. Now Penelope could only see out of her right eye. "Will you tell me when you can see better?"

Looking to the table by her side Penelope saw a large, shallow wooden box resting on it. When Mr. Brough lifted the lid, she saw ranked orderly rows of—lenses. Now she understood.

It took quite a while, and a great many changes of lenses but eventually Penelope could see the shelves and their contents. Mr. Brough made a note of the numbers of the lenses, and repeated the exercise on her left eye. Penelope was fascinated, and after a while enthusiastically joined in. She tried not to squint, or imagine she saw more than she could. It seemed Mr. Brough was pleased, from the satisfied sigh he gave when he finally closed the box and removed the iron contraption from her face.

Going to the large counter in front of the shelves, he rang a small hand bell there, and a neatly attired maid came through from the back of the house, bearing a tray of tea. She poured it out and left. Sev, who had watched the whole process with fascinated eyes, accepted his dish and sat down where he could see her.

"It seems," said the older man, "that one of your eyes is much worse than the other."

Penelope was surprised. "I hadn't realized that."

"When the nearsightedness is as pronounced as yours, ma'am, it can be difficult to tell. It's not surprising you never noticed. That difference may have been contributing to the headaches."

"I can't wear spectacles all the time! I manage quite well without them."

"You do not," Sev said firmly. "You stare at people without seeing them, you can't get much enjoyment out of the theatre. As my wife I shall expect you to wear them."

"People will call me bluestocking."

"What does that matter?" he demanded impatiently. "Promise me you'll try, at least."

Penelope felt ruthlessly cared for, and she loved it. "I promise."

He smiled warmly. "Good." Turning to Mr. Brough, he asked, "When can you have a pair ready for her?"

"For you, my lord, tomorrow," Mr. Brough replied. "I have a supply of lenses to hand. All I need to do is cut a pair down to fit a frame."

"But not horn-rimmed." Penelope pleaded. "May I see what you have in mind?"

What Mr. Brough had in mind was a small pair of fine, gold-rimmed spectacles much like his own. Penelope breathed a sigh of delight. "The horn-rimmed ones are the only ones I've ever had. They're very ugly."

"Unlike their owner," Sev said with great gallantry.

Penelope knew a moment of anxiety. "What will my papa

say?"

"It won't matter soon enough," Sev reminded her. "I'm sure he'll learn to manage with the sight of you in spectacles."

Penelope gazed around the room, wanting it all now. The collection of blurred outlines she had lived with for so long was no longer good enough. She wanted to see the world properly. Now.

Chapter Fourteen

The spectacles arrived the next day, delivered by hand in a pretty, gold-tooled leather case. Penelope was sitting at breakfast with Sev and her father when they arrived. Her stepmother had not yet arrived downstairs. She looked up timorously at Lord Wimbourne. He might not like this.

"I desire my wife to see properly," Sev said mildly. "Of course, she is under your jurisdiction for the next ten days, but after that I wish her to wear these."

Penelope drew the delicate articles out and looked at them. They glittered in the bright morning sunlight. She glanced up at the men, both watching her, but she wasn't close enough to discern their faces.

"Put them on," said Severus quietly.

Penelope put them on. They were much lighter in weight than her horn-rimmed ones, and there was no dark line around the lenses, a frame before her eyes. She stared at the tabletop, which looked no different. Then she lifted her head and looked at Sev. He gazed back at her, warmth and encouragement etched on every feature.

Penelope caught her breath. She could never, never remember seeing as well as this. The two men watched her in silence as she stared around the room. It was a pretty, almost feminine room, decorated in light colors with satinwood furniture. That much she already knew. She hadn't noticed the little china ornaments on the mantelpiece before, or the delicate embroidery on the fire screen in front of the cold fireplace. The paintings on the wall were small landscapes for the most part, interspersed with engravings.

It was a revelation. Colors became more intense now they weren't blurred into vague masses, lines were clear. She hadn't realized she was smiling until she saw Sev's reaction to her pleasure, a warmth on his face she felt down to her toes.

"Even if I have to take them off in public, I have this. My other spectacles must have been badly set, because I can see so much more now. And it's so easy. My eyes don't hurt."

"Do they usually hurt?"

"Mostly," she admitted.

He got up and came round the table to her, lifting her hand and pressing a kiss on the palm. "Then I shall insist that you wear them all the time."

Penelope looked at her father, to see his reaction, but his face was passive. She looked back up at Severus. "If it pleases you."

"It pleases me." He released her hand and went to the buffet, picking up a heated plate. The intensity in the room seemed to subside with the natural movement, and Penelope reached for the teapot. "I'll order you some more pairs," Sev said casually. "I thought I would visit Mr. Brough again while you're at the mantua makers. It wouldn't do for you to break a pair and have nothing to hand."

He brought his plate back to the table, now loaded with chops, eggs and ham. "Thought you might like to come to White's with me," said Lord Wimbourne, with a significant look.

Sev laughed. "Assuredly I mean to put in an appearance there. Oh, don't concern yourself, sir, Penelope knows all about the book. It will be a great pleasure to disabuse them."

Lord Wimbourne grinned. "I thought we might prolong it a little. Keep them guessing for another day."

Sev's eyes gleamed. "Sporting some blunt of your own?"

The older man tutted. "Hardly fair, old man, hardly fair." He glanced at Sev, his eyes full of mischief. "I did think I might go and see my old friend Cornelius Salt, though. He's been a bit strapped for cash recently."

Both Sev and Penelope laughed then. It was true that the aptly named Captain Salt had found living expenses a little difficult since he retired from the navy. He deserved better. Perhaps a little wager at the club might help to provide a portion for his eldest girl, a beauty who hadn't yet found a mate. Perhaps some good would come of that appalling betting book after all.

As Severus had mentioned, the day belonged to the mantua makers. Penelope and her stepmother attended one of the most fashionable modistes in London. Penelope had never enjoyed a visit so much as this one. Despite Marcela's personal preference for dark, somber colors, she proved to have excellent taste, and assisted Penelope in selecting several fabrics for new gowns. Initially, Penelope had decided to order only one new gown, but the temptation was too great, and she spent a delightful day choosing and ordering. She didn't order a Court mantua, as she wanted to think about it properly. As the new Countess of Swithland, she would have to be presented once more, but this time in something more appropriate to her new status. Tedious, but necessary, and the mantua would cost a fortune.

By the time she returned to the house, Penelope was exhilarated and exhausted, drinking several dishes of tea one after the other. She was concerned to find that after his visit to White's with Sev, her father had once more retired to bed to rest. Marcela went upstairs to see him, leaving Penelope alone with Sev.

Suddenly shy, she avoided his eyes, but drawn to him, she looked up. He was frowning. "What is it? Has something upset you?"

"What?" He came back to earth. "No, no, not precisely. That is—is your father often ill?"

"No." To her surprise, a feeling of relief swept through Penelope. She had been afraid her worries were groundless but to hear them voiced by someone else seemed to solidify them. "Just recently. He's complaining of pains in his stomach more than he ever did before."

"Yes. He was taken ill at White's. It was very sudden; one moment he was standing by me, laughing at something someone had just said, the next he doubled up, clutching at his stomach. It's out of his control." He paused. "Penelope, I think it might be suspicious."

"What?" This was something Penelope hadn't considered before, or at least hadn't allowed to impinge on her consciousness. "Not natural?"

His frown deepened; he stood up and took a few agitated strides around the room. "I'm not sure. Penny, you mustn't tell anyone else, I'm not at all sure about any of this. He might have developed an ulcer. They can be very bad, and the pain is, I'm told, terrible, but with the right care, they can heal. They come on very suddenly. So it might have a reasonable explanation."

Penelope paused for a bare moment before she decided to entrust Sev. "I've been worried, too. I've seen his wife—my mother—Marcela administer potions to him. I haven't the faintest idea what is in them."

"I think we should find out."

He had his back to her, facing the window, but she could

tell by the rigid set of his shoulders that he was tense. "It's difficult. He's married her for an heir, hasn't he?"

"Yes." She sat rigidly, hands clasped in her lap. "Toby is an adequate heir, but my mother was always bitterly disappointed that she didn't give Papa a son."

Something in her tone must have betrayed her, for he spun around, the full skirts of his formal town coat rising in the warm air. "Was it bad?"

She didn't dissimulate, but her hands now gripped rather than clasped. Sev stared at her, waiting for her answer. It came in a whisper. "Sometimes."

He stayed where he was. "Tell me." It wasn't a command, more a soft request. He seemed to understand that she couldn't tell him if he came too close; the memory was bad enough.

She lowered her head, stared at her hands. "After I was born the doctor told my mother she might not bear a child again. She refused to believe it. I remember many times when she announced she was expecting, only to lose it in a month or so." She shut her eyes tight, trying to forget, but unable to. All she could see was red, eyes open or shut, spectacles on or off. "The pregnancies drained her, but she insisted on trying over and over again. She wanted a son more than anything. There was one time, at dinner—" She bit her lip in an effort to regain control, seeing it all again in her mind. "I've never seen so much blood."

The silence was deafening. Penelope raised her head, to see Severus watching her, a look of deep concern on his face. Slowly, he held out his hand, palm up. Slowly, she got to her feet, moved across the room and took it.

The offer of comfort, once accepted, was almost more than Penelope could bear. He folded his arms around her and guided her to a sofa where they could sit together. "I've never told anyone about this because it seemed too much like complaining. What were my worries next to that? But I felt unwanted, Sev. Not needed. They sent me to school after Mama complained to my father that I was a thorn in her side. I reminded her of her failure, she said. I was her failure."

In his arms, she was soothed, assuaged, able at last, to talk about it. "I enjoyed school. They let me wear my spectacles, and I met Antonia. I never told her how I felt about life at home, but I think she guessed some of it." His hands smoothed her back in a series of gentle caresses. She relaxed into them, trying not to think about what she was telling him. It still hurt too much. "It killed her of course, but not for many years. She wouldn't stop trying. My father tried to stop her, but she caught him up in her obsession, made him think it was as important as she did." She ducked her head, burying it in his shoulder so he couldn't see her. "Now it will all start again."

"Is that why you accepted my offer? So you wouldn't have to see it again?"

"No!" The answer was vehement but muffled by her mouth against the stiffened moiré material of his coat. "I would have accepted Toby for that, but not you. Never you!"

His arms tightened about her. "Thank God."

The vehemence of his response was such that she looked up in wonder. They stared at each other for a tense, fraught moment. Then he pressed his lips to hers in a fervent embrace that was all passion.

After the first jolt, his lips softened and he seemed to remember the tenderness he had forgotten. His embrace quieted, passion still there but softened by consideration and respect. He finished the kiss and drew back to look at her. "You mean much more to me than that. You know that, don't you?"

"Yes."

"I'd like children, but it's not vital to my well-being. There is an heir, a distant cousin; you'll meet him by and by. I want you, Penny, not an heir."

"I was going to tell you," she said, leaning back against the protection of his arm. "If it's an inherited trait, you should know."

"I don't care. If it happens, we'll try not to get you pregnant again." He drew her close to kiss her again.

Penelope had never felt so wanted. All her life she'd been resented, ignored and despised; her mother had preferred to keep her out of sight, so she wouldn't be reminded of the girl who had cost her the ability to mother an heir. Her father, exhausted by the domestic turmoil, retreated to his club and the coffee-house. It was hard to believe that someone wanted her for herself, but first Antonia and now Severus seemed to do so.

When he drew back, Penelope felt him tremble. "I think we'd better go out to the park. You're far too much of a temptation. I've promised myself I'll wait, and I'm determined on it." His smile was decidedly shaky.

Penelope was indignant. "What about me? What if I haven't promised myself to wait?"

He chuckled. "I hadn't thought of that. I suppose I assumed that you would want to."

She looked at him, studied his face and reached a hand up to touch his cheek. "With anyone else I might, but not you."

He turned his head and kissed her fingers, closing his eyes. "We'll see," he murmured, so low she nearly missed it. "But not now. You need some air and so do I. Walking or driving?"

"Walking," she replied firmly.

Ten minutes later, as they were about to leave, Penelope

put her hand up to her spectacles, but Sev forestalled her. "No. No more. Leave them on."

"But—"

He turned her so she faced the large pier glass set in the hall. "They add a certain piquancy to your face, don't you think?"

It was wonderful to be able to see that far. What Sev said was true: the thin gold frames suited her much better than the thick, horn-rimmed ones. She glanced over her shoulder at him then turned round completely, placing her hand on his arm. "Shall we go?"

Chapter Fifteen

Early the next day Sev, Penelope, and Lord and Lady Wimbourne went to the offices of Grey, Grey & Teacher, in the heart of the City, within sight of the Monument. Penelope didn't give the tall pillar a second glance even though, for the first time in her life, she could see it properly. It was clear that her father disapproved of Penelope wearing her new spectacles out of doors, but since her husband-to-be decreed it, he could only have gainsaid it for a week. Penelope watched the whole journey from the carriage window, marveling at what she had missed before. She could mark items in the shop windows, see expressions on the faces of the people, everything in blessedly sharp focus.

The brass plaque outside the tall, narrow building proclaimed the business that went on inside. Above and below it were other plaques, displaying other businesses there. All were soot-grimed, although this being summer, few chimneys belched the smoke that put London under a blanket of fog. A few active chimneys proclaimed the existence of bake houses, but few houses in this part of London had their own kitchens.

A clerk ushered them through to a large room to Mr. Grey's office. The clerks busily scratching at the high desks barely bothered to look up, much less bow to them as they passed. They were far too busy. The walls of the office were lined, floor to ceiling with shelves holding papers, some of which, judging by the dust on them, hadn't been disturbed for years.

Mr. Grey, tall, sparely neat, stood to welcome them. "A joyous occasion." His voice was dry; he had said the same thing in much the same circumstances many times. This time it was true and his slight smile to Penelope betrayed his pleasure at seeing his young friend so well established. Penelope knew him well enough now to discern what lay behind the slight smile, the dour expression.

Sev's man, Mr. Little, had come right across London for the meeting today and now bowed to them with a great deal of dignity.

Feeling light at heart Penelope sat in the hard chair drawn up for her while Sev stood behind it. They listened to the terms of the contract, drawn up the previous day. Apart from giving a gasp when she heard the amount of pin-money Sev seemed prepared to bestow on her, it was much as she had expected. And the lawyers seemed satisfied.

The quill pen was perfectly sharpened. Without hesitating, Penelope dipped it in the standish and signed the contract. After her, her father, as her legal guardian signed, then Sev. That was it. Penelope was now as legally tied to Sev as if married to him already. If she, or he, broke the contract, the subsequent court case could ruin them.

Just before he signed, Sev glanced at Penelope and gave her a private, warm smile. That was all.

The contract signed, everyone indulged in a glass of wine then the gentlemen shook hands. "Are you busy for the rest of today?" Penelope asked Mr. Grey then.

His smile was warmer than before. "I can spare an hour, ma'am."

Penelope bade the menfolk good-bye and Severus took Lord

Wimbourne off to the club. Lady Wimbourne settled down to chaperone her. Easy to tolerate, now her wedding was imminent.

After a blissful hour with Mr. Grey, Penelope went to the mantua-makers to have her toile fitted. This was a mock-up in plain cloth, which the mantua maker would apply to all the gowns she ordered from this establishment. Her maid could make fine alterations after she took delivery of the gowns. Greatly daring, she ordered two more outfits, because she couldn't resist the fabrics so casually left on show, then, feeling guilty, she left the establishment. Her carriage waited outside to take her back, together with a note from her stepmother. She had been delayed in her own shopping; she trusted Penelope to take the carriage back on her own.

Liberated from the stranglehold of her stepmother's chaperonage Penelope stepped into the carriage and ordered the coachman to take her the long way around. A drive around London's more respectable streets, able to see properly, not obliged to make polite conversation seemed a pleasant way of spending the next half-hour or so.

The passage of the carriage set up a pleasant breeze with the windows open, and Penelope settled back and watched. It was wonderful. Before, she had relied on instinct and guesswork for a lot of her daily life. Now, that part of her could relax. She could see what was going on.

After half an hour, she rapped on the roof of the carriage. It was time she went back. The carriage drove up the length of Oxford Street, and into the West End, through several streets and squares of well kept, neat town houses. All the streets were similar, and only the variations of the squares told her where they were. It was very restful. Penelope thought of the London season, how busy these streets were at that time, full of the great and the good and the foolish.

Jerked out of her daydream Penelope sat up. She saw someone she knew, in a gown she'd seen over the breakfast table that morning. Lady Wimbourne, coming out of a house Penelope didn't know, a man she didn't recognize standing at the door watching her leave. The man was fashionably if soberly dressed, and a total stranger. Penelope didn't know which was odder; seeing her stepmother leaving this house or realizing that she was alone. Servants and protectors always surrounded Marcela. In the short time Penelope had known her she'd learned that her stepmother considered walking alone in the streets tantamount to inviting rape.

Penelope counted houses. The one her stepmother had visited was ten houses from the end of the street. Bruce Street. Penelope knew no one had seen her. Her stepmother must have been very absorbed in whatever she had been doing to miss the crested carriage sweeping past and Penelope's curious gaze from the window.

Once at the house, after discarding her hat and gloves, Penelope went to find Sev. Her stepmother arrived shortly after, but Penelope had already gone to her room, leaving a message for someone to inform her when her betrothed arrived.

Thus a concerned Sev was waiting in the small parlor when Penelope entered. In as few words as possible she told him what she had seen. "So I thought I would tell you at once, considering what you discussed with me earlier."

Sev listened to her in silence. Now he frowned. "It does sound strange. I've been thinking—why should your stepmother want to harm your father? Is he—forgive me—is he cruel, unkind in any way?"

"My mother henpecked him. The begetting of an heir was her obsession, not his, especially after it became obvious the constant pregnancies were damaging her health. He was never cruel to her. I know as much about Marcela as you do. But I haven't seen any evidence of mistreatment there, either."

"You're right. I thought they were well suited. They seemed happy enough. It doesn't look good, Penelope."

"No." She crossed the room to the window.

"In fact," Sev said from behind her, "it looks damned smoky."

"What can we do?"

He slipped his arms around her waist and rested his cheek on her hair. It felt comforting. "You trust Grey, but he's your father's man. I can find out who lives at that house without too much trouble."

"How?"

"Send a servant round to deliver a note. Claim it's the wrong address. No, wait—I'll do it myself. Let's keep this as discreet as we can."

She laid her hand on top of his, loving the gentle warmth. "They'll recognize you."

"Not if I pull my hat well down and wear an old coat. I'll borrow one, say it's a prank I want to play on a friend." He lifted his head and kissed her hair. "Don't worry, not yet anyway. This is my house, and I can vouch for the food and wine."

"Do you think it's the brews?"

"I don't know. I think I'll have her herb chest stolen, and take some samples from it. She'll never know it's gone if I do it while you're in the drawing room after dinner."

"Severus!"

"What else would you have? If we confront her, she'll claim it's innocent. We have to know more before we confront her, warn her that we suspect something."

"If she's guilty."

"Pray that she's not."

Penelope's anxiety began to dissipate, soothed by sharing her problem and his presence. Already she was coming to rely on him. She felt his lips at her temple, whispering a kiss. "Try not to worry. We'll find out and we'll deal with it. Together."

She let her head fall back against him. "Together. I already have so much to thank you for."

"You think I'm not grateful to you?"

Raising her eyebrows, she turned in his arms to face him. "How so?"

"Saving me from a fate worse than death. From Miss Trente. You know she was planning on entrapment?"

She laughed. "What?"

"Trapping me into a compromising situation. Forcing my hand. Peter told me after he heard her boasting about it."

"So you panicked and proposed to me." She couldn't have said that a few days before, but now she felt surer of him, and of herself.

"No panic in it. None at all."

His kiss was soft, gentle, and then he lifted his head again. "Putting it in that kind of focus made me realize what I wanted in a wife and what I didn't want. I was lucky enough to be accepted by my first choice."

He laughed when she blushed. "I'm not used to compliments."

"Get used to them." He kissed her again, another closed mouth, soft kiss. "I have a feeling there'll be more coming your way." He stopped any more comments by bending his head to her again.

After dinner, Sev took them to the theatre. The boxes were

half-empty, but the pit and circles were full. Penelope enjoyed herself thoroughly, and supported by the presence of Severus, ignored the curious stares of people who knew them. The announcement of the marriage would appear in the papers soon, then the lucky Captain Salt's betting would be at an end. The book wouldn't close until Penelope became Lady Swithland, but odds were already shortening.

Penelope was amused to receive some visits at the first interval from people who offered their congratulations when they heard the news. She accepted them serenely but it wasn't until one of Severus's particular cronies, one Lord Datchett, entered with his mother that the unspoken comments were finally voiced.

"Swithland, you dog!" The gentleman grasped his friend by the hand and elbow. "Kept us all guessing!"

Swithland laughed and returned the embrace, slapping his lordship's back. "How much did you lose, Datch?"

Datchett shrugged. "Couple of hundred. Didn't put more on it because I couldn't imagine you making Miss Trente your life's partner."

Sev avoided Penelope's quizzical look. "Why not?"

"Beautiful widgeons aren't your style." He freed himself and bowed low to Penelope. "Miss Makepiece, your obedient." Penelope inclined her head graciously. "Oh I say!" Penelope lifted her chin and let him look. "Never knew you wore spectacles." he remarked, then seemed to come to himself, and muttered, "Beg pardon, ma'am! Shouldn't have said anything."

"I don't mind." To her surprise, she realized it was true. "I've always had poor sight. Sev has given me the courage to wear them."

"Well now I've come this deep I might as well say that you look dashed attractive in them," Datchett told her. "If they all looked as pretty as you it might be a proper fashion next season."

Sev laughed. "Perhaps we'll try. Eh, my dear?"

Penelope looked away in confusion, then back again. "Maybe. I thought I might be labeled bluestocking."

Datchett chortled. "I can think of worse and that wasn't what I thought when I looked at you."

Gallantly he bent over her hand, pressed a kiss to the back of it and left. Penelope turned a laughing face to her betrothed. "Such nonsense."

"But it amused you, I think?"

"Vastly."

Chapter Sixteen

After a pleasant evening, they left in the middle of the afterpiece, a farce, done half heartedly, and since there seemed to be a riot going on upstairs in the gods, they thought to make good their escape before the theatre staff threw the mob out into the street. Drury Lane and its environs were not a place for respectable women to linger after dark. Respectable men, however, often lingered there.

Instead of averting modest eyes from the sights outside, Penelope drank them in avidly. Her sharpened vision took in the tawdry, bright silks, the vast expanses of bosom exposed as wares on sale, the shortened skirts.

When she turned to her fellow passengers in the carriage, she saw Sev watching her, an amused smile curving his lips. She sank back into her seat, primming her mouth up into an imitation of disapproval. It seemed to fool her stepmother. "Shocking!" that lady exclaimed. "Can these people not be cleared away?"

"Hardly noticed them myself," Lord Wimbourne's voice, however, appeared a shade too casual.

"The people of London have a remarkably independent attitude," Sev remarked. "They would resist any attempt to remove them."

Her ladyship made a sound of disgust, but leaned back into

her seat. Penelope suppressed a giggle.

Having escorted the ladies home, Lord Wimbourne took himself off to his club, declaring that London always made him restless. Lady Wimbourne settled down, prepared to wait until her stepdaughter was ready for bed. Sev glared at her irritably. His thirst for Penelope increased with every hour he spent in her company, fuelled by the knowledge of what lay before them. She seemed willing—the more he touched her the more he longed to possess her completely. He'd never experienced this kind of madness before, this yearning, as though her skin held a special addictive magic.

They exchanged a smile. She wasn't at all the kind of woman he'd once imagined making his wife, but recent events had proved to him that he had based all his previous assumptions on shifting sands. Now he was sure he'd found firm ground, something they could build on. If they were ever allowed. Impatience filled him. He'd always prided himself on his address and his gallantry. All gone now, at one look from soft, bespectacled brown eyes.

Lady Wimbourne glared back at him, her dark eyes hard, her mouth set in a straight line and Sev realized she would sit there until Doomsday to prevent him touching her charge. He'd heard how strict they were in Spain, and wondered if they ever allowed respectable young ladies privacy, even after their marriage.

He sighed and gave up, announcing that he would go up to bed. "You do not go out?" Lady Wimbourne asked, hopefully, he thought.

"Not tonight. It's past eleven, and I'm tired. Goodnight." Bowing to them both, giving his wife-to-be a small, private smile, he left and went upstairs.

He lied; he wasn't in the least tired. Once ready for bed he whiled away half an hour reading that morning's newspaper. After perusing the same paragraph five times he gave up and hurled the paper to the floor. He'd heard the doors close upstairs; the house would be quiet. Perhaps a glass of brandy would help him sleep.

Two single candlesticks lighted the hall dimly. With the family in, there was no need to wait up or light it more fully. When Sev glanced down, he saw the hall-boy's bed was up and the occupant already in place, his heavy sleeping breaths lifting the light covers. Sev wondered what it would be like to sleep in the hall every night; not to have a permanent bedroom, roused in the night by the family coming in late and forced to rise early. He knew it was luck rather than design that had landed him where he was, and he was grateful for it.

Putting the hall-boy from his mind, he opened the door to the salon, where he knew a decanter or two resided.

He didn't see her until he was in the room and the door closed. Penelope was dressed, as he was for sleep. A light wrap drifted from her shoulders to float at her feet. She started up from the window seat, hands in front of her, crossed over her bosom. "I'm sorry. Couldn't you sleep?"

She had thrown open the shutters. The light from outside all that lit the room, illuminating one side of her from shoulder to feet, leaving the other side in shadow. Her soft hair lay over her shoulders, brushed into a gleaming mane. The sight made Severus weak. He badly wanted to run his hands over the glossy sheen, thread his fingers through the mass.

"No." He turned to the decanter so the sight of her wouldn't tempt him any more. He must be mad to think that this sweet, innocent girl would be willing to come to him without a ring on her finger. And insulting of him to ask her.

He heard her walk across the room to him, and felt her

place a gentle hand at his waist. "I came down and waited. After what you said—I was about to go, I thought you were asleep, after all."

He froze, unable to think properly. "You want me?" He had to know and now, before he turned to her.

He almost missed her whispered, "Yes."

Forgetting the brandy, he turned around and took her into his arms, just holding her. She felt soft, welcoming and altogether wonderful.

"We're as good as married." His voice shook.

"But we're not married." Her breath warmed his thinly clad chest. "That's why—that's why I wanted to come to you. Sev, I have one thing that's mine, and no one else's. My virginity. It's not much, but I wanted to give it to you. If you took it after we were married, it would be your right, don't you see. I would have already given it to you at the altar, in effect." She paused, and doubt entered her voice. "It's silly, isn't it? I'm sorry. Forget I said anything."

He felt a drop of wetness on his cheek. He put his finger under her chin so he could look at her, and she could see him, and the effect her speech had on him. "It's the most precious gift anyone has ever given me. Shall we go to bed?"

He didn't kiss her, not yet, too afraid he wouldn't be able to stop at just one kiss. With one arm around her shoulders, holding her close, he took her upstairs to his bedroom.

Once inside he released her so he could lock the door. When he turned, she was still standing close to him—an ethereal fairy in flowing, shapeless robes that, because of their thinness, delineated her body better than any tight lacing could do.

"Are you afraid?"

"A little." She shivered, but it wasn't from cold. The summer night was sultry, if anything.

"Don't be. I want to make you happy."

Severus picked up the branch of candles and went to the fire where the tinderbox was kept. Striking a light he carefully lit every candle. He put the candelabrum down on the bedside table. "Come here."

She crossed the room to him and lifted her arms to put her hands on his shoulders. He reached for her and, unable to wait any longer, intoxicated by her nearness, her trust, he set his lips to hers.

He kissed her, trying to seduce her with his mouth, knowing what he wanted her to feel. She responded and lifted her arms to hold him tight. They kissed for a long time, until Sev felt her body soften against him. He had to ruthlessly restrain his desire. All he wanted to do was tear off the ethereal nightwear and hold her as close as she could bear, drive himself into her as far as he could go. The urge to lose himself in Penelope was more primal than anything he'd ever felt before and its intensity shocked Sev. He'd thought he'd be the experienced one, the one to know the path and lead the way, but this was new to him, this intensity, this need. He had to go carefully. One of them should know something of what they were about to do.

He lifted Penelope and laid her on his bed, before following her down, touching her, kissing her, reveling in her luscious curves. He made no effort to remove her clothes until he was sure she was ready. He did, however, remove her spectacles, placing them carefully on the nightstand. Then, trying to conceal the tremble in his fingers, he turned to help her to take off her nightwear.

Penelope lifted her arms so he could whisk her nightgown

off over her head. She lay next to him, her eyes big enough to let him drown in them, still and—so beautiful. Severus felt her vulnerability as if it were his own, and he resolved to do everything he could to make this a joyous experience for her. He might not be able to bring her to orgasm on this, her first time, but he'd try everything he could to bring her happiness.

Severus's greedy gaze passed over every inch of her, lingering at her rounded breasts, her slim waist. She lifted a hand and slipped the first toggle through the loop that held his robe together. Smiling, he helped, releasing the robe so he could shrug it off and show her his naked body.

Penelope seemed as fascinated by Severus as he was with her. She stretched out a tentative hand and touched him, smoothing her hand down his chest. He shuddered and pulled her close. "Penelope!"

Welcoming, pliant, soft, seductive skin caressed his rougher body. She was everything he'd hoped for and more. When he skimmed his hand over her ribs, touched her breast, he heard her gasp, and when he lowered his head and kissed her nipple, took it fully into his mouth she sighed his name. She tasted so good, like raspberries and sunshine. He teased her nipple until it peaked against the roof of his mouth, then he transferred his attention to the other one. Every sigh, every murmur, he took inside himself and treasured it; she was that much closer to where he wanted to take her.

He mustn't rush; he must make this as good for her as it could be, try to transmit some of his joy to her. He wanted to give, to feel her response. He forgot all his own needs as he caressed and kissed her, tried to make her feel as relaxed and ready as possible so he wouldn't hurt her. Much.

He lifted his head and gazed down at her face. Her half-closed eyes glinted in the candlelight. "Sweetheart, you're very beautiful."

Her soft chuckle shook her breasts. He felt one quiver under his hand, and bent his head to her again, unable to resist. When he slipped his hand between her legs and softly caressed, he found she was already wet and ready for him. It sent a surge of need through him.

He didn't think he could wait any longer. Raising himself on one elbow he covered her, urged her to part her legs so he could settle between them. "Open your eyes, Penelope. Look at me."

She obeyed, and he didn't take his eyes from hers as he lowered his body and used one hand to guide his shaft until it rested just inside her. He felt her flinch. "You know I'll do my best not to hurt you," he whispered, and bent to kiss her. He eased himself inside her, felt her stretch and relax for him. Her juices eased his way and he closed his eyes to concentrate on retaining control. Warm, inviting, damp woman. And not just any woman. His Penelope. He moved a little, and felt her give way. She was ready.

He withdrew so he barely touched her, then drove hard inside her, muffling her scream by pressing his mouth to hers. He'd ruptured the membrane in one hard thrust. He stilled, fully inside her, and lifted away. "A cruel trick, but if you'd tensed it would have hurt more. How are you feeling?"

She stared up at him, and took a deep breath. "Surprised."

He laughed, and the vibration reminded him, as if he needed any, how intimately they were joined. "No die away maidenly airs, then?" He dropped a kiss on her mouth.

"I don't seem to be a maiden any more." She shifted under him, making the sweat break out on his forehead. Restraint was hurting him as much as he'd hurt her a moment before. He wanted to plunge blindly inside her, bring himself to ecstasy and hope to take her with him.

He mustn't do that. He needed to show her the pleasures of making love, to try to satisfy her as much as he could. He wanted her to want this as much as he did. He moved, and rejoiced when she moved with him. "Oh love," he murmured, and began to push deeper and with more purpose.

Penelope joined him as if she knew what to do, moving against him and gasping with her efforts. She gripped his shoulders and he brought his mouth to hers, to explore, to bring them into perfect harmony of movement, of invasion. He was no longer sure who was invading whom and he didn't care. With her surrounding him, her legs curved around his, drawing him in, he followed his instincts. He drove her to cry out again into his mouth, this time in pleasure. She stiffened, arched her back and pushed up fiercely to take him into her.

Her cry was abandoned. Sev wasn't sure if she knew she was making any sound. He was lost in her, no longer caring if anyone heard. Triumph and delight filled him completely. Her passage gripped his shaft in spasmodic clenches. His mind spiraled, and he gave a harsh shout, letting his essence surge into her, filling her.

They lay still, wrapped up in each other, absorbing the wonder of what they had just shared. Aware that he'd let his full weight sag on to her, Sev rolled to one side, his arms tight around her and heard her gasp for breath.

He kissed her softly. "I feel marvelous. Better than I've felt for a long time."

"Mmm."

Concerned, he tipped her chin up. "How are you? Not too bad?"

Penelope looked up at him, her expression softer than he could ever remember. "Wonderful. It hardly hurt at all. Sev, I—

is it always like this?"

"No." He kissed her. "Never with anyone else." It was true. He'd never felt this close to anyone. The urge to care for her was, if anything, stronger than ever.

She chuckled. "Surely it's the same with everyone?"

"Not when I've decided to spend the rest of my life with you." He leaned back, his arm around her, and kissed her again. "Now I'll find it even more difficult to sleep alone. I don't think I can do it any more."

"But we have to."

"Do we? Can you trust your maid not to gossip?" She nodded. "And my man won't say a word."

"There's the little matter of getting dressed." She curled her leg around his.

"Then we'll get you to your room before anyone is up. At least until after the ceremony. A strange thing happened to me today. By putting my name to the contract, I knew I was committing myself beyond recall, and I didn't care. No, I welcomed it."

"So did I," she whispered, then yawned and laid her head against his shoulder. She was asleep in minutes.

Penelope stirred, touched warm flesh and came instantly awake. The candles had long since guttered down to their sockets and pale dawn light filtered through the shutters. She couldn't see much. By his regular, deep breathing, she could tell that Severus was sound asleep. Careful not to wake him, she groped in the near dark for her clothes, and found her robe. She clasped it around her naked body, went to the windows and unlatched the shutters, opening them a crack so she could see what she was doing. She must go back to her room. She couldn't bear the ensuing fuss if anyone found her here.

Severus sprawled on the bed, the sheets a tangled mass under him and where she had lain, no need for covers on this sultry night. His hair had come loose and tumbled over half his face. He looked wonderful. Her heart went out to him; sometime in the night he had stolen it, but she didn't know if he had given his to her. It was too late to worry; it was done.

Although she'd moved stealthily, something must have woken him, for he stirred, took a deep breath and opened his eyes. They gazed at each other, both smiling, and then he held out his hand to her. She went to him without hesitation. "I have to go."

"A week. In a week you'll be going nowhere." He tugged on her hand until she was forced to lean down, then he put his arm around her waist and pulled her back down on to the bed. "Mmm," he purred, and pulled her to him for a deep, welcoming kiss. He touched her back, his hand sliding deliciously down her spine. "No regrets?"

"None."

"Good. I certainly have none. Far from it." With a lazy smile he slid his hand under her thin robe, caressed her bare skin. "You're lovely."

"Thank you."

"No, thank you."

With an effort, she pulled away. "I have to go."

He sat up and threw the sheet back, reaching for his robe. "Oh, Lord!"

The bottom sheet was marked with her blood. He flicked the top sheet back over. "Don't worry, I'll deal with it."

"You know how to change a sheet?"

"How difficult can it be?"

He found out after he'd taken her back to her room. They weren't seen, but he didn't care if they were. The contract signed, nothing but death could part them now. Back in his room, he stripped off the bottom sheet and threw the other one over the blanket. That was easy. What he found more difficult was arranging the thing. He had no idea which was the top of the sheet, or where to tuck it in. After a good twenty minutes of trying he gave up and flung the sheet to join its mate on the floor. Thank God for good valets, he thought, lying on the bare blanket.

Chapter Seventeen

At breakfast, Sev silently laid Penelope's spectacles by her plate on his way to his own seat. When she shot a startled glance at him, he smiled beatifically. Another parcel arrived for her with the morning post, and, expecting a spare pair of spectacles, but a little puzzled by the size of the parcel, she opened it.

There was another pair of spectacles, but one or two other items as well. A pair of opera glasses, decorated in delicate pietra dura, flowers laid into the ivory body with precious stones. When she lifted them to her eyes, she found a small knurled knob that she could turn to change the focus. There was an object that looked like a fan, but when she flicked it to open it another pair of spectacles popped out. Lorgnettes, spectacles on a stick, gold framed, with tiny diamonds set in the frames. And a fan, painted with scenes from mythology.

Penelope looked up to see Severus watching her closely. "A toy," he explained. "Turn it around."

When she did, she found a tiny lens set into an extension of the sticks. It was for her right eye, the one she'd learned was her weakest. She peered through it and laughed. "Thank you, my lord. A very pretty conceit."

He smiled back. "A pleasure." She wasn't sure he meant the optical devices. She looked away, blushing, to meet the quizzical stare of her stepmother.

Lady Wimbourne suspected, Penelope was sure. She didn't leave her stepdaughter's side all day, after Lord Wimbourne was borne off by his future son-in-law to exclusively male pursuits. Clapping Severus on the back, his lordship roundly declared it was time enough to dance attendance on Penelope when she became his wife. Now he must enjoy masculine pursuits while he still could. Sev gave Penelope an apologetic look that indicated that he would rather spend time with her.

She spent the day shopping and daydreaming. Also watching Lady Wimbourne as closely as she was being watched. Despite the momentous events of the night before, she hadn't forgotten her concerns for her father. What did she know about her new stepmother, after all?

She met her intended again at dinner, when he suggested a visit to Vauxhall Gardens. Penelope was intrigued; Vauxhall in July would be an interesting change. To her surprise, her mother-in-law agreed to the outing with an attitude verging on enthusiasm. Vauxhall was a risqué place; somewhere to flirt and meet people not encountered in everyday life. It would be easy for Severus to separate her from her duenna; she supposed that was why he'd suggested it.

After changing into a gown more suited to fashionable London, even in the unfashionable summer months, a light silk lavender and lace confection, Penelope went down to find her betrothed alone in the salon. Severus looked resplendent in dark green and cream. She found his eagerness to take her in his arms and kiss her flattering. Her inexperience with the intimate acts of the marriage bed gave her a reticence she found difficult to conceal. So she didn't try. She didn't have any illusions about her allure, she told herself and wondered if, after one intimate encounter, he would be sated with her, at least for now.

He proved her wrong. "How are you today, sweetheart? Could you bear some company tonight or would you prefer to rest?"

His concern soothed her anxiety. "I'm fine. A little—" she looked away for a moment, "—uncomfortable, but it seems to have eased."

He studied her, his gaze anxiously roaming her face. "It would be selfish of me to expect you to receive me, wouldn't it?" He didn't wait for an answer. "It was my eagerness speaking, not my concern for you. Forgive me?"

"For what? For being considerate?"

"For asking you to receive me tonight. I wish I could just come and hold you, but I fear that's impossible." He smiled wryly. "I can hardly touch you without wanting you. I could be a schoolboy again, and I thought I was a sophisticated man of the world."

"I'm very happy, Sev."

"Good; I'll do my best to ensure that continues."

They broke apart when the door opened to admit the older pair. They were soon on their way to the pleasure gardens, a carriage to a river and a short trip in a hired barge.

Water was the best way to approach Vauxhall. Despite the lateness of the season, some fashionables still remained in London, so watercraft of all kinds thronged the approach, waiting to land. It gave Severus's party a chance to admire the gardens. In the winter months, the place was lit by thousands of lamps and candles, twinkling like fairyland in the darkness of the night, but at this time of year it wouldn't grow dark until past ten, and Vauxhall wasn't quite so impressive. However, the trees and carefully arranged groves were in full bloom, showing a face of Vauxhall Gardens very few people saw.

Under the cover of her wide skirts, Penelope held Sev's

hand. Floating on the wide river, cushioned in comfort, she felt supremely happy. If it weren't for the niggling worry about her father's health, she would be completely content.

"Will you be ready to leave tomorrow?" Sev asked Penelope's parents. "If you are not, please feel at liberty to take your time. I can escort Penelope back to Swithland House, and send the carriage back for you."

"We will be quite ready," her ladyship replied firmly, dashing Penelope's hopes of a two-day journey alone in a carriage with her beloved. She consoled herself with the thought that they wouldn't be apart for much longer, although, this side of the ceremony, it felt like an age.

Finally ashore, they headed for the supper boxes, where one had been booked for their use. Penelope enjoyed herself hugely, for once able to observe the crowd closely, as she had at the theatre. She was hungry for it, deprived of it for so long. She turned her head to see Severus watching her with amusement. He handed her a glass of cool white wine. His fingers brushed hers as the glass passed from his hold to hers. She shivered. It wasn't cold.

There was some musical entertainment she hardly registered, so fascinated was she by the audience. After partaking of a light supper, including the wafer thin ham that Vauxhall was so famous for, Severus suggested a walk. Penelope accepted with pleasure and resigned herself to her stepmother accompanying them while Lord Wimbourne amused himself listening to the orchestra and finishing the last bottle of wine.

Penelope and Severus couldn't talk freely with a third person present. Tension thrummed between them for a full ten minutes until her ladyship excused herself to follow a call of nature. "You will go back to the box," she instructed her stepdaughter who promised her she would.

"Just not immediately," Sev murmured close to her ear.

They watched Lady Wimbourne set off along a small, meandering walk, then, to Penelope's surprise, Sev pulled her after her ladyship. Penelope had expected a pleasant interlude in one of the small groves. "What's wrong?"

"It's an assignation, I'm sure of it," he told her tersely. Penelope lifted her skirts so she could move faster.

Lady Wimbourne didn't look back, but they were careful to keep other people between them. She moved purposefully until she reached a fork in the path. There were fewer people about now, and when Lady Wimbourne paused, Sev pulled Penelope back into the growing shadows of the summer evening. With a bare glance behind, her ladyship entered a concealed grove, one of the places set aside for what was euphemistically termed 'private conversation.'

"Oho!" Sev drew Penelope aside.

"You know your way around here remarkably well," Penelope murmured.

He gave her an unrepentant grin. "I do, don't I?"

Behind one of the thin hedges surrounding the grove, Sev and Penelope could hear but not be seen. In front of them was a lump of grey stone, a statue of some sort, blurred by the greenery between them. Sev leant down so his mouth was close to Penelope's ear. "Eavesdropping." She heard the distaste in his voice. "I don't like it, but your father may be in some danger. We have no other choice."

"I agree."

They waited in silence, then at last they heard low voices from the other side of the hedge. A man, English, no accent they could discern. "I hate all this havey-cavey business."

"Did you bring him?" Lady Wimbourne's voice, unmistakably cut glass precise in its enunciation.

"No. He was too tired."

"I'd hoped to see him." Penelope heard despair and yearning in the voice which had been so clipped and controlled. This was someone the lady longed to see.

"I know, I'm sorry. Did you bring the money?"

A feminine sigh, then, "Yes. This should be all right for a month or two?"

Paper rustled. Banknotes. "It should." He sounded reluctant. "I know where to find you if I need any more." A pause. "How long?"

"What?"

Infinite patience in the male voice. "How long before all this is over? You can't continue like this for much longer, Marcela, you must know that. Give it up, or do something more drastic. One or the other, my lady." The man's voice rose at the end of the sentence, hushed by a hissing sound from Lady Wimbourne.

"I don't know. I can't go on much longer without him, I know that. I will arrange something—do something."

"That isn't fair. You have to make a decision. Be happy with what you have."

"I cannot!" The cry was filled with anguish and despair, so unlike the measured tones of Lady Wimbourne Penelope could hardly believe her ears. "I'm doing the best I can—I must bear him a child first."

"His lordship?"

"He requires it; I will do it." There was no trace of doubt in her voice. "I will send for you then. And Paul."

"See that you do." The male voice was rough, but it wasn't

possible for Penelope to know why. At first, she'd thought this man was Marcela's lover, but anything less lover-like in tone was hard to imagine.

"I must go." With a sweep of silk skirts, Marcela left the grove.

Under cover of the sound of movement, Sev gripped Penelope's arm and drew her away, down the network of paths towards the sound of music and laughter. "We must get back, preferably before she does." He set a fast pace. "We can't talk about this now; I'll come to you after they've gone to bed."

Panting and flushed, they entered the box a mere two minutes before her ladyship came in. Lord Wimbourne winked at Sev when he saw Penelope's flushed countenance, but he didn't say anything. Now the contract had been signed Penelope thought her father might have given her a little more freedom, but his new wife obviously thought otherwise. Sev was toasting his betrothed when Lady Wimbourne came in, and slipped into her place as discreetly as she could.

Penelope longed to discuss the incident with Sev, but she had no chance until after she'd retired. She sat up in bed, decorously attired in nightgown and robe, but with her hair brushed out instead of in its usual nighttime braids. When she heard his soft knock, she almost fell out of bed in her haste to get to the door, and was still smiling at her own foolishness when he slipped inside and closed the door again.

Despite his stated good intentions he took her in his arms and kissed her, long and slow, but afterwards put her aside with a sigh. "I'm determined not to make love to you tonight. If it wasn't for what happened at Vauxhall I wouldn't even be here."

"I don't mind."

"I do. I won't use you like that. You need time to get used to it." He gazed down at her, his face softening, and just touched his lips to hers. "I must be mad," he added, as if to himself.

"Why?"

"Because you're temptation personified, Penelope, and it's going to kill me to leave you alone. But I'm determined on it."

Taking his hand Penelope led Sev to the bed and they sat on it, side by side. It was too high for Penelope's feet to reach the ground so she curled them up and leaned into him when he put his arm around her shoulders. "What do you think she's up to?"

Sev didn't need to be reminded who "she" was. He stroked her hair as if he couldn't stop touching her. "I'm not sure. I thought she was meeting a lover, but the man she met was not that."

Penelope loved his petting and resisted the temptation to arch under his hand. "They talked about someone else. Paul."

"Yes, it's likely he's her lover, but I don't see why he couldn't have met her himself."

He wound a lock of dark hair around his finger, tangling it in her hair. "This man seems to have some kind of hold on her. I employed someone today to find out what he can."

"Someone I know?"

He laughed. "I hope not. He isn't a salubrious character." She slipped her hand around his waist, over his robe. He felt hard and warm. A muscle flexed under her hand as he turned to drop a kiss on her hair. "He'll find out who lives at that house in Bruce Street, and follow them. I think we must concentrate on her ladyship and find out what she's up to."

"Have you any ideas?"

He chuckled. "Yes, but very few of them are about Lady

Wimbourne. If I don't go soon I'll be lost. I'm resolved on it, Penelope."

"Leaving me alone tonight?"

"Tucking you up and leaving you to dream."

"Of you."

Another chuckle, another soft kiss. "I'm flattered. And glad. I want to take care of you, make sure you're safe and unhurt."

She lifted her head, looked up at him. "Then stay with me. Please, Sev."

He stared at her for a fraught moment. "You should rest," he said, but his tone grew less sure.

Penelope saw the desire flare in his eyes, the pupils darkening as he gazed at her. "I get more rest with you than I do without. I want you, Severus."

"Oh, love!" Unable to resist any more, he took her mouth in a searing kiss. Penelope pressed herself to him, and then leaned back. He followed her down on to the bed, nestling her in the soft covers. Lying over her, his elbows either side of her arms, he lifted his head and smiled, a sweet, intimate caress.

"I feel fine, I swear it," she assured him. "You were so careful last night."

"Not as careful as I should have been." He gave a small, deprecating laugh. "I have a small confession to make. You were my first virgin."

She laughed, too. "I'm glad I was your first something."

He kissed her forehead. "I wasn't sure how to go about it and in the end I just followed my instincts. It seemed to work."

At the remembrance, Penelope closed her eyes and opened her mouth slightly. Before she could close it again she felt his mouth come down on hers, softly at first, but then deeper, stronger. She responded, throwing her arms around his neck to draw him closer and prevent him going away. When she felt his shaft harden against her through his brocaded robe, she knew she had won. For she had been determined that he would stay with her tonight. She couldn't bear the thought of him so close to her, but not close enough.

It astonished her, this ability to entice, her power over this strong, confident man. A few caresses, a few kisses and he was lost. She felt his need of her in every caress, in the press of his body on hers, and she rejoiced. He drew back, studying her, such a soft smile on his lips she couldn't resist smiling back. "Say no now, Penelope. Or not at all."

She met his gaze, but said nothing, so he captured her mouth again and made himself busy undoing the ribbons holding her robe together at the front. Penelope reciprocated by slipping undone the frogged toggles on his dark blue robe, then sliding her hands inside so she could touch his naked chest. His corresponding shudder shook his whole body.

The soft folds of her robe settled either side of her, and Penelope sat up so she could rid herself of her nightgown. She sat naked in a sea of cream silk and smiled her invitation. Her anticipation tightened her throat; she opened her mouth to help her breathe. All her attention focused on him, Severus, the man she had always loved, now sitting close to her, as naked as she was.

He touched her breast, tracing the soft, full curve. "I said you had an inviting figure. I didn't know the half of it." Raising his eyes to her face, he smiled his pleasure.

She returning his smile. "Don't say I'm the loveliest woman you've ever been with. It's enough that you want me."

He slid his arm around her, drawing her close. "You're the loveliest for me. Something in me responds to you every time you're close. When I touch you I want more, when I see you like this I have to touch you." He caught her up in a fierce kiss. "Believe it or not that is new to me." His mouth was so close to hers she felt his breath whisper over her sensitized skin. "I can hardly keep my hands off you."

He increased the pressure on her shoulders, urging her to lie down, to let him cover her body with his. Wonderingly, Penelope touched him, smoothed her hands down his sides, then, daringly, further down.

His breath hissed when she touched his erection, but he didn't draw away. With increasing confidence, Penelope explored the soft skin covering the male hardness and rounded tip, precisely designed by some divine hand to fit her perfectly. Slowly, he drew away, leaning on one elbow next to her so she could see as well as touch. "It's all yours, love. As is the rest of me."

"So big!" exclaimed Penelope, whose knowledge of the male body had been rudimentary before last night.

He chuckled, though it was a shaky one. "Thank you, sweetheart. I aim to please."

The ridges under the smooth head fascinated her. She traced them with one finger, her touch becoming bolder as he gave no resistance. His breath came quicker now. His head fell back, and the ribbon came loose from his hair, which flowed to his shoulders in dark waves. She glanced up at his face, flushing when she saw his intense gaze on her, tracing her contours with his look as she was touching him with her hands.

With a sudden movement, he grasped her wrist and pulled her hand away. "No more. I'm not made of ice."

He leaned over her, pushing her hand into the robe still lying under her body, and urged her legs apart with his knee. His erection pressed between her legs, then his fingers slipped between them, exploring, opening her up. She moaned and leaned back, unable to do anything except experience the stunning sensations he was introducing her to.

He slid inside her. No pain this time, but an exquisite feeling of fulfillment. Opening her eyes, she saw him watching her closely, concern edging his desire. "Tell me if it hurts."

She shook her head. "It doesn't hurt a bit. It's wonderful, Sev."

With a small sound, he bent to kiss her, and moved inside her. Penelope gave herself to him, arching her back to push up in response. She opened her mouth to him, bent her knees and urged him on. He thrust, then finished the kiss, and drew away. Penelope opened her eyes and met his, watching him as he moved, withdrawing only to drive harder, reach further and further inside her. He set a rhythm, so instinctive, so much a part of her that she wondered how she could have lived so long without it. Warmth grew inside her, spread until it consumed her.

Penelope cried out, forgetting discretion in the powerful surge of excitement that welled up inside her. Every nerve tingled; and she understood the true nature of trust. She wouldn't have given herself this completely to anyone else but Severus, would have fought to retain her essence, but he could have it all, in return for this ecstasy. She felt his lips on her nipple, pulling, sucking, increasing the intensity of her response to him.

He released her breast to move to the other one. His hands held hers, pressed deep into the mattress beneath them. Then, for a few short moments, he seemed to lose himself. His eyes shut tight, he thrust into her one, two, three times and froze, deeply embedded inside her. With a hoarse cry, he found his release. Penelope watched, fascinated and awed that she could have such an effect on anyone so strong.

In a moment, he came back to himself. He smiled when he saw she'd been watching him, and released a hand, flicking his long hair back behind his shoulders. He lay down, taking her with him to hold her close. She lifted her head for his kiss, sweet and long. "So much for good resolutions," he murmured.

Penelope chuckled. "This is better. Sev, I—" She faltered.

Instantly alarm filled his eyes. "Penny? What is it?"

She gathered her courage. "I love you, Sev."

He stared at her, but didn't move away, then let out his breath in one long sigh. "I love you too, Penelope."

"I didn't say it to make you say anything. I just wanted you to know. I think I've always loved you, but I didn't know how to tell you before without seeming silly or pathetic. And I thought you wanted me because you couldn't stand the others. I don't mind, honestly."

He hushed her with a soft kiss. "I've always liked you, but I didn't know you very well. Not until recently, when you let me in to your life. The contrast between you and the hussies gathered to win my fortune and title couldn't have been more pronounced. From the day you rescued that poor animal I couldn't help but notice you but it took a little more than kindness to animals. You think, Penny. You stand your ground when you consider something important, but you don't worry about the petty details. Remember that day when Annabelle Rivers and Caroline Trente sulked because they'd chosen the same color of silk for their gowns?"

She laughed. "So that's what it was! I didn't stop to ask."

"I wish I could have done the same. They complained to me all day but neither would go up to their rooms and change. That was the day I realized I'd made a grave mistake. Then I found you, and your interests, your understanding."

"But that would have made us friends. I would have settled

for that."

He kissed her again. "Dear Lord, girl, you think, once I'd kissed you, that I'd let it stop at that? Don't you know how luscious you are?"

"No, and neither did society when I made my come-out."

"They were blind. But I'm so glad they were." This time the pause was longer. When their lips finally parted, he smiled down at her. "Now I know I love you. If I try to think of reasons, I daresay I can find many, but none of them matter. If you'll let me, I'll try to make you happy."

"Oh Sev!" Unable to hide her tears any longer Penelope buried her head in his shoulder. He stroked her hair, held her close and kissed the parts of her face he could reach until she sniffed and lifted her head again. Then he captured her mouth in a long kiss, holding her to him.

Penelope had found her home.

Penelope didn't wake when Severus left her for his own room, but when she finally stirred it was to see the depression on the pillow where his head had lain next to hers. A sheet was thrown over her, but otherwise she lay much as she had done in his arms, warm and safe. Smiling she turned to see her maid, frowning at her. She came back down to earth with a bump.

"What is it, Collins?"

"You were seen, ma'am." Collins folded her hands primly in front of her, over her crisp, white apron.

Penelope's mind went back wildly to when she had spied on her stepmother the night before. "Who?"

"Lady Wimbourne saw his lordship leave your room this morning."

Penelope sat up, running a hand through her disordered hair. "Oh Lord!"

"You'll be leaving for Swithland House this morning," Collins went on. "And her ladyship wants to see you before you go down to breakfast."

An hour later, dressed for travel, Penelope left her stepmother's room. She'd been lectured on the conduct of young ladies, until she was tempted to shriek back that her behavior was nothing compared to Marcela's, but she'd remained quiet and docile, reminding herself all the time that it could be dangerous for her father if she spoke up now.

Sev stood up as soon as Penelope entered the breakfast parlor, and drew out a chair for her. She grimaced at him, and, correctly interpreting her expression, he dismissed the footman. "You were seen this morning."

He echoed her sentiments exactly. "Oh Lord!"

"I must sleep with Collins in my room until the wedding."

"Damn!" He took her hand and lifted it to his lips. "It was worth it, though," he added with a wicked grin.

"You haven't been listening to Lady Wimbourne for the last half-hour."

He picked up the teapot and poured her a dish. "True. But it would still be worth it."

Penelope was forced to admit that it was well worth it, and received a light kiss.

When he entered the breakfast parlor, Lord Wimbourne said nothing about the incident to his daughter, but when his wife's back was turned, gave Penelope a wink that told volumes. Penelope thought that if it had been left up to her father, he would have ignored the incident. She wished it had, because now she would have to wait for a week before she could share Severus's bed. After what they'd said to each other last night, she wanted nothing more than to lie next to him once more.

They set out for the House soon after breakfast, and spent the rest of the day in travel. When they stopped for the night, Penelope, tired by two broken nights, fell into bed, hardly noticing her maid settling herself in the truckle bed pulled out for her. She slept well, and the next day contentedly sat next to her betrothed on the journey home.

As the distance between themselves and Swithland House neared, Penelope's tension rose. It seemed she was not the only one for, a mere ten miles before they reached their destination, Sev broached the subject that had taxed all their minds. "How do we break our news to the house party?"

Lord Wimbourne chuckled fruitily. "As long as I'm there when you do it, I don't care."

Sev grinned. "There is that compensation." He pulled out his watch from his pocket and flipped up the lid. "We won't get there in time for dinner. We could go to the drawing room and make the announcement."

"Couldn't we leave it until tomorrow?" Penelope asked, not quite keeping the anxious tone from her voice.

Sev shook his head. "I have no intention of undertaking any subterfuge. I want everyone to know."

"They think we left for our home. They don't know we've spent the last few days in each other's—harumph!—company." Lord Wimbourne glanced at his daughter, with a knowing grin. Penelope grinned back but subsided when she caught her stepmother's frosty glare.

"We should get back, dine privately, change and go down to face the music," Sev said. "The sooner the better."

"I can't wait." his lordship declared with glee.

Penelope could have waited.

Back at the House, the Great Hall was quiet. Hutton informed them that the house party was still intact, and was at dinner, so they went to their rooms to change. Collins, aware of the impact her young mistress was about to make, had packed the gown of her choice at the top of the trunk, and folded it so cleverly hardly a crease marred the fabric.

It was a new gown in glimmering dark blue taffeta, the color of a countess's coronation gown. The petticoat was white, embroidered heavily in gold thread, a pattern of twining vines with bees darting into the fruit, highlighted with brilliants. The gown was embroidered down the front robings and the hem in a similar pattern. Once Penelope's hair was up, two gold combs thrust into the luxuriant locks, and a gold necklace clasped about her throat, she looked magnificent. There was no time to powder, but it didn't matter. Penelope put her hand up to her spectacles then slowly lowered it, leaving them in place. She wanted all the confidence she could find, and all her wits about her. And she wanted to see their faces.

She shook the lace at her elbows, making sure the delicate tracery fell gracefully, then picked up her fan and left her room, head high, ready to face whatever was to come.

Severus waited outside her room, looking rather magnificent himself in crimson velvet. He took her hands and held them out, his gaze scanning her from head to foot. "A proper countess," he said, every word a caress, then, after a quick glance around bent forward to place a gentle kiss on her lips. "My countess." Drawing back, he held his arm in a stately gesture. She put her fingertips on it, as a countess should.

Downstairs several servants waited, as though by accident. Severus knew better. "You should know that your new countess will be in place by the end of next week."

Murmurs of appreciation and deep obeisance followed. To Severus's surprise, after the servants had got to their feet, Penelope sank in front of him in a deep curtsey. "I will do my best for you, my lord. Be a worthy countess."

He took her hand and raised her to her feet. Then he leant forward and in front of everyone kissed her softly on the lips. "You will."

It was a moment frozen in time. He drew back and they looked at each other. No one moved.

"You're looking very fine tonight." Lord Wimbourne called, coming down the stairs. He was unaware of the moment, breaking it without noticing it existed. "Where are they?"

Hutton shimmered forward. "In the blue saloon, my lord." He led the way.

A small procession followed; first Severus, with Penelope then Lord and Lady Wimbourne. Hutton threw open the double doors without clanging them against the walls and announced them formally.

The attention of everyone in the room riveted to the incomers. Miss Trente was the first to move. "Why, my lord, how unexpectedly pleasant to see you back. And Miss Makepiece—how, how unexpected."

She surged up to Sev, a vision in pink. Sev regarded her with a smile, a cynical twist predominating when Miss Trente tried to take his hand, cutting Penelope out completely. It was so typical of her and, Penelope thought, her attention going to Miss Trente's parents, so typical of them, too, for they were watching fondly, with no thought of the sheer bad manners of their daughter trying to do such a thing.

Firmly, Severus put her aside. She stared up at him, her blue eyes wide, and then her glance flicked over to Penelope.

She blinked. "Why, Miss Makepiece, *spectacles.*" She looked around the room, inviting everyone to join in her amusement. "I had no idea you were a bluestocking!"

A faint titter of laughter rewarded her, but they noticed what Miss Trent had not. Instead of letting her go, Severus had taken Penelope's hand in his. Now he looked at her and lifted her hand to his lips. "The loveliest bluestocking I have ever met."

Penelope shivered, but only he felt it. She kept her head up. He kept her gaze then turned to face the now silent room, smiling easily. "Miss Makepiece has done me the great honor of consenting to become my wife."

It was done. Penelope watched the reactions with fascination. Miss Trente's mouth dropped open, and the other girls, sitting making a charming picture by the large window, looked equally blankly amazed.

The older guests hid their chagrin better, but Penelope had no doubt they felt it. She couldn't blame them; Sev had kept them hanging on here, waiting on his whim. She loved him, but she wasn't blind to his arrogance, his assumption that everyone would fall in with his wishes. The trouble was, everyone did. So far, if she defied him, her action would have been capricious. He had given her no reason to.

The first person to speak was Peter, who broke the frozen silence by striding across the room to his friend, to clap him on both shoulders. "Well done, Sev!" Sev grinned back at him. He turned to study Penelope. "And well done Penelope!" He took her free hand and kissed it. "Saw them all off," he murmured, so that only she heard, then he straightened up and released her. "I like them," he said frankly, referring to her spectacles. "They suit you. Why didn't you wear them all the time? Is your sight so bad?"

"Terrible. But my mother, and then my aunt, wouldn't allow me to wear them in company." She shrugged. "I had other battles to fight at the time." Deliberately she kept her attention away from Miss Trente. "Sev asked me to wear them all the time. I got headaches, you see."

Peter glanced at Severus, one dark eyebrow raised quizzically. "Yes, I see."

Sev's response was to smile and lead Penelope over to a sofa. After she had sat down, he sat next to her and delivered his next bombshell. "I want the marriage to take place without delay, so I've decided that the ball will serve as a wedding feast. I hope you can all attend."

Penelope watched, her face frozen into immobility as Miss Trente's face went from white to pink. The rosy flush suited her as much as the paleness. Penelope knew an unholy pleasure she would never admit to anyone, but all those good looks hadn't done Miss Trente any good at all in her pursuit of Severus Granville.

Severus seemed indifferent to the double blow he had just delivered to the hopeful Miss Trente and her friends, but he had given them the chance to escape.

To Penelope's surprise, Miss Willis asked Sev, "Have you invited any more people?"

"Miss Willis, I'm sure the invitations include the best people," Sev said smoothly. "Of course, on the occasion of my marriage more of the local gentry must be invited. I'm sure that won't be too much of a problem."

"Of course not," someone muttered.

Penelope longed to get him alone, to talk to him about this effortless command of the situation. She had expected chaos, but by presenting the marriage to them as a done thing, he seemed to take the wind out of their sails. Her father and his wife had settled quietly, happy to let Severus take centre stage. A maid handed her some tea. She hadn't even realized there were servants in the room.

It was wonderful to see properly, people's reactions. Before, Penelope had to guess, and she'd often been wrong. Now she had the confidence of knowing. Severus had given that to her. She would always be grateful for that.

She hoped the news wasn't too much of a blow to Toby. In a few weeks, he'd lost his inheritance and now the woman he'd expected to marry. Although they had always got on, it was nothing like the happiness she found with Severus. She hoped Toby would find a woman who made him as happy, in time.

All evening Severus stayed by Penelope's side, attending to her small needs, making her smile. Penelope knew this was to demonstrate their new status as a couple, to establish it beyond doubt, but she suspected it was also from choice. There was no one else she would rather be with. She bade goodnight to him with a great deal of regret at her bedroom door, Collins waiting within sight of them. Despite that, he took her into his arms and kissed her properly. He murmured, "Good night, my love. Not long now," before leaving her to her solitary bed.

Chapter Eighteen

Penelope woke up to a tray of tea and bread and butter, and several notes, so she left her bed and sat at the little bonheur du jour by the window. Her stepmother hoped she had a restful night. She wrote a dutiful response. Several people had sent her congratulations. She wrote simple thank you notes, knowing that most of them were insincere. Toby had requested a private interview. Sighing she set a time and place for Toby

Putting her spectacles on when she awoke was getting to be a habit. She hardly noticed she was wearing them until she raised her head and looked out over the park. She caught sight of a man who could only be Severus, talking to one of the gardeners and she felt warm inside at the sight of him. How long this would continue, how long she could command his interest she didn't know but she would do her best to keep him all her life. He was in her heart for good now.

Collins busied herself getting her mistress ready for the day. Penelope found herself indecisive as to what to wear. She didn't want to be too frivolous for her meeting with Toby but she wanted to look pretty for Severus. Caught up in her decisions she caught sight of her reflection in the mirror and grinned. Never had she been so foolish about her clothes.

Settling on a gown of apple green, plain but light enough for such a warm day, Penelope sallied forth. She'd arranged to meet Toby before breakfast in the small parlor on the ground floor.

She liked this room. It had been one in which she had spent many hours with Antonia, when visiting in the school holidays. She remembered the last time she had been in here, when she'd been crippled by her last headache, and noticed that the sofa was again restored to its rightful place by the window. Toby was sitting on it, waiting for her. So was her Aunt Cecilia.

Toby stood and bowed. Penelope curtseyed to him and to her aunt. Both Toby and Cecilia wore grim expressions, so Penelope thought it best to let them lead the conversation.

"How could you do this to us, Penelope?" Aunt Cecilia demanded.

"I did nothing to you, Aunt. Perhaps you should ask my father. He received Severus's offer for my hand and gave his permission before we went to London."

"I intend to," Aunt Cecilia said, her mouth a grim line, "but I expected better of you. Your father has always gone his own way but I thought you were a sensible girl."

"I was asked not to tell anyone."

"Who asked you?"

"My father agreed with Severus's request that we didn't tell anyone until we had signed the contract."

"Ah!" Mrs. Makepiece conveyed a great deal of emotion in this one syllable. Penelope watched, cautiously. "Do you know about him?"

"Yes, Aunt. I've been visiting Antonia here this age. I've known Severus for years."

"Not that, foolish girl. His London affairs!"

Penelope inwardly quailed. She'd avoided thinking about

that. "I know about them. He says he will give them up."

Mrs. Makepiece gave her a pitying look. "You know very little about men, Penelope, if you believe that will be anything but a temporary measure." Her look changed subtly, compassion entering her pale eyes and Penelope remembered that however irritating and interfering her aunt was, her motives were sincere.

She had to admit that her aunt's motives were most sincere where they concerned her son. Penelope had entered the room certain of meeting a ruffled mother hen and she hadn't been disappointed. Her Aunt Cecilia was certainly ruffled.

"Swithland will undoubtedly resume his previous life, but you may be glad of it when he does," she told her niece now. "It is true, it is a brilliant marriage and I can quite see why your father jumped at the chance, but you will not receive the same security and devotion that you would have had with Toby."

"Indeed that might be the case ma'am," Penelope said, although she didn't believe it for a minute, "but I must, as you say, make the most of my opportunities. I should in all fairness tell you that although my father preferred the suit with Lord Swithland, he left the decision up to me."

She watched the expression on Toby's face change from anger to sorrow. Perhaps he had cared for her, after all. Studying him, Penelope knew that she would never have been happy with him. His loose lipped, plump face wasn't unpleasant, but it evoked no desire in her. She would have endured, but not enjoyed, and now Severus had introduced her to the joys of lovemaking, it would have been torture with Toby. "I'm sorry, Toby. I thought we wouldn't suit, but other matters intervened before I could explain all of my feelings to you."

"You are making a great mistake, Penelope. You will be disappointed in your choice." Toby sounded lugubriously unhappy. Penelope was sorry for it, but there was little she could do to help him. However, she tried.

"You should look around you. There are several young ladies here for this visit you could approach. Miss Willis is possessed of a very tidy fortune."

Aunt Cecilia covered her eyes, then removed her hand and stared at her son. "I hoped it wouldn't come to this. He's been making sheep's eyes at Miss Trente since he arrived. Haven't you noticed?"

"No, Aunt, I'm afraid not." Penelope frowned. Perhaps Toby had been eager to lead Miss Trente into dinner, walk with her, but Penelope was so used to gentlemen dancing attendance on that young lady that she hadn't noticed one more. "I know it's none of my concern, but I think Miss Trente has a shallow nature. She won't care about her husband, only for herself."

"Well thank you for that, at least," Mrs. Makepiece said. "My sentiments precisely. She would not make Toby a conformable wife, I'm convinced of it."

Toby's mouth took on a thin line. "I'm a grown man, Mama. Please allow me to make my own decisions about my future happiness."

Makepiece and Penelope exchanged a feminine glance of exasperation.

"She won't have him," Penelope assured her aunt.

"I sincerely hope not." Mrs. Makepiece seemed a little mollified, her mouth relaxing into a smile of relief.

"She tried to entice Sev into a compromising situation."

Mrs. Makepiece's mouth grew even longer and thinner and she lost the smile. "The madam!"

"She's likely to try that with Peter Worsley. He's the second son of an earl, you know, and well off in his own right," Toby said, unsuccessful at keeping the sulky tone out of his voice.

"He knows," Penelope told him.

Her aunt frowned. She glanced at her son. "I believe we should take our leave. We wouldn't wish to overstay our welcome here."

Toby shrugged, his pout more suited to a sulky child than a grown man. "You're right, Mama. Lord Swithland has a full house here, so he's unlikely to miss our presence. Penelope has, not unreasonably, chosen the finest prospect for a husband. While I cannot completely condone it, neither can I condemn your action."

Penelope stood dropped a curtsey. "Then I will bid you a good journey. I hope to see you soon. If you'll excuse me now, ma'am, I was on my way to breakfast." She stopped after opening the door, turning back for one last word. "In case you're wondering, ma'am, it wasn't for status that I accepted Severus's offer. I've loved him for years."

Without waiting to see the response, she left the room.

She'd hardly gone three paces when her hand was caught and she was pulled into Severus's arms. Before she could get her breath back, he captured her mouth in a kiss. "I heard that," he said after he lifted his head.

Penelope buried her head in his chest, overcome. "You shouldn't eavesdrop."

"In this case. I didn't mean to. I came to see if you needed any help, but it seems not. I missed you last night."

"Did you?"

He kissed her when she lifted her head. "Not for much longer, love."

Taking her hand, he led her into the breakfast parlor. Penelope knew she would have to get used to everyone looking at her when she entered a room, at least for the time being. For all she knew they had always done it, but now she could see them clearly. Expressions ranged from hostility to polite interest.

Severus handed her to a seat then took his place next to her. He made it clear that he meant to make his affection for her plain. Penelope wasn't sure how she felt about that. She was embarrassed by his attentions, but flattered as well. Putting her chin up, she decided to enjoy it while she could. As her aunt had reminded her, this devotion might not last.

To her relief Don Alfonso was not present, although his sister was. Breakfast was an informal meal, the servants only coming in to replenish the dishes on the buffet, or bring fresh tea and coffee. Penelope liked country house breakfasts. Later, the servants would replace the breakfast dishes with a cold collation, which would serve anyone who couldn't wait to eat again until dinner later in the afternoon.

Penelope recognized her mood as happiness. It was a long time since she'd felt this light-hearted, this joyful. If ever. She smiled at Antonia, seated across the table at her and her friend smiled back, albeit in a more restrained way. Was it obvious then, that they hadn't waited until the wedding? She hoped not. Her stepmother knew, and her father too. It should remain there.

Severus excused himself after making a good meal, to attend to estate matters. "I'm determined to get everything up to date then the estate can run itself for a week or two." He didn't look at Penelope. He didn't need to.

When Penelope left the breakfast parlor, she was at a temporary loss as to what to do. She'd given Mr. Grey control over her portfolio while she was otherwise engaged, and it was too sunny a day to stay immured indoors, otherwise she might have hidden herself in the Old Library with a good book.

The feeling of time to fill didn't last long. A maid hurried up to her and bobbed a breathless curtsey. "Your luggage has arrived, miss, but we don't know where to put it."

"Luggage?"

"From Derbyshire, ma'am." From her father's house. "We don't know where to put it, ma'am, and since his lordship is occupied, we thought we would consult you."

Penelope was at a loss. "I'm not sure, either. I'll go and consult with his lordship, if you take me to him."

The maid took her through the hall, and Penelope recognized some of the cases there. Her embroidery. She might be glad of that. Her nearsightedness had not prevented her wielding a needle from time to time. At the back of the hall was a stone corridor, blessedly cool in the growing heat of the summer morning. The maid took Penelope along it and to a plain, whitewashed door at the end. She knocked and Penelope heard the familiar tones, "Come in."

Inside she found a plain room with a large rent table at its centre. It was covered with papers in neat piles. Sev sat at the table with a man she had never seen. They both stood when she entered. Penelope felt as if she was intruding in something that was none of her business, but Severus's welcoming smile calmed her. "Baxter, I should have done this before. My dear." He crossed the room and took Penelope's hand. "This is my land steward, Mr. Baxter. His family has served ours for generations, to our mutual benefit."

Mr. Baxter, a stout gentleman of middle age, dressed soberly, but in his shirtsleeves, bowed over her hand. "It will be a pleasure to serve you, ma'am."

Penelope stopped him leaving when he moved to the door. "No, I didn't mean to interrupt. It's just that my luggage has arrived and the servants have no idea what to do with it." She glanced up at Sev. "Neither do I."

Severus's smile was reassuring. "I didn't realize. I'd planned for us to choose our apartment together. We can't use mine; it's purely a bachelor suite."

"Isn't there a traditional place we should use?"

He grimaced. "Damned dark and gloomy, and on the wrong side of the house. I've no mind to use it." He glanced back at Mr. Baxter. "Can you manage without me for half an hour?" Smiling, Mr. Baxter nodded and Severus took Penelope out of the room.

"I'm sorry, I didn't want to interrupt you."

"Don't concern yourself. It's a pleasure." He winked, blatantly pleased.

He took Penelope upstairs. Almost immediately, they were joined by the dark, quiet presence of Lady Wimbourne. How she had discovered their presence upstairs Penelope had no idea, but she gained a new respect for her stepmother's spy network.

Marveling, Penelope toured the rooms she could occupy after her marriage. There were more than she had supposed. She turned to Sev. "Will you choose?"

"Don't you like them?" His eyes held anxiety.

She smiled, trying to reassure him. "I like them all, but I don't know the house as well as you do. You know which rooms are better in the mornings, which are warmest in the winter."

He lifted her hand from his arm and kissed it. Penelope had no doubt that if they had been alone, he would have kissed her mouth. "Then did you like the last rooms? The ones before these?"

She recalled the ones he meant. The ones they stood in were decorated in the Chinese style, but needed refurbishment.

The last ones were on the South side of the house, and were decorated luxuriously, but not ostentatiously. Penelope realized they were perfect, and said so. His warm smile told her she'd made the right decision. "I've always liked those rooms. They belonged to my grandparents, but I had them refurbished a few years ago."

Penelope was pleased, and willingly let her lord go back to his duties, while she attended to hers.

The rooms were lovely. The bedroom she chose wasn't too large, but there was room for her books and her private possessions. The bedroom Severus would use was directly next door, and the associated sitting rooms were on the other side. Supervising the unpacking, Penelope wondered if Severus's grandparents had been as devoted to each other as she was to Severus. She hoped so.

Chapter Nineteen

Penelope had some very bad dreams that night. It was unusual for her because she rarely remembered her dreams. A jolt brought her into reality, and she sat up, rubbing her fists over unaccountably sticky eyes.

"Good morning," said a deep voice.

At first, Penelope thought she was still dreaming. Then, cautiously opening her eyes a crack against the glare of the sun she saw Don Alfonso. "Wh-what...?" She swallowed. "Oh!" She winced in pain.

Her head pounded as badly as it had ever done, and nausea threatened. It had to be a dream. Last night, after Severus's long, deep goodnight kiss, she'd taken to her bed, very tired by her satisfying day supervising the maids unpacking her belongings, so she couldn't possibly be here. The jolting and swaying confirmed her suspicions that she lay in a carriage, although how she got there she couldn't immediately recall. And she could have sworn that the Don had left before they set out for London—dammit, he had.

Despite the pain in her head, she sat up and forced her eyes open. She became aware that her hair was still in its nighttime braids, bouncing about her shoulders, and she was bundled in a blanket. "What on earth is going on here?" she enunciated, careful to make her words clear. She didn't want to have to repeat them. It hurt to talk.

"We are going to our wedding, my dear," said the Don, equally clearly. His gaze passed over her in a way that made her draw the blanket more securely around her.

"What? But I'm not marrying you—I'm marrying Severus."

He shook his head, as though admonishing a recalcitrant child. "You were promised to me. I haven't given you permission to go, and so you are still mine."

Slowly, what was happening permeated the wooliness in her head. Then she remembered something else. "My maid—Collins—she was sleeping in my room."

"She still is," the Don said calmly. "It is early yet. I had a sleeping draught put in her tea last night. She will sleep for some time, but she will be well."

"Is that what you did to me?" Penelope demanded. Now she remembered the bitter taste in the tea she had shared with her maid before they settled down for the night. Not enough to stop her drinking the tea, but enough so that she remembered.

"I am afraid that you made it necessary." He sounded regretful. "If you had come with me when I asked you it would not have been needful."

Needful? Necessary? Penelope felt her anger rise, and lifted her hands to her temples, trying to make sense of all this. "I am contracted to Lord Swithland. Please take me back."

"The contract is invalid. You were promised to me first."

She lowered her hands. She felt at a great disadvantage, being so inadequately dressed. "Don Alfonso, my father has no jurisdiction over me. He is my father, and I would not knowingly do anything to distress him, but I do not have to obey him. I am over age. In any case, he agreed to my marriage to Severus."

The Don nodded, steepling his hands and touching his

sensual mouth with his fingers. "He will not be distressed when I send him notice of our marriage."

"I will not marry you, Don Alfonso," Penelope said slowly, and added, "I do not wish to marry you."

"You will marry me."

She was getting nowhere. Looking out of the carriage window Penelope realized two things. They were going quite fast and she didn't have her spectacles with her. This made it impossible for her to see more than a blur of color as they passed. If she squinted and slitted her eyes, she might make out a landmark when they passed, but she had no idea where they were. "Where are you taking me?"

"Portsmouth."

Penelope drew a sharp breath. It had seemed dramatic to describe this as abduction but she realized that was what it was. She was being abducted. Perhaps he hoped to compromise her virtue, force a marriage on her that way. "I wish to go home. I will tell everyone I meet that I wish to go home."

He sighed, spreading his hands wide in a Continental gesture. "I have a yacht waiting at Portsmouth. We will stop long enough to be married, for propriety's sake, and then we will embark for my home. I promise you will not be sorry. Lord Swithland will not want you after this scandal. It will be the only way for you."

Penelope gritted her teeth and, despite the growing heat of the day, drew the blanket closer around her. It would not be the only way. There had to be some other way.

She saw the flash of a building pass her, then another. They must be approaching Portsmouth. Surely she could find someone to help her. As if he read her eager thoughts, Don Alfonso leaned forward until he loomed over her. "Time to sleep again." He gripped her throat and pressed hard on it.

Before she could claw at his hand for release, before she could scream or struggle Penelope felt a great wave crash over her head and she dived back into blackness.

The sharp knock on her private sitting-room door almost made Lady Wimbourne jump, but she was made of sterner stuff than that. "Come in," she said coolly.

The door opened to admit Severus, every inch the Earl of Swithland. Marcela had rarely seen him like that, except in public gatherings in London. She held out her hand for his salute and after kissing the air above it, he released it. "I have come for an explanation. Tell me about Paul."

She gaped. "How do you know about him?"

"I know that you have paid large sums of money to have him cared for." Severus regarded her coolly, dispassionately.

"Who do you think he is?"

"You employed someone from the Bruce Street agency to look after him. I employed someone to discover that fact." Severus's usually friendly eyes were cold. "I think Paul is your husband. I think there is a plot afoot to defraud Lord Wimbourne of money."

Marcela gasped and covered her mouth. Severus watched and waited, but didn't expect was followed. "My husband? Is that what you think? No, my lord, I had no husband before Lord Wimbourne. I am married to him in truth." She paused, staring at him, a wild look in her black eyes. "Paul is not my husband, and he is not my lover. He is my son."

It was Severus's turn to gape. "Your son?" Turning, he took a few hasty steps around the room, blindly staring at her. "How can this be?"

"If I tell you," she said. "You must promise to tell no one else."

"I cannot promise you that until I've heard your story."

She sighed and stared at him. He gave her time to think by drawing a chair up. He needed to sit down.

Now her protectiveness towards the unknown Paul made more sense. He'd thought she'd been slipping him money, either because of extortion or love, he didn't know which. It had to be love. Her face had softened when she spoke his name.

She gave in. "I will tell you, and leave the decision up to you. You may ruin my life by telling my husband. He may never want to see me again, but I cannot keep my secret for much longer."

She stared down at her clasped hands, and watched the knuckles turn white. "I was contracted before, in Spain, to a man I loved very much. He was strong, and powerful, and he loved me. My brother was glad to see me happy. The contract was signed. Then I lost him."

She looked up at Severus, her eyes blank. "He was killed, drowned in a boating accident. We had been so happy, and we had not waited for the marriage to love. When he died, I was pregnant. With Paul." Her eyes became glossy with tears. Severus blinked. "It is why I watch Penelope so closely. She is a good girl and does not deserve the fate that awaited me. What if you die before the wedding ceremony? What then?"

He thought better of Marcela for that, to care for the person and not the convention. She deserved to know something he had not even told his betrothed. "There is provision for that. I didn't love Penelope heedlessly. She might not have noticed, but the clause in the contract is for her and her children. It makes no mention of marriage. If I were to die before the ceremony, she would still be cared for. I haven't told her that, because I don't want to make her unhappy by thinking of the possibility."

"Oh God if he had done that!" Marcela's voice broke in a sob, and she looked down again, letting the tears fall. Fumbling, she found her handkerchief in her pocket.

While she was recovering, Severus went over to the table and poured her a glass of water from the carafe, giving her a modicum of privacy. She took it with a muttered word of thanks and sipped. He waited until she was ready to go on. "If it distresses you too much, we can discuss this at another date." He understood why she would want to keep her son's existence a secret. An illegitimate child could ruin a mother. But she hadn't abandoned the baby, as so many other women would have done, she paid for the child's care.

"No, I wish to tell you. I have kept this secret for so long, it burns me up inside." She took another sip of the water before she went on. "My brother Alfonso went to school here. His mother was English, unlike mine. When I told him I was pregnant he beat me, but then promised to make things right. He brought me to England and put me in a house with a few attendants. I had the baby there. I wanted to give my son away when he was born, never see him again, but Alfonso would not agree to that. He said the baby was one of the family and he would not see him go to strangers. Alfonso has a very strong sense of family and of honor. And when I saw my baby I knew he was right. Paul is a beautiful child.

"Alfonso found someone to care for Paul, gave out that Paul was his son and not mine. A man has a bastard child and pays for its care, he is seen as a good man. People forget what caused the child. Alfonso has been good to us, but it has been hard. I see my son when I can and I miss my home. When Lord Wimbourne proposed marriage I had thought to tell him, but he so badly wants a son I thought I should try to give him one first. Then he might consent to take my son—my brother's son—into his house." She looked away.

Severus watched her and believed her. He had never seen the possessed, controlled baroness so close to tears before. This must be true. Silence settled between them and turned into anticipation. "You have forgotten something."

"What have I forgotten?"

Severus smiled. "Lord Wimbourne wants a son. He is very fond of you. I would say tell him the truth. Tell him. He will understand, Marcela, I'm sure of it. And he'll be glad that you've borne a child already, it's proof for him of your fertility."

"I do not think—"

A new voice came from the door. "He's right. Tell me, Marcela."

Lord Wimbourne came into the room, and Severus got to his feet.

Marcela stared at her husband, terror in her face, horror. Lord Wimbourne walked across to the sofa, on which she sat and held, out his hand. "Tell me, Marcela. Tell me of your own free will. I knew there was something, but I didn't know what it was. Now tell me."

He didn't need to look towards Severus to tell him his presence was *de trop.* Severus left the room, pulling the door closed behind him.

When he went to find Penelope to tell her of the developments, Severus found she was still abed. At least no one answered when he knocked on her door, and when he went outside the house to look he saw the shutters on her windows were still closed. It was only eleven. He must learn not to be so impatient, but he wanted to tell her about Paul before anyone else did.

Grinning at his own boyish eagerness, knowing the desire

to tell her about Paul was only part of it, he went in to breakfast.

It wasn't until after breakfast that Sev began to worry. He started by sending a message to Collins, Penelope's maid. The message came back that no one had seen her that morning. Then Severus grew more concerned. Walking into the hall to find a maid he found Peter instead.

"What is it?" said Peter at once.

"I would have expected to see Penelope by now," Sev said shortly. "I'm trying to find a maid to go into her bedroom and make sure everything is all right."

"I'll come with you."

Severus knew better than to argue, and if truth be told was glad of the support. They found a housemaid in one of the main rooms, busy dusting and after the first confusion she was glad to comply.

The men stood outside in the corridor while the maid went inside. "Don't disturb her if she is asleep," Sev instructed her.

The maid was back outside in a matter of minutes, and the pale expression on her face was enough to make Severus push past her and into the room. Peter followed with the maid.

Collins, Penelope's maid, lay in the truckle bed. Their entrance didn't disturb her in the least, and when the housemaid shook her by the shoulders, Collins merely grunted and groaned. That wasn't a natural sleep.

Peter went over to the windows and crashed the shutters back against the wall. Severus stood in the middle of the room, staring at the empty bed, still rumpled from her body. Penelope hadn't risen that morning. She was gone.

Chapter Twenty

Penelope came to her senses again. She kept her eyes closed, and breathed deeply, in case there was anyone else with her. Her headache had abated to a dull throb, and she could think again.

She smelled fustiness, dirt, and the sweet odor of beer. By this, she guessed she was in an inn. She was lying on a bed; she felt the pillows under her head and the lumps in the mattress. Fear and anger warred in her for control, and anger won. She would kill him when she got out of this. She longed to open her eyes and be back in her room at Swithland House, looking forward to her wedding on Saturday. Oh Sev!

She pushed Severus to the back of her mind. She couldn't depend on him to find her. What clues would he have? All he would know is that she was gone, probably against her will. Don Alfonso had left before they went to London; there was nothing to connect them. She must hope he found her, but couldn't depend on it. By the time he found out where she'd gone she might well be aboard ship. She must at all costs try to avoid that.

Breathing deeply, she listened. She heard no one, and after waiting and listening for a further five minutes, as near as she could make it, she opened one eye.

She was alone. Rolling on to her back she stared at the

beamed ceiling stained with years of badly vented fires. It was broad daylight, and she guessed the same day as when she had last come to her senses. Thursday.

If she was right, she couldn't be very far from Swithland House. Thirty miles, maybe. That meant they were close to the coast. Or, from the sound of the seagulls outside, probably at the coast. Portsmouth.

Grateful for the chance to think, Penelope did her best not to waste it. She had several possibilities she could take, and she would make the most of anything that came her way. She could overpower Don Alfonso, but then she would have to deal with his servants. There would be a coach driver, footmen; burly men she had no hope against. She could try to gain the help of someone here, an innkeeper. She could climb out of the window and run. She wouldn't get very far, especially in her nightwear.

Penelope was ready when the door rattled and her persecutor came in. She sat up, not hunching up as she wanted to, unused used to men seeing her in her nightwear. She felt vulnerable, but she wouldn't show him that.

"Good afternoon, Don Alfonso."

He bowed, as if they were still in a fashionable drawing room. "Good afternoon, my dear. You seem to have recovered from your agitation."

Penelope quelled her rising anger. She had given only one man the right to call her his, and it wasn't Don Alfonso. "I have recovered my senses. I still have a headache. Did you bring my spectacles?"

He frowned. "I regret, no. Does it matter so much?"

"I don't see very well without them."

She saw his shrug. "I will arrange for some for you, but I would prefer it if you did not wear them in public, it does not create a proper impression."

240

Biting back the retort that it had nothing to do with him, as she had no intention of letting him have his way, she said instead, "As you wish. Did you bring me any clothes?"

"Indeed. I will buy you what you need, but I brought something from your room."

Opening a small box at the bottom of the bed, he drew out Penelope's second best riding habit. She sighed in relief. It added one more small weight to her side of the scales. Without proper clothing she would appear mad, and be easily out-argued, out maneuvered.

"May I have a maid to help me?"

He gazed at her through narrowed eyes. "You can manage on your own."

So much for that ploy. He studied her for a moment longer. "I would like you to accept your fate and become my bride, as your father promised me. I do not think you have yet accepted that. My men will be at every door and there will be no escape. If you decide to come to me of your own accord, you will not regret it."

Penelope would have chosen Don Alfonso over Toby. She now realized she would have been wrong. For all Alfonso's dark beauty, there was no yielding in him, no kindness. Toby, whatever his physical detractions, would have been kinder, and tried to give her a better life.

Severus beat them all. Not because he was better looking, richer or kinder, but because Penelope loved him. She was his, wherever she lived, whoever she was married to, she was his forever. She debated whether to tell Don Alfonso that she wasn't a virgin, indeed might be carrying Lord Swithland's child, but decided against it. She was too vulnerable at the moment, but she would tell him if she had to. She wasn't ashamed of it.

The Don bowed and left the room.

He gave Penelope a bare half-hour to dress, but by the time he returned, she'd managed to scramble into her riding habit and fasten her hair up into a simple knot.

The door opened, but without a knock and the Don came back in. "Are you ready?"

Penelope picked up her jacket. "If you insist."

The Don stared at her. "You are beautiful," he said softly, and took a pace towards her. Penelope stepped back. "I will not be unkind, unless you give me reason to be so." To her relief he didn't come any closer. "We must eat before we leave. We will board my yacht soon."

He turned on his heel and left the room. Penelope breathed out a long sigh of relief and went over to the window. The cobbled yard outside told her that she wasn't in a regular coaching inn, more like a small country inn. The carriage she had been brought in filled the yard, and the stables at the end were too small to hold more than four horses. A large coaching inn might contain people who would recognize her, so he wouldn't risk that. She watched a man stride across the yard to the stables and wondered how far she would get if she dropped out of the window and ran. Not very far, probably, but it would cause a delay.

Lifting the sash, she leaned out and stared at the cobbles below. She might break a bone if she jumped, but if she hung on to the sill and dropped, she could get away with it.

She was steeling herself to make the effort when the door to her room crashed open and Don Alfonso strode in. "Don't even consider it."

He came close, spun her around, gripped her chin with his hand, and kissed her hard. She kept her mouth shut, but the kiss was brief and he didn't seek to probe any further. He released her and stood back. "You will enjoy it more if you do not struggle against me. Accept it; you will be my wife before the day is out."

Before she could reply, he strode to the door and left the room. Penelope heard the key turn in the lock.

Chapter Twenty-One

Severus wasted no time, striding down to the kitchen where most of the servants would be at that time of day. Since he sometimes used the back entrance as a short cut, or when he wanted to avoid someone, no one remarked on his presence apart from a curtsey or bow until he opened his mouth and roared: "Everyone stop what they're doing. I want everyone in the main kitchen in five minutes."

They could have heard him above stairs. Servants scurried, and in five minutes Sev got what he wanted.

He decided that in the interests of speed, subterfuge was useless. "Miss Makepiece has gone, against her will. I think she's been abducted. I want anyone who knows anything, who saw anything, to tell me now."

His stern face, his loud voice stilled the room. The collective gasp at the news was followed by a low murmur, as servants turned to each other to discuss the news.

"I saw someone, my lord," said a quiet voice. A little housemaid.

Severus had no difficulty in recalling her name. "Rotherham. When?"

"Late last night, my lord, after dark. I was clearing up in the small parlor downstairs when Don Alfonso came in from the terrace. I thought he'd left the house last week, but maybe he'd forgotten something. I hid. You don't see housemaids unless you want to, and I'm very good at keeping still." Her face grew frightened. "Should I have told you, my lord? I'm sorry, I didn't know."

"No." Sev took care to moderate his voice. "You weren't to know. Did you leave the room?"

"Yes, my lord, as soon as he had gone."

"How long before the door was locked for the night?"

The under-butler stepped forward. "I did the rounds at half past eleven, my lord. I locked all the doors."

Severus nodded. She'd been gone longer than he'd thought, but it was barely noon now. He still had a chance.

A disturbance heralded the arrival of Lady Wimbourne. She couldn't have wasted much time. Severus didn't attempt to cushion the blow. "Your brother has made off with Penelope. Where has he taken her?" His voice shook. It was fear for her, brought to mind when he spoke her name aloud, but Penelope's stepmother wasn't to know this. It might just as well have been fury.

Lady Wimbourne put her hands to her mouth and her face, always pale, grew paler. "Oh God!" Turning, she stared around the room. "How do you know it was him?"

"He was seen."

She turned again, faced Severus. Except for her pale complexion and wide eyes she could be discussing the time of day with a friend; her hands didn't shake and she retained her upright stance. Now Severus recognized the way she donned her mask, the rigid mask she never dropped except in the presence of people she trusted. He was beginning to understand why. "I feared it, but I thought he had accepted his failure. He has done it before, in Madrid. He sees something he wants, he takes it." She grimaced. "I will tell you another time."

Severus nodded. "Go on."

"He has a house in Bath and another in Oxford. He has a yacht on the coast, at Portsmouth."

That was all the information Severus needed. Footmen stepped forward. "When Lady Wimbourne gives you the addresses, I want two men on each route. I will go to the coast myself."

Peter's soft voice sounded at Sev's side. "I'll go with you."

"I think he'll head there. There's no time to be lost. Peter— I'll see you outside in ten minutes." He turned to the butler. "Make sure there are a couple of strong horses saddled and ready."

The spell broke; everyone scattered, to do what they could. Except for Lady Wimbourne. She lingered. "I am sorry. I did not know he would go this far. He gave me to Wimbourne, he said, in return for his daughter's hand in marriage. Wimbourne made it clear he could court her, and he would favor the suit, but he would not compel her to marry anyone. I thought he understood. I should have spoken more clearly at the time, but—"

Sev glanced at her. "It's not your fault."

"He will ruin her."

"No. I will marry her."

"If he—takes her, he could make her with child."

"I don't care. But if he does that, I'll kill him for it." Sev ignored Lady Wimbourne's gasp. He knew full well if Don Alfonso raped Penelope, she could fall pregnant with his child, but he wouldn't have Penelope hurt. He wouldn't wait, he would marry her before anyone could gossip. Anything else was completely unthinkable.

Sev left the room, heading for his own. In ten minutes, he

was out again, dressed for riding in a plain coat and breeches. Pausing for a moment, he went back in the room, took a paper out of a drawer, and tucked it into his coat pocket. When he went downstairs, taking them two at a time, he found Lady Wimbourne waiting at the foot. She handed him a small package. "He didn't take her spectacles."

Severus took them with a word of thanks. "If you can, try to stop word of this getting to the guests. Tell them I've been called away on business and Penelope is sick in bed."

"I can do that. Will the servants be discreet?"

"If they value their positions."

Severus went out to where the horses waited. Peter followed in a few moments, similarly dressed. A footman followed him. Silently each gentleman watched as he packed a saber and a holster containing two pistols on to each saddle. A box of pellets and a horn of powder each were safely bestowed.

While this was done, Sev turned to Peter. "We'll take the main road, but there are others on the less popular roads."

Peter nodded. "Don't worry, we'll find her."

"I don't doubt it. I won't give up. If we fail to stop them sailing, I'll go after them."

"I'll stay with you until you do," Peter turned to mount his horse. "You'll need someone to stop you murdering him."

Severus's lip curled. "If I want to, no one will stop me."

At the pace Severus set it was impossible to talk. All his thoughts fixed on Penelope, desperately trying to send her strength, to let her know he was coming for her. She'd been taken in her night things, and her maid was still too ill to check her belongings, although she had tried.

Severus didn't let himself imagine what might be happening to Penelope. He knew she wouldn't give in. That in itself made the sweat break out on his forehead when he thought what Don Alfonso might do to her to her if she resisted. She was a gently nurtured girl; she could have no idea. He hoped she'd not been made as ill as Collins from the brew they'd ingested—they'd found the remains of the tea on a little table and from the dregs had deduced that there had been more than the tea in it.

Severus went through the plans he'd made and prayed they were enough. If Don Alfonso realized they were on to him, it would be easy to get Penelope away. All he had to do was take the yacht to a more secluded cove and take her there. Oh, God, he couldn't bear it. He would follow until he found her, then he would find out what she wanted to do. However much it hurt him he would never make her do anything against her will. If she felt she had to stay with the Don, if he had compromised her too far, if—please no—he had made her love him, then he, Severus, would stand aside. Otherwise, he would take her back, whatever the world said. Just let him find her.

Chapter Twenty-Two

Penelope heard footsteps on the bare boards outside the little room that formed her cell. In came Don Alfonso. Penelope folded her hands in front of her and met his stare with one of her own.

His gaze raked insultingly over her, and Penelope wished she wore a hooped petticoat, so her form wasn't quite so revealed. His gaze was greedy, showing more than he had so far. She couldn't bear it. "Why do you want me when I don't want you?"

He closed the door, but didn't latch it. "I have never wanted a woman so much before," he said, his voice low. Penelope chilled to hear it. "I want you and I will have you."

Penelope swallowed. "What if I give myself to you here and now—will you go then? Will that be enough?" If he did such a thing she thought she might be able to bear it—if he left. Then it would be her secret, her burden. She would never tell anyone else, never share that particular grief.

Her hope of freedom was short lived. "No. I want you to wife. I will have you, and in time, you will learn to enjoy it. I will do my best to give you all that you need, even if you have to live in Spain forever."

"No!" The cry was involuntary, forced out of her by his cold demand.

"Yes. You will marry me here. Today, before we go any further. Then no man will have the right to take you from me. You will be my wife, my property, and bound to obey. But I want to show you something else."

Without warning, he stepped forward and seized her. His mouth descended on hers, hard and painful in its intensity. It was a travesty of the sweet caresses Penelope had shared with Severus, something unwanted, and wet. Penelope couldn't remember Sev's kisses being so wet, like a slug on her skin. She felt his thick tongue on her mouth, trying to prize her lips apart, but she clamped them shut. She couldn't bear the thought of that thing in her mouth; she knew she would retch if he succeeded.

Nevertheless, Don Alfonso seemed to enjoy the contact. He prolonged the kiss, and when she wouldn't open her mouth to him, he licked down to her neck, leaving what felt like a trail of slime behind him, cold and wet. Penelope held herself stiffly, her hands still folded together before her, trying to deny him access.

The Don drew back, such a fire in his eyes that Penelope had to force herself to stop her instinctive recoil. "Innocent, untried. I feared that you had been violated, but it is not so, is it? You do not know how to respond. I will teach you. You will find it better when you do."

He stepped back, leaving Penelope in free air. "I have sent for the vicar of this parish. We will be married when he arrives."

Penelope couldn't stop herself in time. "Have you a license?" *Stupid, why did you tell him?*

He frowned. "No, I believe the vicar will provide that. I am Roman Catholic, my dear, and when we reach Spain we will be married properly in the sight of the Church, but this will be enough to secure you in English law. Will you do this willingly?"

"No. I do not wish to marry you, Don Alfonso." There was no prevarication in her tone. Even a marriage in law could be invalidated if one of the participants claimed she was coerced into it. If she voiced her objections at the altar, she could claim annulment afterwards. Or she could kill him. She'd do that, if she could be sure of getting away.

"You will. I could take you here and now. If I do that you will marry me." His eyes gleamed again and Penelope became afraid.

"You would take me against my will."

Her calm words stopped him and he stared at her. "If you refuse, I will kill you. No one else will have you."

Turning abruptly, the Don left the room, for once forgetting to bow to her. His formality was intimidating. So was his kiss.

Ripping off her jacket, Penelope pushed up the sleeves of her shirt and went to the washbasin, plunging her arms into the cold water. It was a relief after the hot, slimy kisses. She pushed her hair roughly off her face and splashed the water over it. The soap was a hard, rough tablet, but she managed to get up a thin lather to wash with.

She felt better once she'd removed all trace of him from her skin, able to think once more. Her cold front had been bravado; inside she was shaking with terror. She was constantly terrified he might rape her; nothing would stop him once his ring was on her finger, she saw it in his eyes. He wanted her; that much was true.

There was something else. Last year a new Act of Parliament had come into force. From now on, a marriage was only legal if banns were read for three weeks before the marriage or there was a special license, like the one Severus had procured in London. If the Don hadn't obtained one, any ceremony she went through with Don Alfonso wouldn't be legal.

She knew what she would do.

Chapter Twenty-Three

Severus and Peter stopped at the first village, but no one had seen a carriage pass that day, or at least not that anyone had noticed. Sighing, Severus remounted and they continued on the road to the coast.

They had better luck at Eastleigh. They stopped at the main coaching inn on the High Street, and while regaling themselves with home-brewed and a fine pigeon pie, they asked the landlord if he had seen anyone.

"Strange thing, sir," the landlord mused, not averse to pausing from his labors for a few moments. He leaned against the high screen behind Severus and rubbed his stubbly chin. "A carriage stopped here earlier today. A gentleman's carriage. The gentleman came in and wet his whistle, and he took a basket of food with him. We do that, sir, provide food for the road. Well, he said his lady was ill, but funny thing, sir..."

Severus put two sovereigns down on the counter. "Two more pints, please, landlord. And keep the change." He quelled the anticipation rising in him.

He leaned forward and spoke confidentially. Severus willingly endured the landlord's fetid breath. "One of my ostlers passed the carriage with food for the horses. There was a lady in there, right enough, out for the count. In her nightwear. Now I know the weather's been steamy recently, but no lady would take to the road unless she was really ill and I ask you, what lady would consent to travel if she was that ill?"

"Did your ostler get a look at the lady?"

"Aye, sir, as much as he could. A pleasant armful, he said—" He paused at Sev's low growl, but after a startled look, went over to the barrels and drew their beer, carrying on the conversation over his shoulder. "Pretty, young, but not a young girl. Brown hair in braids. Very pale, he said, and the lady hardly stirred, else he would have asked her if she was all right."

Sev slapped another two guineas on the counter and eyed his tankard.

"How fast can you down a pint, Peter?"

Peter grinned. "Faster than you, that's for sure."

The vicar proved to be a young man. Penelope insisted on talking to him alone. The Don didn't allow her the privilege without a struggle, but Penelope insisted that she needed spiritual guidance.

When the vicar came into the room, they closed the door and Penelope sat down on the bed, since there was only one chair in the little room.

Ten minutes later she came out again. Her clothes were as neat as she could make them, the jacket of her riding habit buttoned up to the chin. Her posture was completely unbending. "I have spoken to the reverend," she said. "I am ready."

The breath left Don Alfonso in one long sigh. "I am pleased. Come, my dear." Holding out his arm, he waited until she placed the tips of her fingers on it then led the procession downstairs to the small parlor, redolent with the stale odor of beer from the taproom across the hall. The flustered vicar followed them.

"Here!" The lane on the outskirts of Portsmouth, outside the gates of the town, had been rough, but on horseback easy to negotiate. At the end of it was a sprawling collection of buildings, and a small, local inn.

There was no one about so Severus swung out of the saddle and secured the reins of his horse over the low branches of a nearby tree. Peter followed. The weather had been warm and dry, otherwise the path to the inn would have been mired and more difficult. As it was, their booted feet stirred up clouds of dust on their way to the front door.

Severus's determined hammering was met by silence. Glancing at Peter, he tried again. He tensed his jaw. "We're going to have to explore a little."

The front door opened to reveal a small woman, dressed in simple country clothes. At least she looked respectable, although appearances were often deceptive.

"Where are they?" Severus demanded.

To his surprise, he met with no resistance. He was ready, his spare hand on his sword and a pistol heavy in his pocket, but the woman stepped aside so they could go in.

Followed by Peter, Severus went in to the dark, narrow hall. A large door was open to their left. Glancing in Severus saw tables, benches, and a row of tapped barrels. No one was inside. To their right was a closed door. Unhesitatingly Severus opened it and went in. To his own personal nightmare.

Penelope was leaning on Don Alfonso's arm. Before them stood a vicar, a surplice and stole thrown over his everyday clothes.

Severus hated dramatic entrances, but in this case, he made an exception. Resisting an urge to shout "Unhand that woman!" instead he simply roared, "Stop!"

Don Alfonso stared, furious but with something else that made Sev uneasy. Complacence. Superiority. It was hard to place but it was there.

Painfully, Severus made himself look at Penelope. She looked agonized, but seemed to be unharmed.

"You are too late," said the Don. "This cleric has just declared us man and wife."

Severus stared, his mouth working but unable to speak. Feeling the panic rise he pushed it down, forced himself back. Before he did anything else, he had to be sure of something. He looked at Penelope. They might as well be the only people in the room. "Did you want to marry Don Alfonso? Think hard. If you say yes, I will let you go. If it is no, you will be a widow before nightfall."

There was no hesitation. "No." The fatal word dropped like ice into the still, silent room.

She wasn't allowed to say any more as Severus strode forward and struck Don Alfonso across the face. "Here, outside, swords," Severus said grimly.

Don Alfonso was still smiling, although the blow had reddened his cheek and knocked him to one side. "I thought the challenged man had the right to choose the time and weapons."

"That is in an affair of honor. You mistake my intentions; that was not a challenge. If you don't fight back, I'll kill you anyway."

The two men stared at each other, their glances unwavering. "Very well," said the Don. "I will kill you. I was leaving the country in any case."

Penelope stepped forward, touching neither of them, only her movement attracting their attention. "You should know that the marriage isn't legal."

All heads turned to her, with varying expressions of disbelief, shock, and blank incomprehension. Don Alfonso made a derogatory sound. "This man is a cleric. I made sure of that. He is entitled to marry us."

The young man moved to stand behind Penelope. "Not without banns or a license. I had strong suspicions that this marriage was taking place under duress, and when I spoke to Miss Makepiece, I found it was so. That alone would have made it invalid. Without the proper documentation, the marriage service means nothing."

Penelope put her hand on Severus's arm. He flinched, but otherwise stayed as still as a man can, staring at her face unblinkingly. "I thought if he thought we were married he would relax the guard on me, and I could get away."

Heedless of the other occupants of the room Severus smiled, an expression of growing delight. "Such a clever love." He reached his hand up to caress her cheek. She moved against it. No one, looking at them, could deny their devotion to each other. No one would deny them the right to be together.

Except for one man. Don Alfonso moved between them and faced Sev, nothing showing on his face and upright figure except perfect aristocratic disdain. "I still consider Penelope to be my wife. When I have killed you, I will take her to Spain with me."

Sev hit him.

The room erupted into action. The two men at its centre engaged in earnest, lost to everything except their dispute. Penelope shrieked, and tried to drag the Don away while Peter tried in vain to restrain his friend.

Then a voice, one well-used to controlling drunken sots when the need arose climbed up out of the chaos and roared, "Gentlemen, I won't have you ruining my best parlor. Outside! Now!"

It was enough. Severus and Don Alfonso allowed themselves to be separated and all turned to the door. In it was framed a woman, perhaps approaching five feet in height, dressed for work. Her overskirt was kilted up over a lighter petticoat and a clean white apron covered it all. She stood, arms akimbo, glaring at the mess of people in her best parlor.

Severus was the first to regain some composure. He executed an elegant bow. "Madam, your pardon. We will naturally obey your wishes."

Straightening his shoulders, he led the way outside. Penelope, knowing he would not be moved from this, followed, resigned to nursing split lips and bruised eyes afterwards. She would still marry him on Saturday, black eye or not.

He paused at the narrow exit to the yard beyond. "You should stay inside, love," he said, his voice a gentle caress.

Penelope wasn't to be deterred. "This is all because of me, and I want to see it through."

Sev sighed. "As you wish."

Penelope was glad Severus knew better than to argue. She would have watched anyway.

Severus removed his coat and gave it to Peter. He remembered something, and drew the slim case out of the pocket. He gave the package to Penelope. "I thought you'd want these."

Never before had anyone realized how vulnerable she felt without proper sight, how helpless and how angry it made her.

Severus had restored her independence back to her. She perched them on her nose and saw the yard come into proper focus. She gazed around and Severus's gaze followed hers, but he was assessing the task ahead of him.

The yard was roughly cobbled and surrounded by buildings in various states of repair. Thatch clumped over one open barn, while another was neatly tiled. The dim shapes of the equine occupants were visible behind half opened doors. The carriage Penelope had arrived in stood to one side, and looking up, Severus saw a small window, glinting in the sunlight. "That's where they put me."

He nodded. While his urge to kill the Don overwhelmed him with its intensity, he knew he must keep his wits, not lose them in blind anger. He needed his judgment intact, the calculating part of his brain ready to serve him. He would thrash this man as near to death as he could take him. For Penelope's sake, he would try not to kill him, but if it became necessary, he was equal to the task.

Severus faced Don Alfonso, who removed his coat and gave it to one of his footmen, who stood grimly by. When Severus took up his pose, feet well apart, fists raised, Don Alfonso held up a hand. "One moment."

Severus didn't relax, but met his opponent's eyes with a determined stare.

"I will not fight with fists. It is not worthy of gentlemen." Turning at his leisure, the Don gestured to one of the men, who went to the carriage and drew a long case out of the boot. "I will not fight with fists. If you choose to do this you may beat me to a pulp, but I will not respond. Can you use these?"

The footman came forward and opened the case. Severus straightened up, his fists dropping to his side. "Yes."

Swords. Not small swords, the usual dueling weapon of a

gentleman, but strongly bladed swords and short daggers. Peter, standing next to Penelope, gave a low whistle. "Rapiers and double-edged daggers." Killing weapons. The rapiers had longer blades that Severus was used to but without picking one up Severus saw the double edge. Each side of the sword was sharpened all the way down to the hilt. Trained in the faster, more athletic school of fighting with a small sword, Severus might have found them a severe handicap, but as luck would have it, he knew how to use a rapier and dagger. Not that he was about to tell that to the Don. A demonic smile curved his lips. He could kill his man with these.

When he lifted his head from contemplating the weapons, Severus saw Penelope wince. Peter placed a gentle hand on her shoulder. Severus was close enough to hear the words of encouragement Peter murmured to Penelope, and he heard a low click, a sound he recognized as the cocking of a hammer on a pistol. "Whatever happens, you won't go with the Don."

Both sounds, the pistol and Peter's voice, reassured him. With the production of the lethal weapons from the coach, the stakes had just risen. If Severus lost his life, or was incapacitated, Peter would save Penelope.

One false move could mean the death of either man. Penelope reached out and clutched Peter's left hand. He responded, clasping hers in a firm grip. Severus gave her a small smile, trying to convey reassurance, then turned back to his task.

Severus chose his weapons and, the dagger lax in his left hand, tried a few cuts in the air with the rapier. It was a sound weapon, properly balanced, sharp and true, the blade tightly fastened into the handle. It would hold. The Don took the sword and dagger left and used them both, whirling them in a deadly arc, first one way, then the other. Severus lifted a brow in faint amusement. He would save his moves until he needed them. No sense in allowing the Don to know how skilled he was.

They faced each other. Severus felt the cobbles of the yard under his booted feet and realized that the terrain was rougher than any meadow. He had noted the obstructions in the yard: the overturned pail in the corner, the pile of sawn wood ready for the kitchen fire.

There was no sound except the shifting of horses' hooves. Everyone in the yard, from earl to potboy, was silent. The air seemed to hold above them until, with a cry of "Engage!" Don Alfonso lunged.

He met steel. Severus acted without thinking, blocking the lunge as the blade flashed through the air. The Don disengaged with a shriek of metal and stood back. With a lithe movement, he swept his weapon towards Severus's right side, leaving the centre of his body open to attack. Severus thrust, as he knew the Don expected, so he was ready when the Don knocked the long blade aside and came at him with the shorter one. Turning his whole body to the side, he avoided the thrust and delivered a blow to the Don's wrist with his clenched fist, not using the cutting blade at all. It served to click Severus's mind into place, to block out everything except the fight. The reasons for it, the concern he had felt all day, even his weariness engendered by the long ride to get here melted away. Severus allowed the necessity to win to dominate his mind. Nothing else, only the calculations that worked through his brain sending information to him.

With a muffled oath, the Don stepped back, his hold on the short blade loosening momentarily. Instantly Severus followed up his advantage, coming in close with dagger and knee, bringing his knee up and his dagger in straight.

Severus felt the Don's hot breath gust against his cheek. Panting, the Don avoided the body blow and threw himself to one side, stumbling on the rough cobbles. Severus followed him, crossing the rapier in front of him in an effort to knock the dagger out of the Don's loosened grip.

Don Alfonso recovered, lunging forward to meet Severus's steel with his own. Light sparked from his eyes, and he became more animated than Severus could ever remember seeing him, shouting, "You are no match for me. Street tricks!" Severus recognized the Don's fury with unholy, cold delight. It was the advantage he wanted. Don Alfonso bore down on Sev, blades whirling in counterpoint.

Severus made no move until the Don was upon him. Then, with two economical sweeps, he knocked the blades aside and stepped back, holding the rapier firmly before him, making small, wicked circles with its tip. Time to taunt his opponent, try to urge him into losing his temper. "I have them both. Street guile and gentleman's habits. Try me." He allowed himself a slow smile.

Inviting the Don to come on, he slid his foot back slowly, aware of the rough cobbles as Don Alfonso had not been. His footing now firm, he twisted his sword in ever-increasing circles. "Had enough?" His voice was soft, almost caressing.

A scurry behind Penelope made both combatants glance around. People were arriving, people they didn't know. Word had got out about the fight. Severus hoped they didn't know who these men were, or there would be a scandal it would be hard to live down. He heard the words, "A guinea on the tall one!" and he thrust the already wagering crowd to the back of his mind.

Severus stayed absolutely still. With a snarl, the Don attacked and Severus burst into action. He spun on one heel, whirling his long blade about his head. Blades clashed and sparked, but none found their mark. The attack didn't stop with

Severus's startling move. He fended the blows dealt him until he felt his wrists ache with the jarring blows. The sensation was reassuring. The Don had not shown him a move he couldn't counter, or turn into an attack. It was time to attack.

Severus moved forward, his sword coming down in a deadly, glittering arc, his dagger hand close to his body. The simple movement changed when Don Alfonso met the long blade with his own, adding pressure intended to put Severus off balance and send him staggering back. Severus expected it. Instead of falling, he ducked under the locked blades and thrust forward, aiming at Don Alfonso's heart.

The Don reacted instantly, pushing Severus's hand aside with his own dagger, letting the sharp blade slide down. It drew a long, red line, but Severus jerked back, preventing the onward drive and brought his sword down, protecting himself from further hurt. He couldn't feel the wound at all, but he knew he must put an end to this soon before the trickle of blood made his grip too slippery to maintain. He held his weapon up a little, and the blood dripped on to the cobbles instead of down on to his hand.

The men stared at each other, both panting. The landlady and her cohorts kept the chattering, shuffling crowd out of the arena. Severus was aware of the dull muttering of the men, placing bets and shouting the odd word of encouragement. He ignored it all.

"You are good," said the Don.

"I can be better." Before Severus had finished his sentence he attacked.

He used science and strength, skill and fury melded together to a white-hot tempest of assault. He knocked Don Alfonso's weapon aside with a series of blows, each scream of steel met by a yell from the now thoroughly excited crowd.

Bringing his superior weight to bear, Severus charged, and brought his knee up high to drive against Don Alfonso's body and bring him tumbling to the ground.

Don Alfonso hit the cobbles with a crash that knocked the wind out of him. Severus blocked the dagger arm with his knee, and dropped his sword, transferring the dagger to his right hand with a short toss. He drew his right hand back and thrust.

The Don shrieked. Severus got to his feet and retrieved his sword. "I'm satisfied." He looked down. "And you?"

A weak voice, panting for breath managed; "Very well. I submit."

Severus kept his attention a moment longer, speaking very low, for his ears alone. "If it weren't for Penelope, you would be dead. It might be thought unfortunate if the first thing I did as her husband was to kill her new uncle."

Severus turned away and went straight to Penelope.

Chapter Twenty-Four

Severus submitted to having his cut bandaged, although he protested it was just a scratch, and he wouldn't be able to get his riding gloves on if she bound it too tightly. Penelope laughed, light-hearted at getting him back.

Now only Penelope, Severus, Peter, and the cleric sat in the small parlor. The spectators had moved to the taproom, where they sat imbibing the home-brewed and settling the bets they had laid as the fight went on.

Food, plain but hot and freshly prepared, was brought to them and they ate in complete conviviality. It wasn't until the meal was finished that anyone broached the subject of their next move. Peter sighed, replete, and sat back. "So—where do we go from here?"

Severus smiled. "I have a few ideas." He picked up his glass and leaned back in his chair. "I think the best thing to do with Don Alfonso is to see him to his yacht."

"How is he?" Penelope asked.

"Resting. His wound's been dressed. I pinked his shoulder. Pretty deep, but he'll recover. I just wanted to stop him causing any more trouble." He shrugged. "I wanted to kill him."

"Why didn't you?" That from Peter, not as casual a question as it sounded.

"I thought of Penelope. If I'd killed him this would all have come out in court. I didn't want anything to touch her."

Penelope sat still, hardly believing what she was hearing. He did it for her. To save her from scandal. No one had thought that much of her before. She stared at a wine stain on the table, not daring to lift her head, her knuckles clenched in her lap.

She felt the warm touch of Severus's hand on hers. "It's over now. I won't let you out of my sight for a while. Not, at least, until Don Alfonso is out of the country."

Lifting her head Penelope looked shyly at him. He smiled, a warm, intimate smile then turned away to the cleric. "To that end, I'd like to ask a favor of you. Will you marry us?"

The cleric flushed red, and wouldn't meet Severus's direct gaze. "I—my lord, forgive me, but the banns haven't been read—"

"No matter," Sev replied. "I have a special license in my pocket. There are enough of us to make it legal, yes?" He waited for an answer.

The vicar looked at Severus, then at Penelope. "Do you truly wish to marry this man?"

"Yes," she said. "I don't care where."

Sev squeezed her hand. "I don't want to let her out of my sight for the next few days, and there are no females available to provide a respectable escort. Since we were marrying anyway on Saturday, a few days won't make any difference?"

Penelope wasn't so sure about that. It was one thing for Severus not to let her out of his sight, but quite another to keep his hands off her. Or hers off him. She did her best not to think about it.

The cleric bit his lip. "If you don't marry, I will be putting Miss Makepiece in harm's way. I think it is my duty."

It wasn't the marriage Penelope had envisaged in her youth. No blossoms, no love tokens sewn on her gown, no guests but the occupants of the little parlor. After the dishes were cleared, they pulled the table to one side of the room to act as an altar, and the vicar set out the things he needed.

For the second time that day, Penelope stood up and gave her hand to a man, but this time it meant something. Before it had been a stratagem, and Penelope had not thought about the vows, hoping God would forgive her the transgression. This time she meant every word. She took her time over the vows and looked up at Sev when she was making them. He looked back, accepting her promises. He made his promises, equally solemn, and Penelope knew he meant every word. When the ceremony was over he kept his kiss short, a brief warm salute, but afterwards he kept hold of her hand.

Peter helped the vicar clear the cloth, chalice, Bible and prayer book away, then they lifted the table and restored it to its previous place in the centre of the room. The vicar produced the parish register, something he had not done in the previous ceremony, and they both signed. Penelope lingered, staring at her new name next to his.

Severus filled the glasses, a motley collection of ill-matched goblets and wineglasses with different patterns on them. The one Penelope held was decorated with a thistle, a Jacobite symbol. She supposed all kinds of people might stop at this place. The landlady had to be prepared for them.

Before anyone could drink, Peter raised his glass. "The bride and groom!"

Everyone drank except Severus and Penelope, who smiled at each other. Penelope thought she was too full to say anything, then Severus toasted her extravagantly. "To my beautiful, brave, clever bride."

Before anyone else could toast her, Penelope stood up. "If I may. To my husband, who never gave up. My handsome, brave, clever husband." She could say that last word forever and never tire of it.

Everyone laughed when the flush rose to Severus's cheeks, but he held his hand out to her once she had drunk. "Enough, flatterer! I can see this turning into a contest, so we'd better stop now."

Penelope finished her wine, and pushed the glass forward for a refill. Peter obliged. "Are we moving to the more salubrious inns on the High Street? We need to make a move if we want to do that."

"I can offer you the hospitality of the vicarage," the young cleric offered. "It would be an honor to have you stay."

Severus smiled. "I think not, though I thank you. I don't want to advertise our presence here any more than we have done already. If no one has any objections, we'll remain here tonight, see Don Alfonso on his way in the morning, then return to Swithland House. If we're careful, no one need know that we went anywhere. You, my love," he told his wife, "are ill in bed, according to everyone except your father and stepmother."

"Now we're married, what do we do on Saturday?"

"Go through it again, unless you have any objections. This was insurance, in case anyone discovers we've been here." He turned a soft look on her. "And because I want to look after you myself for the next few days, and this is the only way I can do it." His look was a caress, and said so much more than the words. Penelope smiled shyly back. He lifted her hand to his lips, and retained it afterwards. "We'll hire a chaise at one of the inns and make our way home. If anyone sees us, well then, we went for a drive when you began to feel better."

"In a hired chaise?" Peter said.

"We can stop it outside the gates," Severus never took his gaze from his wife.

Peter shrugged. "As you say, you are married. If anyone notices, you have your explanation ready."

When the cleric took his leave, Peter and Severus saw him to the door.

Severus and Peter returned, followed by the landlady with a taper to light the candles in the various sconces and stands scattered about the room. Severus looked at his wife. "The lights are on upstairs, and I want you in bed before too much longer." He laughed when she blushed. "You've had a tiring day."

"Oh! Oh yes, of course," Penelope wished that the earth would swallow her up for her obvious assumption when Severus mentioned bed. "I suppose I am tired." She stood and curtseyed to the others. "I will go up now."

Climbing the wooden staircase, she wasn't aware of Severus behind her until he reached across her to set open the door to the room. "My dear."

Penelope went in.

Severus closed the door and put the latch down. Penelope waited until he turned around, but didn't know what to do. She wasn't sure if he meant them to sleep or—something else. She was tired and happy just to sleep in his arms, if that was what he wanted.

Severus removed Penelope's spectacles and put them on the high oak chest of drawers which, together with the bed and a small washstand, was all the furniture the room offered. The bed was of oak and very old, with carved posts and headboard. The drapery wasn't so old, but was thin and well worn. Penelope noticed these things in passing, and then all she could see clearly was Severus.

It would do. He closed his arms around her and she lifted her face for his kiss. It was long and sweet, and when he had done, Penelope had no doubt of Severus's plans for the next hour or so. He began to undo the buttons of her jacket. "There are many things I could say, but I'd lose myself in the telling. I'm happier than I thought possible, especially when I remember what I felt like earlier in the year. Then, I looked on marriage as a life sentence, something I could no longer avoid." He looked up from his task to meet her eyes. "Now I wonder why I wasted so much time."

He finished the jacket and drew it off her, then lifted his arms to undo the buckles holding her stock in place. That came off too. "You know your way around a lady's garments," she commented, as his arms went around her waist to the tapes of her skirt.

"I do, don't I?" He turned her around. She felt his hands at the laces of her stays. "Ill-gotten knowledge, I'm afraid." Her stays loosened, and he drew them off to join the majority of her clothes on the floor. She only wore one petticoat, and he undid the tapes to that and her pocket.

When she felt his hand on her waist, gently urging, she turned back to him wearing her shift. At first, she couldn't look at him, but he waited, his hands resting on her hips, and eventually she looked up.

Immediately he claimed her mouth. His hands moved to her back, drawing her closer. She opened her mouth, let him in, resting her hands on his shoulders. It was difficult to realize that this was to be hers for the rest of her life. Perhaps she should take it one day—or night—at a time.

The kiss went on until, with a sudden movement, he swept her up and carried her across to the bed. She looked at him now, and his smile warmed her down to her toes. She no longer cared about her state of undress. He could do anything he wanted with her.

After he shrugged off his coat, he knelt and lifted her shift to just above her knee, concentrating on untying her garters. Penelope hadn't been aware that the mere action of sliding down a stocking could be so sensuous. He smoothed down her legs, kissed the soft flesh behind her knee, then ran his hands up her body, pulling her shift up. Penelope sat up to discard it and realized he was, apart from his coat, fully clothed.

It didn't seem to matter any more. He sat up, and took her hands, looked at her face. The lace at the end of his sleeves tickled her thighs. "Not the wedding night I thought we'd have, but I'll make it memorable for you."

"For us both." Penelope kissed him. Desire lanced through her when he caught her face between both his hands, kissed her mouth, her cheeks, and moved down to her throat. She leaned back, taking him with her and began on the buttons of his waistcoat.

It didn't take as long to strip him as it had her and soon they lay naked together on the old bed, lost in each other. Kisses and caresses blended into each other, and Penelope was no longer sure where she ended and he began. She tasted him in his kiss, and felt his touch on her skin.

Tentatively, she touched his chest, hard muscle under smooth skin, broken by springy black hair. It thickened when she dared to move lower. She daren't look now, caught by bashfulness. Very strange, since she'd been here before, seen him naked before, but true.

"I like it when you do that. Kiss me, love." He leaned forward and pressed his lips to hers. She conquered her fleeting shyness and responded, moving closer, exploring him with her hands and mouth.

His lips stiffened against hers when she touched his erection, wrapped her hand around him, then he relaxed, moved closer, caught her in his arms and deepened the kiss. She felt the delicious pressure of his chest against her breasts, and she moved a little to increase the sensation. He felt the wriggle and chuckled, after his lips left hers. "We'll find out what you like. We have a long time to discover each other, love. A lifetime."

The caresses she bestowed on him had their inevitable effect. Sev moaned low in his throat, moved back a little and mounted her, rolling her on to her back. "Another time," he whispered, his breath hot on her lips. "I can't wait any longer." She felt him slide between her legs, opened herself to him. His heat burned into her.

He found his way without guidance, as though they were made to fit together. Penelope bit her lip when she felt him insinuate himself into her. Then he thrust, hard, and his breath hissed out above her head.

Seeking her mouth with his he murmured, "Oh Penelope, oh love!" then caught her lips in a searing kiss, entering her, body, mind and soul. At that moment, she gave herself up to him. Everything that was hers to give she gave.

He paused, deep inside her and drew his head back. He gazed at her for a taut minute and his voice shook when he spoke. "Sweetheart, this is our night, our moment. I don't deserve this, any of it, but I'll try to be worthy of you, to be what you want me to be. I love you, Penelope, tonight and always."

"Oh, Severus, I love you so much."

He found her lips once more, showered kisses on her face and drove deeply within her. She froze, her moment upon her, and arched up to him, unthinkingly inviting him to do more, then cried out, not caring who heard her.

He drank her cry with his lips, mercilessly drove her harder. Incredibly, the warmth inside her increased after her first peak, instead of receding as it had before. She squirmed, felt him hold her hips steady so he could plunder her, wring every color of ecstasy out of her.

She was left gasping, "Oh God, Severus, Severus!"

"Hold on to me, my love. Hold tight!"

All Penelope could manage was to gasp his name, over and over while he brought her to a shattering climax, one that made her shiver uncontrollably, but she felt safe in his arms, safe to let herself enjoy what he gave her.

Perhaps enjoy was the wrong word. This went deeper than enjoyment. In giving herself into his care, Penelope received far more than she ever imagined possible. He kissed her, his tongue exploring and stimulating her, inviting her to join him.

To her surprise she did, one more time, shuddering in his arms when he gripped her tightly, and pushed deep, filling her.

For a few seconds he lay on her, his full weight pressing her into the lumpy mattress, but then he groaned and rolled to one side. Since he was still holding Penelope, she followed, to lie sprawled half across him.

They lay entwined, their only movement that of breathing, sated, replete.

Penelope recovered first. When she tried to pull away Severus pulled her closer, and she stayed, content there. Lifting her head a little she managed; "Is it always like this?" Because every time he made love to her, she ended up completely unable to move, wanting nothing more than to stay in his arms.

His short, breathy gasp of laughter told her it wasn't so. "You can do this for companionship, for a thrill, for something outside the act, for any number of reasons. But I tell you true, I've never done it for love before you. Never. If I thought I had, I was wrong."

Up until then Penelope had been unsure that he had felt the same way. For a man of his experience might encounter this all the time with umpteen different partners. She had no way of knowing that until he told her. Her inexperience made her unsure. Her heart told her he was as affected as she, as deeply involved, so engrossed they lost track of where they were.

"Severus, that was wonderful."

"I know." His arms settled about her. Happier than she had ever been before, Penelope fell asleep, surrounded by her husband, lost in him.

Chapter Twenty-Five

At dawn, Severus woke Penelope and made love to her again. Sleepily, she accepted his embrace, and then she wasn't sleepy any more. He loved her gently, until the end, when he seemed to forget, and drove her to joyful release.

Afterwards, he held her close, then, with a slight sigh, threw back the bedclothes.

She lay back, replete and at her ease, and watched Severus shave in cold water. It was something she'd never seen before, a man, shaving, although she realized that Sev didn't do this often for himself he managed pretty well. Afterwards he poured the shaving water into the slop basin and refilled the washbasin. He proceeded to give himself a thorough wash. Penelope watched in fascination, watched the strong muscles of his back, recently so blissfully engaged, flex when he stretched to reach the washcloth around to the more inaccessible parts. When he turned he saw her watching him, and to her delight, he flushed.

She laughed. "I think I'm going to enjoy being married."

"I know I am." He crossed the room to kiss her.

Regretfully, he laid her down on the bed. "Get some sleep, love," he told her. "I'll make sure you're woken when the coach is ready to take us home." Penelope snuggled down, and only dimly heard the quiet click of the door.

She was jolted awake about two hours later when the door opened again. It was still early, but she felt gloriously refreshed. Severus entered and came over to sit on the bed. It was only then she saw his expression wasn't the happy one she expected, but concerned. He wasn't smiling, he was frowning. Perhaps he wasn't able to get a traveling vehicle. She sat up, pulling the sheet up with her. Somehow, she realized nudity wasn't appropriate. "What is it?"

"Don Alfonso is proving difficult. He won't leave until he's spoken to you. I told him no, but to be frank, it would be easier if you heard what he had to say. Then he'll leave peacefully. Or so he says. I don't want you to do it, and so I told Peter, but I promised Peter I'd ask you."

"I'll do it. What can he do to hurt me now?"

Severus took a little more persuading, but eventually he reluctantly accepted her reasoning. And Peter's, she had no doubt. Don Alfonso was a wealthy and respected man so if he could be persuaded to leave in peace, or at least, under a flag of truce, the outcome would be much better for Penelope, and for Marcela and her son, too. The Don could create a lot of trouble, even from Spain, if he wished.

Penelope let the sheet drop, and watched Severus's eyes darken, delighted she had this effect on him. She was only beginning to explore what she could do, and she loved it.

With an effort, he raised his gaze back to her face. "It seems an age until bedtime." He leaned forward, bestowed a gentle kiss on her lips, then drew back, lifting the sheet again. "You'd better keep hold of this, if you want us to go anywhere today, except back to bed." She held the sheet in place, but was tempted to let it fall again to see that wonderful desire in his eyes again.

Penelope jumped when someone knocked on the door, but Severus just called, "Come in!" and explained, "Hot water. How quickly can you dress?"

"Twenty minutes," she said firmly.

"The sooner the better. I want to get you back home by nightfall." He leaned forward and gave her one quick kiss before he left.

Penelope was as good as her word, turning up downstairs on time, as neat as she could make herself. She found Peter in the small parlor and made a quick breakfast of bread and cheese with tea. Sipping the brew, she commented, "This is good tea for a place like this."

Peter grinned. "You've forgotten where we are, m'dear. Doubtless they get their largesse straight from the coast."

Penelope sighed. She couldn't approve of smuggling, but while duties were so high it must be difficult to resist. And the tea was very good.

When Severus came in, he looked grim. "All ready?"

"Completely."

They followed him outside.

For the first time since she'd arrived, Penelope caught sight of the tall masts and church spires of the busy city. Portsmouth was an old and vital part of England's defenses, busier than it had ever been.

Severus helped Penelope mount the lively chestnut mare he'd procured for her. The town was so crowded, that carriages would take a long time to pass through the narrow streets. He paused, and studied her face before he cupped his hands for her. "Are you sure you're up to riding, my love?"

She knew immediately what he meant. After he'd made love to her. She wasn't accustomed to being so well-used, although she'd like to be. "I'm fine, honestly." In fact, she was a little tender, but she wouldn't have admitted that to him, or he might have insisted on her staying behind. Or worse, not made love to her for a while.

The inn was on the outskirts of the town, outside the town gates, one of the straggling line of buildings servicing the overcrowded city, so they were on the heights before the land swept down into the natural bay.

The great city lay below them like an intricately detailed model. Portsmouth projected into the sea, with the docks to one side of the thumb-shaped promontory. Two highways, bustling with traffic of all kinds, lay below them. Severus told them that they were the Southampton Road and the London Road. They watched the slow progress of the carriages, carts and horseback passengers heading for the city, and then Severus led the way down the gentle slope towards one of the bridges.

There was a great deal of traffic queuing up to use the bridge, but the queues were orderly and everyone was passing across in good time. Despite this, Penelope saw Severus's gloved hand tap on his saddle while they waited. She glanced at him and smiled, receiving a warm tribute in return. "You're right," he told her. "I hate waiting for anything."

Eventually they were over, and into the city. Severus took them at a reasonable pace down the large streets and they attracted no undue attention. Penelope smelled the sea, the sharp tang of salt, but apart from that, it was similar to many other cities in England. Modern buildings jostled older, tumbledown structures, and people went about their business as though they were alone, not surrounded by humanity of various stages of respectability.

Penelope allowed Sev to lift her down with relief, not just pleasure at being in his arms again, however briefly. His concern for her was evident in the way he steadied her, and his anxious scanning of her. "Not long now," he said. "Chin up!"

Chapter Twenty-Six

They left the horses at an inn, and dismounted. Penelope accompanied Severus down to the docks

Penelope stood with Peter and Severus within sight of the well-equipped, beautifully turned out private vessel in the smaller dock. Beyond them lay the great dockyards, filled with ships, their thrusting masts vying for space in the blue, white-scudded sky. They stood back against a convenient wall, but despite trying to keep out of the way, the dock was full of people, mostly men, about their business. Several passed them loaded with roped up bundles of cargo. Sometimes the ships held human cargo, although the bulk of that particular trade passed through Bristol and Liverpool. Every port had its share.

After a while one of the footmen, Barnes by name, approached and murmured in Severus's ear. He turned to Penelope. "We're going aboard the yacht. The master's willing, and we don't want to make our affairs public. The crew seem amenable to our wishes."

"Do they think you're officials?"

"Most of the crew will do as they are told. The master knows who we are, and he vouches for our safety." Sev took Penelope's hand. "Promise not to leave my side. I need to know where you are, love."

Penelope gave her word and stepped forward towards the

vessel. She was not at all used to boarding sea going vessels, but ropes supported the gangplank, so she didn't look down for the short journey from the port to the ship. The deck was smooth and beautifully polished. The master, a jovial looking gentleman, was there to greet them. He looked askance at Penelope, but said nothing. Penelope gazed curiously about her before the master took them below.

There another surprise awaited her. The master took them to a stateroom, a large, well-appointed room. If the furniture hadn't been firmly bolted to the floor, it might have been a comfortable parlor almost anywhere. Politely the men waited for her to sit until seating themselves. She chose a wooden chair with an overstuffed seat, quite high, and Severus took one next to her. "Don Alfonso will be here very soon now," the master said. His voice, more accustomed to filling the deck, boomed out in this relatively small space. He had that halting inflection Penelope noticed in her stepmother.

"We only want to know what he wishes to tell us," Severus said. "Then you may be on your way."

The master shrugged. "I have been ordered to ready the sails for immediate departure. I do not expect to stay here for much longer."

Peter crossed one leg over the other, on the surface the negligent, English gentleman but his words were far from that. "You leave with us on board and you answer to the British government. Penalties can be extremely severe."

The master paled. "I am fully aware of that."

All they heard for half an hour was shouted orders, muffled by the planking between them, and the slap of gentle waves against the hull. Penelope wished she could see more of the ship. This was her first time aboard such a vessel, and she longed to see more, but she knew it wouldn't happen. Not this time, at any rate.

After about half an hour, they heard the sounds they were waiting for. Shouts heralded the arrival of the Don. Penelope stood, and Severus stepped just in front of her, a protective gesture she saw no need for but appreciated all the same. The sound of several feet descending the stairs outside followed, and almost at the same time the double doors to the salon swung open. Don Alfonso stared at her, his arm in a sling, but as rigidly upright as ever. On either side of him stood two burly guards. Severus nodded to them and they nodded back.

"My wife," said Don Alfonso.

Only her pride prevented Penelope from shrinking back. The thought of what she might have suffered under his hands made her stomach turn, but she made sure nothing showed on her face.

"You are mistaken, sir." His voice was low, but held an edge of menace.

"Not in Spain," the Don said. "Today we will leave for my country."

"The man's deluded," Peter said.

Severus frowned, but Penelope thought he looked more exasperated than angry. "Penelope is my wife now, beyond doubt. The ceremony you went through with her was not valid in law."

"I shall marry her again in Spain."

Penelope had had enough. This was getting ridiculous. "Don't I have anything to say to this? I wish to be Lady Swithland and so I have become her. That is my last word on it. If that is all you have to say, Don Alfonso, we'll be on our way."

"No." He reached into the deep pocket of his frock coat. Penelope watched as he drew out a beautiful dueling pistol, the butt and stock damascened in gleaming, well-polished silver, winding like a spider's web over the black base. He studied the weapon for a moment then leveled and cocked it. He aimed at a window on the far wall, then slowly swung the weapon to point at Severus. At the same time, the men either side of him drew large, brutal pistols from their belts and trained them on Severus, Peter and herself.

Penelope watched in horror, unable to do anything. Peter was swiftly disarmed by the master, who now stood behind him, pistol leveled at Peter's head.

"Now," said Don Alfonso, "you will come."

Deliberately she avoided Severus's gaze, kept her attention on the Don. He met her gaze with a heated one of his own. "You are mine. By every law of nature, you are mine."

Penelope was taken aback. His obsession verged on insanity. But she wouldn't give in to it.

She shook her head. "I am my own. In law, I was my father's and now I am my husband's, but I give my affections and loyalty where I choose. That does not belong to you, Don Alfonso, and never will."

"You will come to me," said the Don steadily, "because I will kill your so-called husband if you do not."

"You will not," said Severus.

"Believe me," the Don said in a low voice that filled the room, "I will."

Outnumbered, outflanked and outbribed, Penelope knew they could be in real trouble here. Her one concern was to get Severus safely ashore. Then she'd use the small pistol Peter had given her at breakfast and kill Don Alfonso.

"Very well," she said. "If you let Severus and Peter go, I'll go with you."

Sev ignored him, looked straight at Penelope. "Don't do this. I love you, I can't think of living without you."

Penelope caught her breath. For Severus to say this in front of all these people meant more to her than she could ever tell him. It was a moment she would remember forever, whatever happened next.

"I love you too, Sev. I won't let this come between us." She tried to tell him what she planned to do, pleading with her eyes, but only Peter knew she had the pistol.

Don Alfonso cut in to their last moments. "You say you are married. I married her first."

"Not legally. Since last year there are certain conditions to a valid marriage. I had a license, you did not." Severus put the case clearly, then lifted his chin, daring Don Alfonso to challenge it.

He didn't. He rubbed his chin thoughtfully, looking from Severus to Penelope and back. He must have seen what was evident to everyone in the room; the adoration neither of them wanted to hide any more, for he said, "Then I will kill your husband, and make you a widow.

"By the time your bodies are found, we will be at sea. I will swear it was a duel, two duels. Enough people saw us fight at the inn to confirm the bad blood between us. You will not come between me and my wife, Lord Swithland."

"You think I will marry you after this?" Penelope demanded. Before Severus could prevent it, Penelope stepped in front of him. "You will not kill him without killing me, and I will not marry you willingly. A marriage under duress is no marriage, is it not?"

With a choked "Penelope!" Severus tried to move her aside, but she stood her ground.

Don Alfonso's eyes went wide. "You would do this for him?"

"Undoubtedly."

The Don kept the pistol trained on them. "You have no choice. After this we set sail. We will remarry in the Faith in Spain. Your reputation will be ruined by the time we get there if you don't."

Penelope stared at him, her mind reeling. She had no time to reach into her bodice for the pistol. She'd tried everything she could think of to persuade this madman of his stupidity, and nothing worked. One more thing remained, a hopeless, perhaps useless thing, but she didn't care. If Severus died, then so would she.

Slowly, so slowly it seemed to Penelope he steadied the pistol, took his aim.

When it came, the explosion was deafening in that small space, the noise rocketing off the walls. The room filled with black smoke. Penelope fell to her knees, unable to support herself any more.

Severus was dead. Nothing mattered any more.

Chapter Twenty-Seven

Penelope curled into a small ball on the floor, her head resting on her bent knees. She forced the tears back; they would come later, in private. This moment was necessary if she was to control herself and appear arrogant and blank faced before her tormentors.

She lifted her head when the sounds of a violent scuffle reached her ears. Falling bodies shook the deck beneath them and splintering wood heralded the destruction of the furniture in the elegant salon. Penelope was in the middle of it.

Smoke from the discharged pistol filled the air still, but there were no more shots. The close, hand-to-hand fighting in the room precluded that. Penelope made to stand up, move back and get her bearings but something stopped her, a heavy weight on her skirts at the back.

The Don had fallen just behind her. Penelope yanked her skirts from under him, making his body turn. Something wet struck her face, and she put her hand up to her cheek. It came away red. When she stood, the floor under her feet was already slippery with it. All around them was a maelstrom of charging, shouting figures.

When she saw Severus's bloody hand, she forgot everything else. "Oh my God, Severus!"

"It's not my blood. It's his." His dark look burned into the still figure on the floor.

By his side Peter spoke. "You weren't the only person with concealed weapons, my dear. Did you think we'd come aboard this vessel with one sword and pistol each?"

She should have guessed but when she'd seen the men who were supposed to be their allies turn against them her mind had spun into confusion.

She squinted in an effort to see what was going on but although the smoke had cleared all she could see was a turbulent mass of men, all dressed similarly. They moved too quickly for her to make them out.

Severus dragged her close and held her, and she was content to feel her heart against his once more, both beating strongly. "We have to take stock, love. And quickly, too. None of the blood is ours. It's Don Alfonso's."

"What happened, Sev?" Her voice almost broke, so she bit her lip. Weakness wasn't permitted now.

Severus.

The furniture lay in splinters, delicate chair legs shattered, china in pieces. The instigator of this mess, Don Alfonso, lay on the floor in a pool of blood. A man crouched next to him, pressing hard on his chest, where the wound must be. Not dead yet then, Penelope thought dispassionately. Penelope saw how alive Peter looked, how his eyes sparkled. "Best mill I've had in years."

Penelope wondered how they would get off the ship.

Peter surveyed the room. "What now? Are we all safe?"

"The only person seriously hurt seems to be Don Alfonso," Severus told him.

"Good thing too," came the response. "The man must be mad."

Severus gave him a wry grin. "If he is then I am too. I think we share the same obsession." Things were settling down now, smoke clearing and the low groans of the wounded subsiding. "If he's still alive, Don Alfonso will need help," Sev said

"Why should we care? The idiot deserved it."

Despite his friend's callous remarks, Sev unlocked the door to the stateroom and let the crewmen in. Penelope shrank back as a man came through the door feet first and collapsed on the floor, on top of one of his compatriots. "Must have been trying to kick the door down," Peter commented, not at all put out.

Two other men came in after him, brandishing dangerous looking pistols. The master glanced up and snapped a few sentences in Portuguese. The men put their pistols down and Penelope sighed in relief. Severus took command. "You two. Stay there. You'll be needed to see to your master. He's been injured, we may have to take him ashore."

The men looked at Severus, but didn't move. "Hurry or he'll bleed to death." snapped the Earl of Swithland.

The master said a few words.

That seemed to do the trick. They knelt down by their master and lifted him, one at the shoulders and the other at their feet. "Take him up to the deck," Severus said. "We'll be able to see better there."

The two men carried Don Alfonso up the narrow staircase. As he passed them, Penelope heard him groan slightly. Still alive, then, and perhaps even conscious. Penelope was still finding it difficult to hold on to reality. Severus wasn't dead. The Don had no more hold over her. The sudden changes were making her head spin.

The world spun even more. There was a whooshing sound in her ears and her sight went dark. Penelope fainted.

She came to on the deck of the ship, cradled in Severus's arms. The first thing she saw was his face. She was in no hurry to sit up. He bent and brushed his lips on her forehead. "Better?"

"Perfectly. I don't think I've ever fainted before."

"Perhaps you got to your feet too quickly. Anyway, I got to hold you, which is what I badly needed to do."

"Oh Sev, I thought you were dead!"

"So did I when the gun first went off." He grinned. "Peter, the consummate politician had another pistol concealed in his waistband and I had one about my person, too, but he got to his first. He fired the shot, not the Don."

It seemed Don Alfonso was alive. He had been laid on a door, a makeshift stretcher. "We'll have a doctor see him and keep him closely watched."

"Will he die?"

"He might."

A faint movement from the stretcher brought her to step forward. Ignoring Severus's hand on her arm, she went to the Don's side.

"Why did you go to such lengths?"

Don Alfonso looked up at her and the pain in his face softened. "I have wanted you since the first moment I saw you, at a ball last year. I sold my sister to get you."

Penelope was amazed. "I never gave you any encouragement."

By her side, Severus spoke, his voice grim. "You didn't have to. He wanted you; therefore you belonged to him. He couldn't imagine it any other way."

Penelope frowned. "That's ridiculous."

"I wanted you," the Don said.

Then Penelope remembered what he'd said before the mêlée. "What did you mean about my father?"

The Don gave a sinister smile, soon wiped out when he tried to move and cried out with pain. "My dear, your father is probably dead already. Remember the tisanes my sister is so fond of giving him? All those strange herbs, a few more wouldn't make any difference to their appearance, would they?"

She didn't need Severus's sharp intake of breath to realize the full implications. Her father was taking those tisanes more and more, and Marcela would be blamed for his death.

"I heard," Peter said, joining them at what was probably Don Alfonso's deathbed. "Go, both of you. I'll see to matters here."

"He could be lying," Severus murmured.

Peter snorted. "No he isn't. He's dying and he won't risk his immortal soul on a lie. Just on murder. Ride for Swithland House, or you'll regret it."

Penelope spoke before Severus. "Don't think you can persuade me to stay behind. I can ride, especially now I can see properly." She touched her spectacles, still miraculously perched on her nose. "If I lag behind, go ahead of me."

"On one condition," Severus said. "We hire a groom for that eventuality."

She had to agree to that.

They still had the mounts they'd hired to bring them to the shore and they were fresh. Thirty miles to Swithland House. They could do it by nightfall if the weather remained fair and someone knew the road well.

Chapter Twenty-Eight

Severus set a tearing pace; such that made Penelope fear for his life until she saw how well he handled his horse. She followed with the groom and found that if she kept him in sight, she generally caught up with him. She didn't like to admit that the ride, after the stresses of the morning, was pushing her more than she liked, but with every jolt, every moment her horse stumbled, she reminded herself of the importance of the ride.

In the interests of speed they stopped every ten miles to change horses. Severus explained at one of the stops that he'd taken this journey many times, especially in his youth, when the excitements to be had in the town drew him to taste its pleasures. "Mainly drinking," he explained with a shame-faced grin. "And there are some choice gaming hells if you know where to find them."

"Oh!" Penelope felt the hot blood rush to her face. "I thought you meant—"

Severus laughed and kissed her, heedless of the ostlers, busy about their business in the inn yard. "Not a chance, love. Even at seventeen I knew the dangers of dockside whores. I was never that desperate. I was waiting for you."

Penelope was surprised to discover that she could laugh, despite her anxiety.

Severus heard her laughter with relief. He still wanted to leave her behind, but she'd kept up with the punishing pace he'd set, so he had to keep his word and let her come. He knew how much this meant to her; she was close to her father, and he was the only close blood relative she had. Unlike his own, he thought with a grimace, remembering the stern, distant man who looked rather like all the other stern, distant men in the picture gallery at Swithland House. That was what had made him determined to find another kind of wife for himself, to be a different kind of father to his children. If he had any, of course.

The weather held out and before the end of the afternoon, they reached Swithland House. Sev dismounted and threw the reins to a startled groom before helping his wife tenderly from her mount. After a small stagger, Penelope held herself upright. Severus swelled with pride for her, that she had the backbone to endure all this, but at the same time his heart ached for what must lie ahead of them. Taking her hand, he led her in through the back door.

Servants milled about the kitchen, preparing the dinner due to take place that evening, but word spread that his lordship was back, and when Severus got to the back hall, the butler was waiting for him. Not by a glance did he betray his surprise at his master's precipitate arrival, with Penelope in tow. "Wimbourne—where is he?" Sev snapped out.

"He is abed, milord. He has suffered rather a severe attack of stomach cramps."

Ignoring maids and guests who stared after them in astonishment they passed through the lushly carpeted corridors to the suite of rooms assigned to Lord and Lady Wimbourne.

Severus flung the door of the sitting room back to be

confronted by an astonished Lady Wimbourne. "Did you give him any tisane?" Severus demanded without preamble, wishing he'd received the results of the tests he ordered made on the samples he'd taken.

"He had a cup an hour ago," her ladyship stood, and when Severus strode towards the bedroom, she hurried in front of him, blocking his way.

"Madam, if you don't get out of my way, I will put you aside." Severus growled.

Her ladyship stood her ground, glancing at Penelope. "I will not have you disturb him. He is sleeping now."

Severus laid hands on her, and instead of screaming for help, she said, calmly. "It is my own tisane. Not my brother's."

The earl stopped, his hands still gripping her shoulders. "I beg your pardon?"

"If you are fool enough to think that I would give him anything my brother has tampered with, you are sadly mistaken," she said. "Do you think I do not know my herbs? Or my brother?"

"You mean you knew he'd poisoned your herbs?"

Her ladyship shook herself, and with a muttered apology, Severus released her. "I suspected it. I threw them out and bought new. I have kept these locked up, and the old ones in plain view. My brother may poison these as much as he likes. I never use them."

All the tension went out of Severus, and Penelope let out one long sigh. "Thank God!"

A sentiment Severus fervently echoed. But he had something else to tell her ladyship. Two something elses.

He took her cold hand between his warm ones. "Your brother is probably dead, Lady Wimbourne. He threatened to take Penelope to Spain with him, against her wishes, and he was shot in the resulting struggle."

Lady Wimbourne fixed him with a perceptive stare. "Did you kill him?"

"No," Severus told her, not without a twinge of regret. "Peter Worsley did."

"Then I owe Peter a favor," said his new mother-in-law. "My brother has become more and more unbalanced in recent years. What he wanted, he must have. Nobody could gainsay him."

"What about Paul?" Penelope blurted. Severus recalled that when she'd left Swithland House, the boy's future was still uncertain. "We can take him if you wish, and then you may visit him whenever you want to."

This time her ladyship smiled and Severus caught his breath. Marcela was truly beautiful when she smiled, all her chilly loveliness swamped by Spanish sunshine. "My lord wishes to bring Paul into our household. We will say that he was the son of my first marriage. If anyone discovers the truth, my lord says that we will defy them. I have sent for him and we will not be parted again."

"I'm so glad!" Penelope said with the impulsiveness Sev now knew she had and wanted to encourage. He wanted to give her the confidence to say whatever she wanted to, not to think about her every movement, or speech.

"I will welcome your son, my dear." The new voice came from the door where Lord Wimbourne stood, dressed in a light banyan over his shirt and breeches. "Don't you realize that you have given me proof that you can bear a son?" Lord Wimbourne glanced up and saw Sev. They exchanged a smile, and Severus no longer felt *de trop.* "But I no longer care about an heir," he continued, looking back at his wife. "That obsession always belonged to my first wife, anyway. I have found a treasure far above anything I hoped for."

She was sitting on a wide sofa; he dropped her hands only to walk around it and sit next to her.

"I heard most of it," he confessed. "I knew there was something wrong. I've never been so subject to stomach pain before."

He glanced at his daughter and smiled. She dropped a light curtsey and smiled back. Warmth welled in Sev's heart to see Penelope so happy. He'd do it all again to see that smile. But concern crossed Penelope's face. "But if you weren't taking the poisoned herbs, why did you get the stomachache?"

To their surprise, Lady Wimbourne looked down at her lap, flushing hotly. "I fear that is my fault. I have stopped using it now. I know how much you wanted a son, that is, people told me you did, and I had a—potion—I knew had worked."

It took a few moments for them to catch up with her, then it was Lord Wimbourne who said, in a choked tone, "You mean—Spanish fly?"

The blush deepened. "Yes, my lord. Only very small amounts."

Lord Wimbourne exchanged a speaking look with Severus and neither man could hold back any longer. Relief combined with amusement and produced a great roar of masculine laughter. When Penelope would have spoken, Severus grasped her arm and stopped laughing enough to inform her that he would tell her later.

Lord Wimbourne prevented his wife standing and leaving the room by holding her hand. He was the first to recover. "And have you stopped dosing me with the stuff?"

"Can you not tell?"

"To be truthful, no. I knew something gave me the stomach

pains, but I trusted your good sense, my dear. And I was right, wasn't I?"

Wiping his eyes, Severus made to leave, but was prevented by a shake of Lord Wimbourne's head.

Lady Wimbourne looked up at her husband. "You will not punish me?"

"No, of course not. You were anxious for me to have what you thought I longed for. A son no longer seems as important. Besides, you have a son I can share, don't you?"

In a flash, Severus realized where Penelope got her generosity of spirit. Father and daughter had never looked so similar than in that moment.

His hand still holding his wife's, Lord Wimbourne looked up at Severus. "And my daughter? I trust you with her. I hope you will not abuse that trust."

"Her happiness is far too important to me for me to do that, sir."

One of her rare smiles lit Lady Wimbourne's face. The news seemed very welcome to her, and Severus was glad of it. "I am so glad. You are right for her." The smile broadened slightly. "The house is in an uproar. You were to have been married in the chapel tomorrow morning, or had you forgotten?"

He grinned back. "Not forgotten exactly, ma'am, just put it to the back of my mind. With your permission, we will proceed with the ball tomorrow night. We'll make the announcement there. Too many people saw us arrive together for us to hope to hide the fact that we've been together for the last few days."

Her ladyship gave an imperious wave of one hand. "I shall deal with it. Miss Trente insisted on continuing with the ball. She hasn't given up hope of you yet."

Severus laughed again, all anxiety banished. "She'll have to look somewhere else for her title and fortune. That's all she ever wanted from me."

"She'll probably attempt to cancel the ball or at the very least sabotage it if she knows you are married," his lordship said.

Sev gave an unholy grin. "Then don't tell her. Let her speculate. When we inform them tomorrow night, all speculation becomes null, so let her have her fun. But not for long." With a wink, he took Penelope's hand and led her from the room.

Chapter Twenty-Nine

Severus took Penelope to the suite she would share with him. The servants had moved her things there. It looked more like hers now, with her familiar dressing case on the floor and hairbrushes on the dressing table. Even better was that Collins was in residence.

She bobbed a curtsey, as she always did, and regarded her mistress with clear signs of disapproval. "I shall order a bath, my lady." Penelope knew her sense of propriety had been outraged, and her maid had been cozened out of a prestigious society event when she could expect to be the centre of attention belowstairs. She would recover from her disappointment.

"No, leave us for now," Severus told her. "Inform the servants, if you please, that no one is to gossip to the guests. I expect loyalty from my staff, and I would appreciate it if my wishes were respected now."

Tight-lipped, Collins left the room.

"I've been longing to do this for an age," Severus murmured and without further ado, took her in his arms for a long, sweet, kiss.

Penelope forgot everything else in his kiss. At first gentle, considerate, it escalated into something more, passionate and needy. Penelope recognized Severus's need of her through her own, surging through her with an intensity that would have shocked her, had she not been so taken with the moment.

The riding habit was disposed of, together with Severus's clothing. Shirts, stays, petticoats and breeches lay in a jumbled heap on the floor. When Penelope touched him, she felt so thankful to find him warm and whole, apart from a few bruises. She pressed a kiss to the marks on his chest. He moaned, the sound rumbling through him, then he swept her up and on to the bed.

He wasted no time. "I'm sorry, Penelope, I need you so much!" he managed to gasp before touching her to ensure she was ready for him. Then he plunged inside her. Penelope arched up to meet his frantic thrusts, to take him deep inside her.

He took her nipple into his mouth, drawing her in, kissing, sucking and nibbling. She responded, cried out and put her hand to the back of his head, pressing him into her, feeling her body respond to the frantic tempo.

At that rate, it couldn't last long. Sev straightened up, and hung for a sweating, pulsating moment above her before catching her to him. She felt the warmth gush into her, and made a strangled cry, holding him tightly.

Almost immediately, he rolled off her and pulled her close to lay her head on his shoulder. They lay together for some time in dreamy satisfaction, happy to be with each other again.

Eventually Severus turned his head and kissed Penelope's forehead. "I was so afraid in that room. Afraid I wouldn't know this again, or not know it for a long time." He kissed her, leaned back and gazed at her, anxiety shading his eyes. "Did I hurt you, love?"

She reached a hand up to caress his cheek. "Not a bit. I needed it too. I needed you close. I don't think you could have got much closer."

He chuckled and kissed her again. "We may try. Sometime in the future, but for now we'll rest."

"Mmm." Sleepier than she'd thought, no doubt encouraged by the lovemaking, Penelope fell asleep in her husband's arms.

Penelope woke alone and to daylight. She was warm and hungry. She became aware of the sound of pouring water and she smiled. She would love a bath.

Severus, dressed in a loose robe she couldn't remember seeing before, entered her field of vision and sat on the bed. "Good morning, sleepyhead." He leaned down to give her a gentle kiss. "I've ordered a bath and some clean clothes. And some food. You are staying in this suite today."

Penelope sat up. "Thank goodness for that, I'm famished."

He smiled, took his time looking her over before reaching out to cup her breast. Penelope smiled back, and reached for him, but he pushed her away gently. "No time for that. Come. Breakfast is served."

After breakfast Severus took her back to bed, and to her surprise she slept again, only to wake to his hands on her body. She could get used to this. But after caressing her, he flung back the covers and got out of bed.

He picked up a light silk robe. "Time to bathe, my love," he said, but the light in his eyes promised more. Wondering what he was up to, Penelope let him help her into the robe. She thought he might like to bathe her. Her loins turned soft at the thought.

Severus led her out of the bedroom and into a smaller room she hadn't noticed earlier, even when she had investigated the apartment and chosen it with Severus the previous week. The room was empty except for a large bath, half sunk into the floor. It was filled with steaming, hot water. Herbs floated on the surface. Penelope smelled the fresh, sharp tang of lavender. "Goodness!"

He turned and undid the sash of her gown, grinning. "I had it built after I returned from the Grand Tour. All those Roman baths gave me ideas. "After you, my love.""

Keeping hold of his hand for balance Penelope stepped over the side and sat on the tiled wall above the bath. The water was at a comfortable temperature. She allowed herself to slide in, and leaned back, closing her eyes and breathing in the delicious scents of the herbs.

Severus joined her, taking his place opposite hers and allowing their legs to twine together. There was plenty of room for two in the big bath. "How do they empty it?" Penelope asked, curious.

Sev moved a little and Penelope saw a small opening, presently plugged. "It goes into barrels below," Severus said. "I believe they use the water for the garden."

"I like this," Penelope said.

He lifted his head and regarded his wife, so nearly lost to him. How could he have borne it if he'd lost her? He had never given himself this fully, and he doubted he could ever do it again. Without her he would be more lonely than he'd thought possible before.

On an impulse, he reached out, closed his hands about her waist and pulled her around so she leaned against him. After a first, startled resistance she acquiesced, and settled against him with a small sigh of contentment. "Oh yes, I like this."

He released her with one hand so he could reach the soap, then lathered his hands, and began to wash her, ignoring the washcloths in favor of a gentle massage. Lifting her forward, he rubbed the soap in ever-increasing circles over her back, feeling the hard bone and muscle under the soft, delectable skin, reveling in the sensation and the pervading feeling of deep peace and ease.

He felt his wife relax, and continued his ministrations. "Where did you learn to do that?" She lifted her hair so he could soap her shoulders.

"Nowhere. It just seems natural with you."

"I shall have to practice on you, my love."

Sev glowed. "It will be a decided pleasure."

There was silence for a while, punctuated by low moans of pleasure when he reached a tight muscle or a pleasure point. He took his time over her breasts, enjoying the way her nipples responded to his touch, the way they floated in the deep bath. Eventually he reached the seat of her pleasure. Leaning her back against him he circled and teased, noting with fascinated delight how different she felt under water, insinuating his fingers deeper into her. Her moans increased in volume, and she unashamedly allowed him full access to any part of her he cared to reach. Severus had to work hard to resist the urge to turn her and take her there and then.

He felt her swell with desire under his hands, held her hard against him and played with her, circling her, pausing before plunging his fingers deep into her. When she came, it was with a sweet, single cry of yearning delight. He waited until the pulses died away before he removed his fingers from inside her, resting them on her stomach and pulling her close.

"Oh my," she whispered, snuggling closer.

Feeling she might drift off to sleep in his arms, Severus decided it was time she washed her hair and, without further ceremony, dunked her head underwater. She came up spluttering, but when she turned, the light of battle shone in her eyes.

"My turn, my lord," she announced.

Severus was delighted to submit. After washing his hair and hers, leaving them both dripping, she soaped her hands and circled his chest. Severus discovered how pleasant it was to receive such ministrations. Closing his eyes, he gave himself over to her completely. She could do whatever she wanted with him.

It seemed his wife relished a challenge. She washed him efficiently, but combined it with teasing, near-accidental touches that brought him to straining attention before she was done. Then she made him sit on the side of the bath and came up on her knees. Soaping her hands, Severus saw where all her attention was focused, and groaned in anticipation.

He wasn't wrong. "You must tell me if this isn't to your taste," she said, before touching him. "I have a lot to learn."

She circled the base with one soaped hand, lathering the hair into suds. "In my opinion," Sev managed, "you have nothing to learn at all. You will, my love, drive me mad with wanting you."

"That's the general idea," she replied, before starting on her task in earnest. She cradled his balls in one hand, massaging them before swirling one soaped hand up and around and down, in a never-ending figure-of-eight pattern. Severus put his hands down on the broad, tiled edge of the bath in an attempt to steady himself. He was as tense now as he had been relaxed when she had rubbed his back. Penelope could play him like a harp. He must ask her if she played the harp, he thought, in an effort to hold his reaction back just a little longer but realized that he was playing the part of a human harp, and dissolved into the unbelievable sensations once more.

This was wonderful. She could do this forever. Severus let himself concentrate on what she was doing for him, let his world revolve around the incredible feelings she was evoking.

When he felt himself tense, he knew his moment was nearly upon him.

Without warning, he seized Penelope and pulled her away, sliding back down into the water and lifting her over him to impale her and put himself over the edge. Gripping her close, he shuddered with his release, as though he was giving her his life-blood, which, in a way, he was.

Penelope held on to him, and incredibly, he felt her pulse around him. He did what he could, thrust himself back into her, willed himself not to subside until she had felt it too. It seemed he succeeded. After a few breaths of rigidity when she threw her head back and cried out, she leaned forward on to him and rested her head on his shoulder, soft and warm. Despite the ridge of hard tiles at his back, he supported her weight. "Sweetheart, that was wonderful."

"I enjoyed it too." He felt her breath on his neck when she spoke.

Regretfully Severus realized the water was cooling, and they would have to get out. Leaning forward he yanked out the plug. "Can't have you catching cold."

She giggled. "In this weather?"

"You'll catch a chill from the water." He climbed out and found a heap of fresh towels. Shaking one out, he held it out to her. "Be careful when you get out. The tiles are a mite slippery."

They lay on the freshly made bed, Severus holding her while they drank the cool white wine brought to their room while they'd been in the bath. His care warmed her.

Sev leaned forward and pushed the edge of her robe aside. He caught his breath and just like that, Penelope's desire rose hard and swift within her,

She watched him pour wine over her, and then lean forward and lick it off. Delicious. "My love, I think we've
304

discovered a new way to play," he murmured, his mouth hot against her skin. "I shall order a fresh bottle to be in the room later." When he looked up at her, his arrested expression stilled her. "Let the world go hang," he said. "Forget the ball."

Recalled to the present, she laughed and pushed him away, "No, Sev, that would be unspeakably rude. We must dress. We'll have time for that later."

"Hmmm." He tried to draw her close again. "Lots of time." Reluctantly he released her. "I'll go to my room and change. But that's all I intend to use my room for in the future. I'll come for you an hour. We should be there to lead people in to dinner, if we're to attend."

Penelope smiled and watched him cross the room and go through the connecting door. It was wonderful that he was so close. Perhaps he'd be closer later.

Penelope was barely ready in an hour, with Collins' able help. Her hair was powdered; she was arrayed in one of her new gowns, a symphony of expensive lace and gleaming pink silk, the petticoat an elaborately embroidered confection. It was pleasant to watch her maid preparing her for the evening.

She was ready when her husband returned to escort her downstairs. He looked wonderful. He wore a wig for the formal occasion, and a suit of clothes she'd never seen before. The coat was green, embroidered in gleaming gold, and the waistcoat a miracle in white embroidered silk, the raised flowers twining lovingly around the buttons and buttonholes. White silk breeches completed the ensemble, with diamonds at his knee and buckling his shoes. Every inch the proud aristocrat. He looked as though he'd never lifted a finger in his life except to call a servant.

In obedience to an elegant gesture, Penelope turned slowly, letting him view her from all angles. She flicked open her fan and shaded her cheek with it in the gesture that meant, "I love you."

He chuckled. "Be careful who you say that to." He crossed the room and offered her the support of his arm. "Time to face the music."

Just as they were leaving the room, she gasped and put a hand up to her face, removing her spectacles.

"Leave them. I was forgetting. Wait a moment, love." He dipped his hand into his pocket and drew out a long, slim case. Out of it, he took a pair of spectacles. These were embellished by diamonds, sparkling around the rims and down the temples.

Penelope burst into shocked laughter. "Severus, you can't want me to wear those."

"Why not?" he said lightly. "Throw it in their faces, do something so outrageous no one can miss your spectacles."

Laughing she took them from him and replaced the ones she wore with the new ones, thanking providence that he had thought to keep the diamonds small. The extravagance of her gown balanced them, though she wouldn't have dreamed of wearing them with ordinary day wear. She didn't care, as long as he was by her side. He flicked the lace at her low cut bodice. "I'll wager this is more difficult to get out of, my lady. I like a challenge!" He leant over and kissed her forehead. "Let's get this over with."

Happily, Penelope went with him to the drawing room.

They were greeted by stunned amazement. Penelope wasn't sure if they knew, or if it was her new eyewear. "Good evening," said Severus blandly.

"Oh, my lord, we had quite given you up!" gushed Miss Trente, surging forward, ignoring Penelope completely. "When you weren't here to prepare for your wedding, we thought something dreadful had happened." Lady Annabelle, behind her friend as usual, nodded acquiescence. Penelope noted with delight that they were not as well dressed as she. They had been leaders of fashion; Severus had made it clear that she could be one too, if she wished. On the whole, she thought not, but it was pleasant to be thought of in a frivolous way after so many years being castigated as a clumsy dolt. She sought for her father and stepmother in the crowd, and was warmed by their smiles. Beside them stood Antonia, also smiling. They exchanged an entirely private smile.

"As you can see," Severus replied gravely, "We are here. We had urgent business, but all is right. We have been married for just over a day, instead of less than one, that is all."

In front of them all he lifted Penelope's gloved hand to his lips and touched his lips to her knuckles. Then he drew away and bowed to her. The bow was far too low, a bow he might give to royalty, so she curtsied low in reply and allowed him to raise her to her feet once more. "My lady," he said, then, equally loudly, "my love."

It warmed her, that public declaration. She felt it to the tips of her elegantly shod toes. Her smile would have lit a bonfire.

About the Author

"Compelling and stylish are the words I would use to describe Lynne Connolly's historical books. Once you read one, you can't wait for the next!" – Anne Herries, writer of best selling romance for Harlequin.

Winner of two EPPIEs, Lynne Connolly is the best-selling author of sensuous romance, including the Triple Countess series and the Secrets trilogy. Lynne fell in love with the Georgian era at primary school, and neer fell out of it, visiting historical sites, towns, battlefields and houses in her home country of England.

Lynne writes sensuous historical romance, and gives the reader a real flavor of what it was like to live and love in the eighteenth century. But she likes the twenty-first century fine, and she also writes paranormal romance set in bustling, modern cities. She lives in England with her family and her Muse, a cat called Jack. She writes surrounded by the doll's houses she enjoys making and filling.

She has a website at www.lynneconnolly.com and a blog at www.lynneconnolly.blogspot.com . She'd love to hear from you – write to her at lynne_connolly@yahoo.co.uk

A feisty auto mechanic and a hunky chef cook up chaos!

Kitchen Matches
© *2008 Marianne Arkins*

Cori Weathers is a wizard with a torque wrench, but the moment she lays eyes on her cooking teacher, Micah DePalma, her lessons turn into a klutzy symphony of flying poultry and burning aprons. It makes no sense. He couldn't be less her type: tall, skinny, and born with a silver spoon in his mouth. So why is her heart sputtering like a badly tuned engine?

Despite family pressure to date only women of his own social class, something about the cooking-challenged spitfire lights all Micah's burners. Cori's a complex dish inside a deceptively simple coating, one he's willing to risk tackle football and jealous ex-boyfriends to sample.

His every attempt to crack her stubborn heart strikes sparks. Will they ignite the flame of love—or explode into just another kitchen disaster?

Warning: This story contains flying poultry, annoying older brothers, the occasional quote from Shakespeare, and enough sexual tension to overheat ovens—and engines.

Available now in ebook from Samhain Publishing.

Tracking her was easy.
Staying out of her bed—that's the hard part.

Dance of Seduction
© *2008 Elle Kennedy*

On the run from her past and her overprotective brother, Ellie has had a taste of freedom—and likes it. Nothing can make her go home. Not even when the man she's always longed for shows up to drag her there. His wicked grins and irresistible dimples won't work.

But she knows something else about Luke: He doesn't give up easily. Luckily, Ellie's not above resorting to naughty tactics. Seduction, she's certain, will make him so uncomfortable he won't be able to flee fast enough.

And boy, is it going to be fun.

The last thing Luke expects is for his best friend's sister to launch an erotic assault. He'll go along with her sexy games, but he's sure that when things get too hot, she'll come to her senses and come home. Except resisting her isn't as easy as he thought it'd be.

And suddenly he's wondering if maybe there can be more than one winner in this dance of seduction...

Available now in ebook and print from Samhain Publishing.

GET IT NOW

MyBookStoreAndMore.com

GREAT EBOOKS, GREAT DEALS . . . AND MORE!

Don't wait to run to the bookstore down the street, or
waste time shopping online at one of the "big boys." Now,
all your favorite Samhain authors are all in one place—at
MyBookStoreAndMore.com. Stop by today and discover
great deals on Samhain—and a whole lot more!

WWW.SAMHAINPUBLISHING.COM

Printed in the United Kingdom by
Lightning Source UK Ltd., Milton Keynes
141665UK00001B/57/P